I0649870

Table of Contents

ACT I: THE SLAG AND THE CHROME 5

Chapter 1: The Rust 6

Chapter 2: The Gilded Cage 15

Chapter 3: The Cattle Call 22

Chapter 4: The Meat Grinder 28

Chapter 5: First Contact 35

Chapter 6: The Beast 42

Chapter 7: The Interview 52

Chapter 8: The Selection 60

Chapter 9: Room Service 67

Chapter 10: The Rules 74

Chapter 11: The Dress Code 82

Chapter 12: The Ambush 90

Chapter 13: The Bathhouse 98

Chapter 14: Steam 106

ACT II: HIGH TORQUE 114

Chapter 15: Sparring 115

Chapter 16: The Snooping 122

Chapter 17: The Bargain 133

Chapter 19: The Club 150

Chapter 20: The Alley 158

Chapter 21: The Morning After............ 166

Chapter 22: The Ball 173

Chapter 23: The Dance...................... 182

Chapter 24: The Balcony 190

Chapter 26: The Mission...................... 206

Chapter 27: One Bed...................... 216

Chapter 29: The Massage 239

Chapter 30: The Attack 248

ACT III: RUST AND RUIN...................... 259

Chapter 31: The Revelation...................... 260

Chapter 33: The Betrayal 276

Chapter 35: The Dungeon...................... 296

Chapter 36: The Rescue Plan 304

Chapter 37: The Breakout 312

Chapter 38: The Sacrifice...................... 321

Chapter 40: The Guilt 337

Chapter 41: The Execution Decree.................. 345

Chapter 42: The Rally 354

ACT IV: HEAVY METAL 362

Chapter 43: Siege...................... 363

Chapter 44: The Throne Room............ 372

Chapter 45: The Reunion...................... 379

Chapter 46: The Release 390

Chapter 48: The Finish 404

Chapter 49: The Final Stand 413

Chapter 51: The Aftermath 430

Chapter 52: Rust Free (Epilogue)....................... 439

ACT I: THE SLAG AND THE CHROME

Chapter 1: The Rust

Sara

The air in the Slags tasted like pennies. Like old blood and wet iron. If you breathed too deep without a filter, you could feel the heavy metals settling in your lungs, coating the alveoli until you drowned on dry land.

I adjusted the strap of my rebreather, ignoring the way the rubber bit into the bridge of my nose, and dug my gloved hands into the pile of refuse.

"Come on," I muttered, my voice muffled by the mask. "Give me something shiny."

The heap I was standing on was a geological layer cake of the city's history. Bottom layer: concrete and rebar from the Before times. Middle layer: plastic and glass from the Collapse. Top layer: the good stuff. The cast-offs from the Chrome City floating above us.

My fingers brushed against something cold and smooth. Not the jagged bite of rusted steel, but the sleek, arrogant curve of alloy. I yanked it free.

It was a servo-motor. Probably from a servant droid or an automated carriage. In the city above, this was trash because it had a hairline fracture in the casing. Down here? This was dinner for a month.

"Jackpot."

I shoved the part into my rucksack, the weight of it a comforting thump against my spine. I didn't linger. In the Scrapyard, lingering got you mugged, or worse—it got you Rusted.

I scrambled down the trash heap, my boots finding purchase on shifting debris. I moved like water—or as much like water as you could when you were wearing steel-toed boots and a utility belt heavy with pry bars.

"Yo! Sara!"

I didn't stop. I didn't even look back. I knew that voice. Jinx. A scavenger with more ambition than teeth.

"I saw that!" Jinx scrambled down after me, sending a cascade of tin cans rattling down the slope. "Split it with me, or I tell the Warden you're holding out on the tithe."

I stopped then. I turned slowly, letting my hand rest casually on the hilt of the jagged pipe I used as a baton. "Jinx. You couldn't catch a cold in a plague ward, let alone catch me."

He stopped ten feet up, panting. He looked bad. His skin had that gray, sickly sheen that meant he hadn't seen the sun in weeks. Or the Rust was setting in.

"Fifty-fifty," he wheezed. "I need credits, Sara. My mask filters are shot."

I looked at him. Really looked at him. His filter cartridge was blinking red. He was breathing raw smog.

I sighed, the sound harsh in my own ears. I hated my conscience. It was an expensive liability.

I reached into my belt and pulled out a spare filter. It was used—scrubbed clean with vinegar and hope—but it had a few days of life left in it. I tossed it to him.

"Catch."

He fumbled it, nearly dropping it into a puddle of toxic sludge. He stared at it, then at me.

"Keep your mouth shut about the servo," I said, turning away. "And wash your face, Jinx. You look like death warmed over."

I didn't wait for a thank you. I didn't want one. Gratitude was just another debt I couldn't afford to collect.

Home was a shipping container stacked three high in a swaying tower of corrugated metal. It wasn't much, but it had a lock I'd modified myself and a ventilation unit I'd stolen from a decommissioned factory.

I climbed the rusty ladder, the familiar creak of the rungs the only welcome I ever got. I keyed the lock—a triple-tumbler mechanism that would confuse most pros—and slipped inside.

The air inside was cleaner. It smelled of lavender and ozone. Elara's smell.

"Sara?"

The voice came from the pile of blankets in the corner. My chest tightened. She sounded worse today. The rattle in her chest was deeper, wetter.

I stripped off my outer gear—the heavy coat, the utility belt, the boots—dumping them by the door. I washed my hands in the basin of recycled water before I went to her.

"Hey, bug," I said, kneeling beside the cot. "I got a servo. A big one. We eat real protein tonight. Maybe even get some of those lyophilized strawberries you like."

Elara smiled, but it didn't reach her eyes. She was seventeen, three years younger than me, but she looked frail as a bird. She sat up, the blankets falling away from her arm.

I froze.

The silver patch on her forearm, the one that had been the size of a coin last week, was now the size of a saucer. The Rust. It wasn't just a disease; it was a colonization. The metal spores in the air settled in the blood, replacing organic tissue with living iron. It started on the skin, looking like beautiful, filigreed jewelry.

Then it went internal. It calcified the lungs. It turned the heart into a paperweight.

"It barely hurts," Elara lied. She pulled her sleeve down quickly, wincing as the fabric snagged on the jagged edge of the metallic scab.

"Don't," I said, my voice shaking. I reached out and gently pulled her sleeve back up. I traced the edge of the silver patch. It was cold to the touch. "It's spreading fast, El."

"It's fine," she whispered. "I'm fine."

"You're not fine. You're turning into a statue." I stood up, the anger flaring hot and sudden in my gut. Not at her. Never at her. At the world. At the Chrome City floating above us, casting its shadow over our slow deaths. They had the cure. The Elixir. They drank it like wine at their parties to keep their skin soft and their blood red, while we scrapped for filters to keep from turning into tin cans.

I walked to the small table where I kept our stash of credits. It wasn't enough. Even with the servo, it wouldn't be enough for a single dose of Elixir on the black market.

My eyes landed on the flyer I'd crumpled up in my pocket earlier. I smoothed it out on the table.

THE IRON TRIALS *For the Glory of the Crown. Winner receives: A Place in the Royal Guard. Unlimited Credits. One Wish.*

One wish.

Everyone knew what the "Wish" meant. It meant access. It meant the King's personal vault. It meant the Elixir.

"Sara, no," Elara said. She was watching me, her eyes wide and terrified. She knew what I was looking at. "You can't. It's a slaughter. They feed Slags like us to the beasts just to warm up the crowd."

"I can fight," I said, staring at the stylized drawing of a knight on the flyer. "I'm better than half those pampered knights. They fight for honor. I fight dirty."

"You'll die," she said, her voice cracking. "And then I'll be alone. Please, Sara. I'd rather rust out with you here than live without you."

I turned back to her. I sat on the edge of the bed and brushed the hair back from her forehead. She was burning up. The fever was the body's last ditch effort to burn out the metal. It never worked.

"You're not going to rust out," I said fiercely. "I promised Mom I'd look out for you."

"Mom died," Elara said softly. "Dad died. That's what happens here, Sara. We die."

"Not us." I leaned down and kissed her forehead. "I'm going out. I need to sell the servo."

"Sara—"

"Sleep, El. I'll bring back strawberries."

I didn't go to the fence. I went to the workshop.

It was a small alcove in the back of the container where I did my tinkering. I pulled my boots over to the light.

They were standard issue scavenger boots—heavy leather, reinforced toes. But the heels were special. I grabbed a screwdriver and popped the false heel off the left boot.

Inside lay my inheritance.

It wasn't money. It was a set of lockpicks made from aerospace-grade titanium. My father had taught me how to use them before the Rust took his fingers, and then his lungs.

"Locks are just puzzles made by men who are afraid," he used to say. *"And every man is afraid of something."*

I checked the picks. Tension wrench, rake, diamond, hook. They were slim, deadly, and illegal in three sectors.

I slid them back into the heel and snapped it shut. I wasn't going to the Iron Trials to win a duel. I wasn't going to defeat the King's champions with a sword or a spear.

I was going to cheat.

I stood up and caught my reflection in the polished steel of the ventilation duct. Dark eyes, messy hair tied back with a grease-stained ribbon, a face that was too sharp angles and not enough softness. I didn't look like a hero. I looked like what I was.

A rat.

And rats survived where lions starved.

I grabbed my coat. The Trials started at dawn. The line for registration would already be forming at the base of the Elevator.

I took one last look at Elara, sleeping fitfully, the silver creeping up her wrist like a beautiful, deadly vine.

"One wish," I whispered to the empty room.

I stepped out into the toxic night, leaving the door unlocked for the first time in years. I wouldn't be needing it tonight. Tonight, I was going to the Palace.

And I was going to tear it down, brick by gilded brick, until I got what was mine.

Chapter 2: The Gilded Cage

Dorian

There is a specific kind of silence that only money can buy.

It's not the quiet of a forest or the hush of an empty room. It's a vacuum. It's the sound of walls so thick they block out the screams of the city below. It's the sound of air that has been scrubbed, filtered, and scented with jasmine until it smells like nothing at all.

I hated it.

"Flex the digits, Your Highness."

I looked down at the doctor. He was a nervous little man with a clipboard and a sweat stain spreading on his collar. He was terrified of me. They all were. Not because I was the Prince, but because of the arm.

I lifted my left hand. The metal plates shifted with a soft, hydraulic hiss. The chrome caught the light of the chandelier—perfect, polished, cold. I made a fist. The servo-motors whirred, a sound like a microscopic drill boring into bone.

"Grip strength is at four hundred percent," the doctor mumbled, scribbling. "Neural integration seems stable. Any... phantom pain?"

"No," I lied.

It always hurt. It felt like dipping your arm into a bucket of ice water and leaving it there until the nerves screamed and then went numb, only to scream again. The metal didn't just replace the flesh; it ate it. The infection—the Gilt—stopped at my shoulder only because the mages pumped me full of suppressants every morning.

"Good. Good." He tapped the needle against a vein in my right arm—the human one—and drew a vial of dark red blood. "Your father will be pleased. The weapon is operating at peak efficiency."

The weapon.
That's all I was. A battery charger for the Crown. A shiny hood ornament on a rotting car.

"Get out," I said.

The doctor didn't argue. He bowed so low his nose almost brushed the marble floor, packed his kit, and scurried out like a cockroach caught in the kitchen light.

I sat up on the exam table, buttoning my shirt. Silk. White. Immaculate. I poured myself a drink from the crystal decanter on the sidebar. Amber liquid, eighty years old, tasted like smoke and oak. I drank it in one swallow.

"Leave me," I said to the shadows.

Two Royal Guards stepped out from the corners of the room. They were dressed in full plate armor, their faces hidden behind gold visors.

"Sir, protocol dictates—"

"Protocol dictates that I am your superior officer," I said, pouring another drink. "And I want to be alone. If anyone tries to kill me, I'll consider it a favor."

They hesitated. Then, with a synchronised clatter of boots, they left.

I counted the seconds. One. Two. Three.

I walked over to the balcony doors. They were locked, of course. For my protection. I pressed my metal palm against the glass. The cold didn't register.

I was bored. A bone-deep, marrow-sucking boredom that made me want to jump off the spire just to feel the wind. I was twenty-three years old, and I had everything a man could want: power, wealth, women, fear.

And I would have traded it all for a cheap cigarette and five minutes where no one looked at me like I was a ticking bomb.

Scritch.
A tiny sound. Like a mouse in the walls.

I didn't turn around. I watched the reflection in the glass of the balcony door.

A panel in the ceiling shifted. A shadow dropped down.

It was graceful, I'll give him that. The assassin landed in a crouch, silent as a whisper. Dressed in matte black, twin daggers drawn. He moved toward me, his eyes locked on the back of my neck.

I swirled the whiskey in my glass.

"You're putting too much weight on your left foot," I said.

The assassin froze.

I turned around slowly, leaning back against the glass. I didn't raise my hands. I didn't draw the sword resting on the table three feet away. I just looked at him.

"The floor is marble," I explained, swirling my drink. "It amplifies vibration. If you want to sneak up on a Chrome, you need soft-soled boots. Those are... what? Leather? Amateur."

The assassin's eyes narrowed behind his mask. He was confused. Victims were supposed to scream, or beg, or fight. They weren't supposed to offer a performance review.

"Prince Dorian," the assassin hissed. "For the Liberation."

"Yeah, yeah. Liberation, death to the tyrant, down with the Gilt. I know the script." I took a sip. "Well? Come on then. Stick me. Aim for the heart, though. The metal deflects off the ribs if you go too low."

I meant it. I lowered the glass, opening my chest to him. A clean death. A martyr's exit. It would piss my father off so much.

The thought made me smile.

The assassin roared—a rookie mistake—and lunged.

He covered the distance in a heartbeat. The dagger tip was an inch from my throat. I didn't blink. I waited for the bite.

Thwip.
A crossbow bolt took the assassin in the throat.

He gagged, the dagger clattering to the floor, and collapsed at my feet, choking on his own blood.

I sighed. "Dammit."

I looked up. Standing in the doorway, lowering a hand-crossbow, was Captain Voss.

Voss was the only thing in the Palace that wasn't polished. He was old leather and scar tissue, with a gray buzzcut and eyes that had seen too many wars. He didn't wear the gold visor. He didn't need to.

"You're ruining my fun, Voss," I said, stepping over the dying assassin to refill my glass.

"You have a strange definition of fun, Your Highness," Voss said, his voice like gravel in a blender. He walked over, checked the assassin's pulse, and then efficiently put a second bolt into the man's heart to end it. Mercy, not cruelty.

"He was sloppy," I said. "I was critiquing his form."

"He was three seconds away from slitting your throat."

"Two seconds. And I would have let him."

Voss looked at me then. Really looked at me. He was the only one who knew. He knew I wasn't reckless because I was brave; he knew I was reckless because I was checking out.

"Not today," Voss said quietly. "The King needs you."

"The King needs a battery." I downed the drink. "Clean this up. It clashes with the rug."

I started to walk past him, toward the bedroom. I needed to sleep. Or pass out. Whichever came first.

"The Iron Trials start tomorrow," Voss said to my back.

I stopped. "So?"

"So, the King expects you in the Royal Box. To choose a champion."

"I hate the Trials. It's just a bunch of shiny tin cans hitting each other with sticks until one of them falls over."

"There's a rumor," Voss said, holstering his crossbow. "Word from the Slags. They say the turnout is different this year. More... desperate."

"Desperate is boring, Voss. Desperate people beg."

"Desperate people fight," Voss corrected. "Like they have nothing to lose."

I looked at my metal hand. I clenched it, feeling the hydraulics whine. Nothing to lose. I knew what that felt like.

"Fine," I said. "I'll go. But if I die of boredom, I'm holding you personally responsible."

"Understood, sir."

I walked into my bedroom and slammed the door. The assassin's blood was already staining the white marble in the other room. I hoped it would leave a mark. I hoped it would rust.

But I knew the servants would scrub it clean before morning. In the Chrome City, nothing was allowed to be dirty. Not even death.

Chapter 3: The Cattle Call

Sara

The sun in the Chrome City was a liar.

Down in the Slags, the sun was a vague, bruised purple bruise behind the smog layer. Up here, three thousand feet above the poverty line, it was a blinding, white-hot spotlight that bounced off every polished surface and stabbed you right in the eyes.

I squinted, pulling the hood of my coat lower. The air was too thin. It lacked texture. I missed the taste of copper and soot. This air tasted like ozone and expensive perfume—the smell of people who had never had to scrub black grease out of their cuticles.

"Name?"

The clerk at the intake desk didn't look up. He was a drone, his face illuminated by the blue glow of a holographic slate. Behind him, the massive iron gates of the Colosseum loomed, swallowing the line of contestants one by one.

"Sara," I said.

"Surname?"

"None."

He paused, his stylus hovering. He looked up then, his nose wrinkling as if I'd just opened a sewage line. He took in my patchwork coat, the rebreather hanging around my neck, and the steel pipe strapped to my hip.

"Slag," he muttered, typing it in as if it were my last name. *Sara Slag.* "District 12?"
"District 14," I corrected. "The Scrapyard."

He snorted. "Sign here. It releases the Crown from liability in the event of dismemberment, incineration, or death."

I scrawled an X on the glass screen. "Do I get a copy?"

"Next!"

I was shoved forward by a wall of metal. I stumbled, catching my balance on a stanchion. Behind me stood a man who looked like a walking tank. He was encased in full plate armor, engraved with lions and eagles. His helmet had a plume of red feathers that probably cost more than my sister's life.

"Watch it, rat," the tank grumbled. His voice echoed inside his helmet.

I looked him up and down. "Nice suit," I said deadpan. "Did it come with the feathers, or did you have to pluck a giant chicken yourself?"

He bristled, his hand going to the jeweled hilt of his broadsword. "You don't belong here, trash. This is a contest for warriors. Not scavengers."

"You're right," I said, stepping out of his reach. "But when you trip in that sixty-pound can, you're going to look like a turtle on its back. I'll be sure to wave."

I slipped into the crowd before he could escalate.

The holding area was a cavernous stone chamber beneath the arena stands. It smelled of horse sweat, unwashed bodies, and adrenaline. There were five hundred of them. Five hundred hopefuls, idiots, and glory-hounds.

I leaned against a damp pillar, making myself small, and watched.

It was a sea of chrome. Plate mail, chain mail, scale mail. Shields polished to mirrors. Swords that had never chipped a bone. They were preening, stretching, practicing their forms. They moved in stiff, rehearsed patterns. *Hack, slash, parry.*

They were fighting the air. They were fighting the idea of an opponent.

Tin cans, I thought. *Waiting to be crushed.*

They didn't understand the terrain. I looked past them, up at the massive gears turning the ceiling vents. I looked at the floor—sand over stone, meaning traction would be loose. I looked at the shadows.

In the Slags, you didn't fight fair. You threw sand in eyes. You kicked knees backward. You used the environment. These guys? They were waiting for a bell to ring.

"Weapon check!"

A squad of Royal Guards moved through the crowd, confiscating unauthorized items. No firearms. No explosives. No poisons.

I stiffened. My hand drifted to my boot heel. The lockpicks were safe—they were part of the boot structure—but I had a serrated shiv taped to the inside of my belt that was technically "non-regulation."

A guard stopped in front of me. He held a magnetic wand. He waved it over my chest. Beep. My zipper.

He waved it over my hip. Beep. The steel pipe.

He frowned at the pipe. "Blunt force only?"

"It's a tool," I said. "I'm a mechanic."

"It's garbage," he sneered, but he moved on. He didn't check the waistband. He didn't check the boots. He saw a Slag girl with a piece of plumbing and assumed I'd be dead in the first round anyway.

Why waste time frisking a corpse?

A trumpet blast shook dust from the ceiling. The crowd went silent.

"Citizens of the Chrome! Welcome to the Iron Trials!"
The voice boomed from invisible speakers, magnified by magic. The floor beneath us rumbled. The massive portcullis at the far end of the chamber began to rise, grinding metal on stone.

Sunlight flooded in, slicing through the gloom. The roar of the crowd hit us like a physical wave—thousands of people screaming for blood.

"Here we go," the Tank from earlier muttered, drawing his sword. He marched forward, chest puffed out.

I stayed back. I watched the herd move.

I wasn't here to win a trophy. I was here to survive long enough to steal a key, break into a vault, and disappear. I didn't need to be the strongest gladiator in the pit.

I just needed to be the one they didn't see coming.

As the mass of bodies surged toward the light, I spotted something near the entrance. A loose grate in the floor, half-covered by sand. A tripping hazard.

The Tank marched right over it. His heavy boot caught the edge. He stumbled, flailing, his armor clanking loudly, but he caught himself.

I smirked and adjusted my gloves.

Terrain advantage: Sara.

I took a deep breath of the fake, perfume-scented air, gagged a little, and walked into the meat grinder.

Chapter 4: The Meat Grinder

Dorian

The Royal Box was designed to offer the best view of the carnage while shielding the nobility from the smell of perforated bowels.

It was soundproofed with a thick layer of aeromancy, turning the screams of the dying into a distant, muted hum, like a tea kettle boiling in another room. The glass was one-way and reinforced, so we could sip our sparkling wine and watch men butcher each other without worrying about a stray arrow ruining the hors d'oeuvres.

"Magnificent turnout," my father said.

King Aric stood at the edge of the glass, his hands clasped behind his back. He was wearing the Ceremonial Armor—solid gold, useless in a fight, but excellent for blinding peasants. He didn't look at me. He was watching the massacre below with the detached interest of an accountant auditing a ledger.

"Five hundred souls," I said, swirling the ice in my glass. "Statistically, three hundred will be dead by lunch. Magnificent efficiency."

My father turned his head slightly. The gold servos in his neck whirred. His infection—the Gilt—had taken his throat years ago. His voice was synthetic, a deep, buzzing baritone that vibrated in my teeth.

"Efficiency is how we survive, Dorian. The city needs energy. The blood spills, the mana rises. It is the ecosystem."

"It's a slaughterhouse, Father. Let's call a spade a spade."

"Watch your tone," he buzzed, turning back to the glass. "And drink less. You look sloppy."

I raised the glass in a silent toast to his back and drained it.

I hated the Trials. Not because of the violence—I was used to violence—but because of the pretension. Look at them down there. A sea of shining metal, clashing and banging. Knights from the High Districts prancing around in armor that cost more than a Slag family earned in a generation, practicing forms they learned in fencing school.

It was a ballet of ego.

"Voss," I muttered.

Captain Voss stepped out of the shadows, silent as a ghost. "Sir."

"Refill. And put something stronger in it. I'm starting to feel feelings."

Voss took the glass without a word. He poured from a flask on his belt, not the crystal decanter. Good man.

I leaned forward, resting my metal arm on the velvet railing. The weight of it threatened to crush the fabric. Below, the melee was in full swing. It was a mess. A chaotic swirl of steel and sand.

I watched a knight in blue enamel armor decapitate a gladiator who was armed with a fishing net. The crowd—the real crowd, in the open stands—roared.

"Boring," I whispered.

I scanned the arena, looking for something, anything, to break the monotony. A monster, maybe? They usually released the chimeras in the second round.

Then I saw her.

She was hard to spot amidst the flash of chrome. She was a smudge of brown and gray in a field of silver. No armor. No shield. Just a heavy coat, tactical pants, and... was that a piece of pipe?

She was cornered against the northern wall by a behemoth in red-plumed plate mail. I recognized the crest. House Sterling. Rich, pompous, and notoriously brutal.

"Another Slag about to be pasted," I thought. "Five seconds. Tops."

The Sterling knight raised a massive greatsword, winding up for a killing stroke that would cleave her in half. It was a textbook execute. Flashy. Slow.

The girl didn't back away. She didn't cower.

She dropped.

It was so fast I almost missed it. She hit the sand in a slide, kicking out with both boots. Not at his legs—at the sand.

A cloud of grit exploded upward, right into the knight's visor.

The knight faltered, blinding flailing. The greatsword swung wide, sparking harmlessly against the stone wall.

The girl was up before the dust settled. She didn't go for his sword arm. She didn't try to pierce the plate. She stepped inside his guard, grabbed the plume on his helmet with one hand to yank his head down, and drove her knee squarely into the codpiece.

Even through the soundproof glass, I flinched.

The knight folded. Armor or not, physics was physics.

As he crumpled to his knees, wheezing, she didn't pause to monologue. She didn't wait for applause. She spun around him, swung that rusty pipe like a baseball bat, and cracked it against the back of his helmet.

CLANG.
The knight went face-down in the dirt and didn't move.

I sat up straight.

"Well, hello," I murmured.

She wasn't done. While the knight was unconscious, she didn't kill him. She knelt quickly, her hands moving with a blur of dexterity. She patted down his belt. She cut a pouch free. She snatched a dagger from his boot sheath.

Then she stood up, kicked sand over his visor for good measure, and sprinted away before his allies could close in.

"Voss," I said, not taking my eyes off her. "Give me the scope."

Voss handed me a brass spyglass. I snapped it open and focused on the girl.

She was panting, backed into a shadow of a pillar. She wiped sweat and grease from her forehead. She wasn't pretty in the way the court ladies were pretty. She was sharp. fierce. Her eyes were darting around the arena, calculating angles, checking exits.

She looked at the other knights not as opponents, but as obstacles. Or prey.

"Who is that?" I asked.

Voss squinted. "Entry 412. No surname. Slag from the Scrapyard."

"She fights like a gutter rat," I said, a grin tugging at the corner of my mouth.

"She fights like she wants to live," Voss corrected.

"Look at her." I pointed. "She just tripped that guy with a length of chain she picked up off the ground. She's not fencing. She's brawling."

My father turned from the window, his golden faceplate impassive. "She is fighting without honor. Disgusting."

"Honor gets you dead, Father," I said, lowering the spyglass. "She just took down a Sterling knight with a handful of dirt and a plumbing fixture. That's not disgusting. That's art."

The girl—412—vanished into the chaos of the melee, weaving between two dueling giants to let them hit each other instead of her.

I felt a spark in my chest. A tiny flicker of something that wasn't boredom or self-pity.

I needed someone who could get into the Vault. I needed someone who could bypass the magical wards, pick the physical locks, and fit through the ventilation shafts. I didn't need a warrior who would challenge the guards to a duel. I needed a thief. A rat. Someone who understood that the only rule that mattered was survival.

I watched her reappear on the far side of the arena, tripping a heavy lancer and stealing his water skin while he struggled to stand up.

I took another sip of the whiskey. It tasted better this time.

"Keep an eye on Number 412, Voss," I said quietly.

"You think she'll make the finals?"

"I think," I said, watching her kick a man in the shin so hard he dropped his shield, "that she's going to be a massive pain in my ass. And I can't wait."

Chapter 5: First Contact

Sara

I didn't walk out of the arena. I limped.

The portcullis slammed shut behind me, cutting off the roar of the crowd and the smell of fresh butcher's work. The silence of the tunnels hit me harder than the Sterling knight's shield.

My hands were shaking. That was the adrenaline dump. It was a chemical crash, the body realizing it wasn't about to die and deciding to panic retroactively. I leaned against the cold stone wall, gasping for air that didn't taste like kicked-up sand.

"Three hundred," a voice echoed from down the hall. A medic, dragging a body by the heels. "Dead or incapacitated. Pit crew is going to be scrubbing gore out of the grouting for a week."

I ignored him. I checked my ribs. The Sterling knight's knee had caught me a glancing blow. Bruised, not broken. My knuckles were raw, split open from where I'd punched a squire's helmet visor. Stupid. Never punch metal with bone.

I needed water. I unclipped the stolen waterskin from my belt and took a swig. It was warm, but it was wet.

"Round Two in one hour!" a guard bellowed from the intersection. "Survivors to the Holding Pens!"

Holding Pens. Like we were livestock. Which, I suppose, we were.

I didn't go to the pens. I needed a minute where I wasn't smelling other people's fear. I pushed off the wall and ducked into a side corridor. The layout of the Colosseum was old—pre-Collapse architecture. The main paths were lit by magelights, but the service tunnels were dark, narrow, and unguarded.

I moved fast, my boots silent on the flagstones. I was looking for a vent, a alcove, anywhere to sit down and re-wrap my hands.

I rounded a sharp corner and ran face-first into a wall.

Not a stone wall. A wall of black silk and muscle.

"Oof." The breath left my lungs.

I bounced back, my hand instinctively going to the shiv in my waistband. I dropped into a crouch, teeth bared.

The obstacle didn't move. He didn't stumble. He didn't even flinch.

He was tall. That was the first thing I noticed. Annoyingly tall, with the kind of lean, predatory build that usually belonged to expensive fencing instructors. He was dressed in black—shirt unbuttoned at the collar, sleeves rolled up to the elbows—and he looked... clean.

Offensively clean.

His hair was dark, swept back in a way that looked like he'd just rolled out of a bed with thousand-thread-count sheets. And he was staring at me. Not with fear, and not with the bloodlust I'd seen in the arena.

He looked amused.

"You're in my way," I snapped, straightening up but keeping my hand near the knife.

He tilted his head. He had strange eyes. One was dark, almost black. The other caught the dim torchlight in a way that looked fractured.

"I believe you ran into *me*," he said. His voice was low, smooth. It sounded like expensive whiskey poured over gravel. "Usually, people apologize."

"Usually, people don't stand in the middle of service tunnels like lost tourists," I shot back. I stepped to the left to go around him.

He stepped to the left, blocking me.

I stepped to the right.

He stepped to the right.

I stopped. The adrenaline spike was back, hot and sharp. "Are you trying to get stabbed? Because I just put a guy in a coma for less."

He laughed. It wasn't a mocking laugh, exactly. It was surprised. "I saw. The Sterling knight. Very creative use of sand. Although, the knee to the groin was a bit... low brow."

"It worked."

"It was effective," he conceded. He leaned a shoulder against the wall, crossing his arms. He took up too much space. "You're Number 412. The Scrapyard girl."

"Sara," I corrected automatically, then regretted it. Names were power. "And who are you? Did you get lost on the way to the VIP bathroom?"

I looked him up and down, making a show of it. The silk shirt. The polished boots (leather, not steel). The lack of weapons.

"You're a spectator," I realized, sneering. "One of the Chrome bloods who likes to watch the animals bleed."

"I've seen better shows," he drawled. "The pacing in the first act was sluggish."

"Sorry we didn't die fast enough for you." I stepped forward, invading his personal space. In the Slags, you didn't back down. You pushed until the other guy broke. "Now move, pretty boy. Before I decide to make the second act more interesting."

I shoved him.

I meant to push him into the wall, to knock him off balance so I could slip past. I put my full weight into it, planting my hand in the center of his chest.

It was like shoving a statue bolted to the floor.

He didn't budge an inch. But beneath the silk of his shirt, under the heat of his skin, I felt something... wrong. It wasn't the give of muscle and bone. It was hard. Unyielding.

And for a split second, I felt a hum. A vibration against my palm. Like a machine idling.

I snatched my hand back as if I'd touched a hot stove.

He looked down at where I'd touched him, then back up at me. The amusement in his eyes sharpened into something colder.

"Careful," he said softly. "You don't know what you're touching."

"I know I'm touching a roadblock." I masked my unease with a scowl. "You think because you're rich you can just stand here? There are fifty killers walking down this hall in five minutes. If they find you, they'll peel that silk shirt off your corpse."

"Let them try," he said. And the terrifying thing was, he sounded like he meant it.

He finally pushed off the wall, clearing the path. He gestured with one hand—his left hand, I noticed. He moved it stiffly, or maybe just deliberately.

"Go ahead, 412. Run along. I think they're releasing the hydra next. You'll want to find a bigger pipe."

I hesitated. My instincts were screaming at me. *Predator. Danger. Wrongness.*
But I had a sister to save and a vault to rob. I didn't have time for cryptically arrogant rich boys.

"Thanks for the tip," I spat. "Try not to get blood on your shoes."

I brushed past him, making sure to shoulder-check him as I went. He felt like a rock.

I didn't look back until I hit the end of the corridor. When I finally glanced over my shoulder, the hallway was empty.

He was gone. Silent as smoke.

I rubbed the palm of my hand against my pants. I could still feel the ghost of that vibration. That low, mechanical thrum beneath the skin.

Weird, I thought. *Rich people are weird.*
I pushed him out of my mind. I had bigger problems.

Somewhere above me, gears were grinding. The Beast was waking up. And I needed to find a weapon that wasn't a piece of rusted plumbing.

Chapter 6: The Beast

Dorian

"It's sloppy engineering," I said, popping a grape into my mouth. "Look at the hydraulics on the neck joints. They're leaking fluid. If that thing turns its head too fast, it's going to decapitate itself."

My father didn't look away from the arena. "It is a marvel of bio-thaumaturgy, Dorian. The Clockwork Hydra is the pinnacle of the Guild's work."

"It's a giant, three-headed lizard held together with duct tape and prayer," I corrected.

Below us, the massive portcullis groaned open. The crowd screamed—a mix of terror and ecstasy.

The Hydra slithered out into the sunlight. It was a nightmare of flesh and industry. Its central body was organic—scaled, green, massive—but the three heads were grafted onto long, segmented necks made of brass and copper. Steam hissed from vents along its spine. Its eyes were glowing red lenses.

It roared, the sound amplified by a vox-caster embedded in its throat. A cloud of black smog belched from its jaws.

"Showtime," Voss muttered from the shadows.

In the arena, the remaining contestants scattered like roaches when the kitchen light snaps on. There were maybe forty left from the initial five hundred. They dove behind pillars, scrambled up the walls, or just curled into balls and prayed to gods who weren't listening.

I scanned the chaos for Number 412.

I found her near the eastern gate. She wasn't running. She was crouching behind a fallen statue, watching the Hydra's movement patterns. Calculating.

Smart girl, I thought. *Stay low. Let the idiots draw aggro.*

The Hydra lunged. The central head snapped up a knight in full plate mail like he was a piece of popcorn. *Crunch.* Metal crumpled. Red mist sprayed the sand.

The crowd went wild.

"Turn up the containment field," my father ordered the mage standing beside him. "The beast is agitated."

The mage, a sweating man in velvet robes, twisted a dial on his control amulet. "Field integrity at ninety percent, Your Majesty. It's... the beast is fighting the control collar. The pain receptors seem to be misfiring."

"Fix it," the King buzzed.

Down below, the Hydra swung its massive tail. It didn't aim for a gladiator. It aimed for the containment barrier separating the arena from the lower stands—the cheap seats, where the squires, the water-runners, and the poor sat.

Crack.

A web of blue lightning sizzled where the tail hit the invisible wall. The barrier held.

"Eighty percent," the mage squeaked.

The Hydra recoiled, shook its heads, and struck again. Same spot. Harder.

CRACK.

The air rippled violently. Sparks rained down on the screaming peasants in the front row.

"Father," I said, setting my glass down. "Shut it down. The inhibitor is failing."

"Let it play out," the King said, unmoved. "The barrier will hold. It was built by the finest—"

SHATTER.

The sound was like a cannon blast. The magical barrier didn't just fail; it exploded. The sheer kinetic force of the Hydra's third strike shattered the containment spell.

The crowd's scream shifted from excitement to primal terror.

The Hydra didn't hesitate. It ignored the gladiators. It surged toward the breach, its brass necks extending into the stands. It wanted fresh meat. Soft meat.

"Containment breach!" the mage shrieked, backing away. "I can't control it!"

"Useless," I hissed.

My father didn't move. He watched the chaos with mild annoyance, as if someone had spilled wine on the tablecloth.

I didn't ask for permission. I didn't think.

I vaulted over the velvet railing of the Royal Box.

"Dorian!" Voss shouted.

I fell forty feet.

The air rushed past my ears. I didn't use magic to slow my descent. I used physics. I aimed for the stone archway above the arena gate, tucked my knees, and landed.

The impact shattered the stone beneath my boots. I rolled, absorbing the momentum, and dropped the remaining ten feet to the sand.

Dust billowed around me. I stood up, straightening my cuffs.

The Hydra was fifty yards away, its massive body thrashing, dragging itself toward the screaming crowd. One of the brass heads was already snapping at a group of squires huddled against the wall.

I started running.

I wasn't fast like Sara. I was heavy. Every step dug a trench in the sand. I diverted power from the core in my chest to the arm. The metal plates shifted, locking into combat mode. The hum became a roar.

Output: 200%. Safety limits disabled.
The Hydra saw me. The central head turned, fixing those red lenses on the new threat. It recognized the signature of the Chrome. It recognized the enemy.

It hissed, a sound like a steam pipe bursting, and lunged at me.

I didn't dodge.

I planted my feet. I raised my left hand.

The massive brass jaw slammed into my open palm.

CLANG.
The force of the impact drove me back three feet, carving furrows in the ground. The metal groaned. My

shoulder screamed as the shockwave traveled up my skeleton.

But I held.

I gripped the Hydra's lower jaw with fingers that could crush diamonds. The servos whined, high and piercing.

"Down, boy," I grunted.

I torqued my body and slammed the head into the ground. The stone beneath the sand cracked. The head dazed, gears grinding in protest.

But it had three heads.

The left head swung around, aiming to bite me in half while I was grappling the center one. I couldn't block it. I braced for the impact.

Then I saw a flash of gray.

"Hey! Ugly!"

Sara.

She was standing on top of a fallen pillar, twenty feet away. She wasn't running for the exit. She was holding... was that a shield?

She hurled it. She threw it like a frisbee, putting her whole body into the spin. The shield sailed through the air and clang-banged off the Hydra's left eye lens.

Glass shattered. The left head shrieked, thrashing blindly.

It turned its attention away from me. It turned toward her.

"Sara, run!" I roared.

She didn't run. She looked past the monster.

I followed her gaze.

Trapped in the rubble near the barrier breach was a kid. Maybe twelve years old. A water-boy. His leg was pinned under a piece of masonry. The Hydra's right head—the one nobody was fighting—was snaking toward him.

Sara looked at the exit. Then she looked at the kid.

I saw the calculation in her eyes. *Self-preservation vs. Stupid Heroism.*

She swore—I saw her lips move—and sprinted toward the kid.

"Don't be an idiot," I growled, releasing the central head and charging forward.

Sara slid under the Hydra's swaying neck. She reached the kid, grabbed the rock pinning him, and heaved. She wasn't strong enough. The rock didn't move.

The right head reared back, opening its jaws. A jet of flammable gas hissed from its throat. It was charging a flame breath.

She couldn't move the rock. So she did the only thing she could.

She stood over the kid. She planted her feet, raised that pathetic piece of rusty pipe, and prepared to hit a ten-ton mechanical dragon in the nose.

She was going to die. She knew it. And she stood there anyway.

Finally, I thought, the adrenaline flooding my system like liquid gold. *Someone worth saving.*
I didn't run. I burned.

I pushed the output to 400%. The metal casing on my arm glowed white-hot. I leaped.

I hit the Hydra's right neck mid-air, tackling it like a linebacker. The sheer weight of my arm dragged the head down. The flame breath discharged harmlessly into the sand, turning the silica to glass in an instant.

I landed on top of the brass neck. I grabbed a loose heavy cabling near the base of the skull.

"Look away!" I shouted at Sara.

She looked up at me, eyes wide. She covered the kid's face.

I ripped.

With a sound like a train derailing, I tore the hydraulic lines and the main power conduit out of the Hydra's neck. Oil sprayed like black blood, coating me. Sparks showered the arena.

The head went limp instantly, crashing to the sand inches from Sara's boots.

The rest of the beast thrashed once, then shuddered and died as the system shock cascaded through its neural web.

Silence fell over the arena.

I stood on the carcass of the machine, oil dripping from my white shirt, my metal arm smoking in the cool air. I looked down.

Sara was staring up at me. She was covered in dust, holding a terrified kid, and clutching a bent pipe.

She looked from the dead mechanical head to me. Her gaze snagged on my face, then dropped to the glowing, smoking metal of my arm.

Recognition dawned.

"You," she breathed.

I wiped a splatter of oil from my cheek with my human hand. I smirked, though my heart was hammering against my ribs.

"Told you to find a bigger pipe," I said.

Guards began to pour into the arena, shouting orders, surrounding us. Voss was leading the charge.

I hopped down from the beast, landing softly in the sand. I walked up to her. She didn't back away this time. She stood her ground, shielding the kid behind her legs.

"You're the Prince," she said. It wasn't a question. It was an accusation.

"And you," I said, lowering my voice so only she could hear, "have a terrible survival instinct. Why save the runt?"

She wiped dirt from her nose, chin lifting defiantly. "Because he's not Chrome. He's one of us."

I looked at her. Dirty. Defiant. Alive.

"Get him out of here," I said, nodding to the kid. "Before I change my mind and let them arrest you both for trespassing."

She hesitated, then grabbed the kid's arm. "Come on."

She took two steps, then stopped and looked back at me. "Nice arm, Your Highness. Try not to rust."

Then she was gone, melting into the confusion of the crowd.

I stood there, surrounded by the wreckage of my father's toy, and for the first time in years, I didn't feel like dying.

I felt like hunting.

Chapter 7: The Interview

Sara

The room didn't smell like blood. It smelled like lemon verbena and judgment.

I sat on a velvet chair that cost more than my entire neighborhood, my boots resting on a mahogany table that was polished to a mirror shine. I kept my hands in my lap, mostly to hide the fact that they were shaking.

There were five of us left. The "Finalists."

The other four—three knights and a mercenary who looked like he chewed gravel for breakfast—had been taken into separate rooms for "evaluation." I'd been left here to marinate.

I checked the door again. Locked. Not a mechanical lock—I could have picked that with a hairpin—but a mag-lock. A humming blue seal that would probably fry my nervous system if I touched it.

"Great," I muttered, leaning back. "Survive the Hydra, die in a waiting room."

The door hissed open.

I didn't stand up. In the Slags, standing up when authority entered the room was an admission of guilt. I stayed seated, crossed my ankles on the table, and looked bored.

The Prince walked in.

He'd cleaned up since the arena. The oil-stained shirt was gone, replaced by a pristine charcoal tunic with silver embroidery. The metal arm was polished, gleaming under the harsh lights. He held a file in his human hand.

He didn't look at me. He walked to the other side of the table, pulled out a chair, and sat down with the slow, deliberate grace of an apex predator settling in for a meal.

He opened the file. He frowned. He flipped a page. He flipped another.

"It's blank," he said.

"I lead a private life," I said.

He looked up. His eyes—one dark, one fractured light—pinned me to the chair. Up close, he was devastatingly symmetrical, except for the jawline where skin met chrome. It made him look less like a man and more like a weapon wearing a human suit.

"No surname," he read. "No address. No employment history. No birth records." He closed the file. "You don't exist, Sara."

"I'm sitting right here, Your Highness."

"Are you? Because according to the City Census, the only things living in Sector 14 are rust-mites and refuse."

"I have a lot in common with the refuse," I said. "We're both good at finding things you people throw away."

He leaned back, studying me. He wasn't angry. He looked... entertained. That was worse. Anger I could predict. Amusement was a trap.

"You fought well today," he said. "Sloppy. But effective."

"I survived," I said. "That's the only metric that counts."

"You saved the water-boy."

"He owed me five credits."

Dorian actually laughed. It was a short, sharp sound. "You risked being incinerated for five credits?"

"Interest rates in the Slags are brutal."

He stood up and walked around the table. I tensed, my hand drifting toward my boot, but I stopped myself. I had been disarmed at the door. My pipe, my shiv, everything but the hidden picks were gone.

He stopped right next to my chair. He was close enough that I could smell him—soap, expensive leather, and the faint, ozone tang of high-voltage magic.

"Let's cut the crap," he said, his voice dropping an octave. "You're not a warrior. You didn't swing that pipe like a soldier. You swung it like a crowbar."

I kept my face blank. "I'm a mechanic. I fix things."

"You break things," he corrected. "You fight dirty. You cheat. You steal."

He reached out and tapped the heel of my boot with the toe of his polished shoe.

"And you walk like you're hiding something. My guess? Lockpicks. Or a knife."

My heart slammed against my ribs. He knew.

"If I'm such a criminal," I said, meeting his gaze, "call the guards. Have me arrested. Why are we talking?"

"Because I have plenty of knights," Dorian said softly. He leaned down, placing his metal hand on the arm of my chair. The cold radiated through my sleeve. "I have armies of men who follow orders, fight with honor, and die exactly when I tell them to. They are boring."

He brought his face closer to mine. "You fight like a stray."

I didn't flinch. I leaned in, narrowing the gap between us until I could see the pores of his skin and the rivets in his neck.

"And you dress like a disco ball," I snapped. "We all have our flaws."

For a second, I thought he was going to kill me. His eyes widened. The metal hand on my chair tightened, the velvet groaning under the pressure.

Then, the corner of his mouth twitched.

"A disco ball," he repeated.

"Solid silver embroidery?" I gestured at his tunic. "It's a bit much, don't you think? You look like you're trying to signal a landing craft."

He straightened up, stepping away. He wasn't offended. He looked delighted.

"It is traditional Royal garb," he said, adjusting his cuff. "But I appreciate the fashion advice from a woman wearing trousers made of tarp."

"It's canvas. And it's durable."

"It's hideous." He walked back to the other side of the table. "What do you want, Sara? If you win. What's the Wish?"

I hesitated. This was the test.

"Money," I lied. "Enough to buy a ticket out of the city. To the coast. Where the air is clean."

"Liar," he said instantly.

"Excuse me?"

"If you wanted money, you would have stripped the gems off that Sterling knight's hilt before you ran. You didn't. You took his water." He watched me closely. "You don't want to leave the city. You want something *inside* the city."

He was too sharp. I had to pivot.

"My sister," I said. It was half-truth. "She's sick. I want the best doctors in the Gilded Sector to look at her."

He paused. The amusement faded slightly, replaced by something unreadable. "The Rust?"

I didn't answer. I didn't have to.

"Doctors can't fix the Rust, Sara. You know that. There is no cure."

"There's the Elixir," I said. The word hung in the air between us. "That's what the King takes, isn't it? To stay golden? To keep the infection from eating his brain?"

Dorian went very still. The hum of his arm increased in pitch.

"The Elixir is a myth," he said flatly. "A fairy tale for the poor."

"Then why are you still alive?" I asked, looking pointedly at his arm. "Because by all accounts, with that much metal in you, you should be a statue by now."

The tension in the room spiked. This was dangerous ground. I was accusing the Crown of hoarding the cure. People disappeared for less.

Dorian walked to the door. He placed his human hand on the panel.

"The interview is over," he said.

I stood up, my legs shaky. "Did I pass?"

He looked back at me. "You insulted my clothes, lied to my face, and accused my family of treason."

"So... no?"

"Go to the barracks, 412," he said, the mag-lock disengaging with a hiss. "Get a shower. You smell like a landfill."

"You smell like a battery," I shot back, walking to the door.

I paused at the threshold. I couldn't help it.

"Hey," I said.

He looked at me.

"Thanks," I said gruffly. "For the Hydra. You hit hard for a disco ball."

"Get out of my sight, Rat."

But as the door slid shut between us, I saw it.

He was smiling.

Chapter 8: The Selection

Dorian

My father didn't sit on the throne. He docked into it.

The Golden Throne wasn't a chair; it was a life-support system masquerading as furniture. Thick cables, braided with gold and copper, snaked from the backrest and plugged directly into the ports along King Aric's spine.

When he moved, the room hummed. When he spoke, the sound vibrated in the fillings of your teeth.

"Review the candidates," Aric commanded.

A holographic array flickered to life in the center of the room, projecting five spinning busts of the finalists.

First was Ser Kaelen of House Sterling. The tank Sara had humiliated. He was conscious again, looking bruised and vengeful.

"Strength: 9/10," the automated readout droned. "Loyalty: Absolute. Combat Style: Heavy Infantry."

"He is the logical choice," my father buzzed. He didn't have facial expressions anymore—his face was a frozen mask of gold alloy—but I could hear the approval in his synthesized voice. "House Sterling has served the Crown for three centuries. He will make a fine addition to the Guard."

"He's a moron," I said, leaning against a marble pillar, swirling a fresh glass of scotch. "He moves like a glacier. The Hydra would have eaten him for a snack if the girl hadn't intervened."

"Durability is a virtue," Aric countered. "He takes orders."

"He takes up space." I waved my hand. "Next."

The hologram cycled. A mercenary from the Eastern expanse. A battle-mage from the Guild. Another knight. All of them strong. All of them disciplined. All of them Chrome.

Then, the hologram flickered to the fifth slot.

Entry 412. Sara.

The projection was grainy. It showed her scowling, a smudge of grease on her cheek, that ridiculous coat pulled tight.

"Zero combat training," the readout stated. "Criminal record: Probable. Status: Slag."

"Remove her," Aric said instantly. "She is a contaminant."

"She's the winner," I said.

The hum of the throne spiked. The cables hissed as coolant cycled through my father's veins. He turned his head slowly, the gold servos grinding.

"Explain."

I walked toward the hologram, walking through the projection of the Sterling knight to stand next to Sara's flickering image.

"Look at them, Father. Look at your 'logical' choices. They fight because they were trained to. Because they want glory. Because they want to wear the white cloak and stand in the hallway looking pretty."

I gestured to Sara.

"She fought a ten-ton mechanical beast with a piece of plumbing because she didn't want to die. She doesn't care about glory. She doesn't care about you. She hates us."

"And this is a selling point?" Aric asked, his voice dropping to a dangerous, sub-bass rumble. "A bodyguard who hates her charge is a liability."

"A bodyguard who loves her life is an asset," I corrected. "She's paranoid. She watches the exits. She checks for traps. These knights? They expect a duel. They expect the enemy to bow before attacking. She expects a knife in the back."

I took a sip of the scotch, letting the burn settle in my chest.

"We have enough soldiers, Father. We have an army of tin soldiers who march in lockstep. I don't need a soldier. I need a survivor."

I need a thief, I thought, but I didn't say it.
I needed someone who could pick the triple-tumbler lock on the Vault. I needed someone small enough to fit in the ventilation shafts of the Power Core. I needed someone who looked at a impossible system and saw the cracks.

I had seen her eyes in that interview room. She wasn't looking at me; she was looking at my pockets. She was casing the joint.

"She is trash from the Scrapyard," Aric said. "She will steal the silverware."

"Let her," I said. "I have plenty of spoons."

"She is unrefined. She will embarrass the Crown."

"Good," I smiled, sharp and cold. "The Crown could use a little embarrassment. It keeps us humble."

My father stared at me. The red lenses of his eyes brightened. He was calculating. Running the numbers. He didn't care about my safety—he cared about the asset. The Prince. The Battery.

"You are trying to provoke me," Aric concluded. "You choose the rat to mock the tradition."

"I choose the rat because she's the only one who won't bore me to death before the assassination attempts start."

A long silence stretched between us. The only sound was the rhythmic *thump-thump* of the pumps circulating the Elixir through the King's body.
"Very well," Aric said finally. "It is your life to risk. If she fails to protect you, the cost comes out of your allowance."

"Understood."

"However," the King added, raising a golden finger. "She is Slag. She carries the risk of rust. She will be scrubbed. She will be uniformed. And she will be watched. If she steps out of line, Dorian... if she becomes a threat..."

"I'll kill her myself," I promised.

And I meant it. If she got in the way of the plan—if she tried to sell me out, or run away before I got what I wanted—I would end her.

But until then? She was my ticket to the blackout.

"Make the announcement," the King ordered the unseen scribes in the shadows. "Prince Dorian selects the Scrapyard girl."

I turned to leave. I had what I wanted.

"Dorian," my father called out as I reached the heavy doors.

I stopped, hand on the latch.

"Do not mistake amusement for affection," the King buzzed. "Pets are entertaining. But when they bite, they are put down."

I looked back at him—a man who had traded his humanity for immortality, piece by piece, until there was nothing left but gold and hunger.

"She's not a pet, Father," I said. "She's a tool. And I intend to use her until she breaks."

I walked out.

In the hallway, Voss was waiting. He looked tired.

"You picked her," Voss said. It wasn't a question.

"I did."

"She's going to be trouble."

"I'm counting on it," I said. "Get her out of the barracks. Move her to the East Wing. Put her in the suite next to mine."

Voss raised an eyebrow. "That's a security risk."

"No. That's a leash. I want her where I can see her. I want to know when she sleeps, when she eats, and when she tries to pick the lock on the window."

"And the others?" Voss asked. "The knights?"

"Send them home with a commemorative ribbon," I said, starting down the hall toward my chambers. "The game has changed, Voss. We're not playing soldiers anymore."

I flexed my metal hand. The servos whined.

"We're playing Cops and Robbers."

Chapter 9: Room Service

Sara

The bed was a lie.

It was the size of my entire apartment back in the Scrapyard. It had four pillows, a duvet that felt like it was stuffed with clouds, and sheets so white they hurt my eyes.

I hated it immediately.

"Your quarters, Miss... ah, Sara," the steward said. He was a thin man with a pinched nose and a uniform that looked stiff enough to stand up on its own. He stood by the door, refusing to step onto the carpet.

I didn't blame him. I was still wearing my arena clothes. There was dried hydra oil on my sleeve, dust in my hair, and I smelled like burnt ozone and sweat. If I stepped on that pristine white rug, it would probably scream.

"It's... spacious," I said, keeping my back to the wall. Never stand in the middle of a room you haven't swept for traps.

"The East Wing is reserved for the Royal Guard and high-ranking guests," the steward sniffed. "You have a private bath"—he gestured to a door on the left—"a wardrobe"—he gestured right—"and a direct line to the kitchen."

He pointed to a small brass panel on the wall with a speaking tube.

"You mean I yell into the wall and food appears?"

"You speak clearly into the receiver, and the kitchen staff will accommodate reasonable requests." He looked me up and down. "Within dietary restrictions, of course. The Royal Physician will be by later to administer your... vitamins."

Vitamins. He meant the suppressants. The stuff they gave Slags to keep us from infecting the furniture.
"Is that all, Jeeves?"

"It's Reginald."

"Right. Thanks, Reggie. Don't let the door hit you."

He pursed his lips so tight they disappeared, gave a stiff bow, and backed out. The heavy oak door clicked shut. I heard the lock engage.

I waited five seconds. Ten.

Then I moved.

I didn't go to the bed. I went to the window. It was floor-to-ceiling glass, offering a stunning view of the Chrome City. Spires of glass and gold pierced the sky. Floating platforms drifted lazily between towers. It was beautiful.

It was also a sheer drop of two hundred feet to the next terrace.

I pressed my hands against the glass. Sealed. No latch. Reinforced panes.

"Fishbowl," I muttered. "Great."

I turned my attention to the room. If I couldn't get out, I could at least see what I could loot.

I started with the desk. Mahogany. Heavy. I opened the drawers. Stationary. Wax seals. A letter opener that looked like solid silver.

Swiped. The opener went into my boot.

I moved to the small dining table in the corner. It was set for one. Crystal glasses. Porcelain plates. And—jackpot—silverware.

Real silver. Heavy. Hallmark stamped on the back.

I grabbed a spoon. It weighed as much as a servo-motor. This single spoon could buy Elara enough meds for a week.

I shoved it into my pocket. Then the fork. Then the knife. Then the napkin ring.

I felt a twinge of shame—just a small one. I was the Prince's personal champion now. I technically had a salary. I shouldn't be stealing cutlery like a common thief.

But old habits didn't die; they just got better opportunities. In the Slags, you took what you could, when you could, because you never knew when the luck would run out.

I did a sweep of the bathroom. It was bigger than the community showers in Sector 14. Marble everywhere. Gold faucets. A tub deep enough to drown in.

There were little bottles of soap and shampoo lined up on the counter. *Lavender and Honey. Sandalwood and Myrrh.*

I swept them all into my pockets. Soap was currency.

I was just weighing a heavy crystal perfume bottle in my hand, wondering if it would fit in my coat, when I noticed the other door.

It was in the far wall of the bedroom, obscured by a heavy velvet tapestry. It didn't have a handle on this side. Just a keyhole.

I walked over to it, stepping carefully on the white carpet, leaving faint dusty boot-prints that satisfied a petty part of my soul.

I pressed my ear to the wood.

Silence.

But not total silence. There was a hum. A low, rhythmic thrumming sound. Like a generator. Or a very large, very powerful engine.

The Prince.

My stomach dropped. This wasn't just a guest suite. This was the adjoining room. I was sleeping ten feet away from the monster who had crushed a hydra's skull with his bare hand.

"Leash," I whispered.

He hadn't picked me because I was good. He picked me because he wanted to keep an eye on me.

I knelt down, pulling the lockpick from my boot heel. It was a reflex. I needed to know if I *could* open it. I didn't intend to go in—I wasn't suicidal—but a locked door was an itch I had to scratch.

I slid the tension wrench into the keyhole. I felt for the pins. One. Two. Three...

Click.

The lock turned.

I froze. I hadn't expected it to be that easy. Royal security was a joke.

I didn't open it. I just sat there, staring at the brass knob, knowing that on the other side was Dorian. The Chrome Prince. The man who looked at me like I was a fascinating insect.

My stomach growled, loud and angry, breaking the tension. I hadn't eaten since yesterday morning.

I pulled the picks out, re-locked the door (safety first), and stood up.

I walked over to the brass speaking tube on the wall. I felt ridiculous. I pressed the button.

"Kitchen," a tinny voice responded instantly.

"I want..." I paused. What did rich people eat? "I want a steak. Rare. And potatoes. And bread. Lots of bread."

"Beverage?"

"Water. In a bottle. Sealed." I wasn't drinking anything they poured into a glass.

"It will be up shortly."

I slumped onto the ridiculous bed, boots still on. I pulled the silver spoon out of my pocket and twirled it through my fingers.

I was trapped in a gilded cage, sleeping next to a living weapon, surrounded by people who wanted to scrub the Slag off my skin.

I looked at my reflection in the back of the spoon. Distorted. Dirty. Sharp.

"One wish," I whispered to myself.

I tucked the spoon back into my pocket and patted the shiv in my waistband.

Let them send the food. Let them send the tailor. Let them send the Prince.

I wasn't going to rust. I was going to eat their steak, steal their silver, and burn this whole pretty palace to the ground.

Chapter 10: The Rules

Dorian

I waited until she finished the steak.

I could hear her through the wall. Not the chewing—the walls were thick enough to block that—but the *movement*. The restless pacing. The thud of heavy boots on the velvet carpet. The distinct, metallic *clink* of silverware being slid into a pocket.

She was predictable. A magpie in a combat coat.

I sat at my desk, staring at the blueprints of the City Vaults. The containment specs for the Heart of the City were complex. Triple-warded, physically locked, and guarded by a construct that made the Hydra look like a wind-up toy.

I needed a thief. I had one. Now I just needed to make sure she didn't get herself arrested for petty larceny before the main event.

I stood up, rolled the neck of my tunic to release the tension in my shoulders, and walked to the adjoining door.

I didn't knock. It was my palace, my suite, my door.

I turned the handle. It opened smoothly. I noted with a smirk that she had re-locked it after picking it earlier. Considerate.

I stepped into her room.

Sara was sitting cross-legged on the massive bed, surrounded by a fortress of pillows. She had the remnants of a T-bone steak on a plate in her lap and a piece of bread in one hand.

She didn't scream. She didn't drop the bread. She went instantly still, her eyes snapping to me, tracking the threat level. Her free hand drifted toward her waist.

"Don't," I said, leaning against the doorframe. "If you pull a knife on me, I'll have to take it. And I really don't want to get grease on my boots."

She swallowed the mouthful of bread with a grimace. "Knocking is polite. Even for Chrome."

"This is the Royal Wing, Sara. Privacy is a privilege, not a right. And considering you're currently hoarding half the Crown's silver service in your cargo pants, I'd say your privileges are suspended."

She wiped her mouth with the back of her hand. "I don't know what you're talking about."

"The left pocket," I said, pointing. "It's clinking. Unless you have a very noisy hip bone, that's a soup ladle."

She glared at me, defiance radiating off her like heat. Slowly, reluctantly, she reached into her pocket and pulled out the silver ladle. She tossed it onto the bed.

"It fell in," she said deadpan.

"And the salt shaker?"

She pulled out a crystal shaker. Tossed it.

"And the napkin ring."

She pulled out the silver ring. Tossed it.

"The soap?"

She hesitated. "The soap is consumable. I'm allowed to be clean."

"You're allowed to *use* the soap, not run a black market beauty supply out of your coat." I sighed, walking further into the room. "Keep the soap. But the silverware stays."

She scowled, but she didn't argue further. She knew she was caught.

I stopped at the foot of the bed. She looked small in the middle of all that white linen. Small, dirty, and dangerous. Like a razor blade hidden in a wedding cake.

"We need to set some ground rules," I said. "If you're going to live here without getting executed."

"I'm listening," she said, tearing off another piece of bread.

"Rule One," I said, holding up a finger. "Do not touch me. Do not shove me in hallways. Do not tackle me. The only reason you aren't dead from the first time is because I was amused. I am no longer amused."

"Fine," she mumbled around the bread. "You're cold anyway."

"Rule Two," I continued. "Do not speak to the staff. Do not speak to the guards. Do not speak to anyone unless I tell you to. You are my bodyguard, not a diplomat. If someone asks you a question, you glare at them until they go away. Can you manage that?"

"Glaring is my primary language."

"Good. Rule Three." I stepped closer, looming over the bed. "Stop trying to map the vents."

Sara froze. Her eyes darted to the desk on the far side of the room.

I walked over to it. She had stolen a piece of heavy cream cardstock—probably an invitation to a gala—and flipped it over. On the back, drawn in charcoal (likely from the fireplace), was a crude but accurate diagram of the suite's airflow system.

She had marked the intake vents, the outflow, and the service access.

"I like to know my exits," she said defensively from the bed.

I picked up the card. I studied the charcoal lines.

"You have the intake flow reversed," I said.

"What?"

"Here." I tapped the paper. "This shaft? The one you marked as an escape route? That's the heat exchange for the lower boilers."

I reached for the quill on the desk. I dipped it in the inkwell.

Sara scrambled off the bed, abandoning her food. She crossed the room in three strides to stand next to me, watching suspiciously.

"If you crawl into that vent," I said, sketching a heavy X over her line, "you will be vaporized by superheated steam in approximately four seconds. There won't even be a body left to bury. Just a smell of burnt canvas and bad decisions."

She stared at the paper, then up at me. Her eyes were wide.

"Why are you telling me this?"

"Because I invested time in you," I said, my voice flat. "And I hate waste."

I moved the quill to the north wall of the diagram. I drew a new line. Precise. elegant.

"The servant's passage runs behind the vanity mirror," I explained, drawing the latch mechanism. "It's narrow, but you'll fit. It drops out into the laundry chute three floors down. It's dirty, but it's cold. You won't cook."

I handed the card back to her.

She took it carefully, avoiding touching my hand. She looked at the drawing. Then she looked at my hand—the human one—that held the quill.

I saw her gaze linger. She was looking at my fingers. Long, unscarred, stained slightly with ink. She watched the way I twirled the quill before setting it down.

It was a look I wasn't used to. Usually, people stared at the metal arm with horror, or the human arm with relief. She was looking at the human hand with... calculation. Like she was wondering if it could hurt her as much as the metal one.

"Why the laundry chute?" she asked, her voice quiet.

"Because if the Palace is breached," I said, turning to face her, "that is the only exit the guards won't be watching. They protect the gold. They don't protect the dirty linens."

I stepped in close. The air between us crackled. She smelled like the steak she'd just eaten and the stolen lavender soap in her pocket.

"I'm not keeping you here to polish my armor, Sara," I said low. "I'm keeping you here because you see the cracks in the walls. Keep looking for them. But don't use them until I say so."

She looked up at me, clutching the diagram to her chest. Her chin went up. Defiant to the end.

"And if I decide to leave tonight?"

"Then you can take your chances with the steam," I said.

I walked to the door. I paused with my hand on the knob.

"Oh. And Rule Four," I added over my shoulder.

"There's a Rule Four?"

I glanced back. "The cleaning staff comes at nine. If you're still hoarding that soup ladle, they *will* report it. Put it back on the tray."
"It's a nice ladle," she muttered.

"Goodnight, Rat."

I closed the door. I listened.

I heard her exhale, a long, shaky breath. I heard the rustle of paper as she hid the map.

Then, after a long pause, I heard the soft *clink* of the silver ladle being put back onto the porcelain plate.

I smiled, staring at the closed door.

Obedience, I thought. *We're making progress.*

Chapter 11: The Dress Code

Sara

The next morning, my door didn't open. It was breached.

I was awake before the lock clicked—sleeping in a strange place meant sleeping with one eye open and a hand on a weapon—but I wasn't prepared for the assault team.

It wasn't guards. It was worse.

Three women and a man swept into the room like a tactical squad armed with measuring tapes and judgment. They were Chrome staff—immaculate, silent, and terrifyingly efficient.

"Up," the man said. He held a garment bag like it contained the Crown Jewels.

"I'm not decent," I growled, pulling the duvet up to my chin. I was wearing a tank top and boxers I'd stolen from a clothesline in District 12 three years ago. They were comfortable. They were also gray with age.

"We have seen worse," one of the women said, stripping the duvet off me with a strength that suggested she wrestled bears on her days off. "The King has ordered the asset be scrubbed and uniformed."

"I'm not an asset," I snapped, scrambling out of bed and reaching for my pants. "And I have clothes."

"You have rags," the man corrected. He snapped his fingers. "Burn the coat."

My head whipped around. One of the women was holding my coat—my heavy, patch-work, grease-stained coat with the secret pockets and the hidden shiv.

"Touch that coat and you lose a finger," I said. My voice dropped to that low, dangerous register that usually made junkies back off in the Scrapyard.

The staff didn't even blink. They were palace trained. They probably dealt with tantrums from inbred dukes daily.

"Sanitation protocol," the woman said, dropping the coat into a bio-hazard bag. "It carries spores."

I lunged. "My tools are in there!"

Two of the women intercepted me. They didn't hit me; they herded me. They used their bodies to block my path, steering me relentlessly toward the bathroom.

"The Prince has provided replacements for all necessary equipment," the man said, unzipping the garment bag. "Now. Scrub. The gala is in two hours."

"Gala?" I dug my heels into the carpet. "I thought I was guarding a door, not attending a party."

"The Prince is the door," the man sighed, looking exhausted. "Wherever he goes, you go. And he cannot be seen with a bodyguard who smells like... what is that? Diesel and regret?"

"It's character," I spat.

They shoved me into the bathroom. They didn't lock the door, but the implication was clear: *Come out clean, or we come in with scrub brushes.*

I turned on the shower. The water was hot enough to boil a lobster. I stood under it, watching the gray water swirl down the drain. I scrubbed until my skin was pink and raw, trying to wash off the Slag.

It didn't work. You can't wash off where you come from. It's in the blood. It's in the way you look at a room and count the exits before you count the people.

When I came out, wrapped in a towel that was softer than my bed at home, the assault team was waiting.

"Arms up," the man ordered.

I dropped the towel. He didn't react. He just started dressing me.

First came the under-layer. A body suit made of some black, moisture-wicking material that felt like a second skin. Then came the armor.

It wasn't plate. It wasn't chain. It was leather—black, boiled leather, reinforced with steel ribbing. It was a corset, essentially, but weaponized. They cinched it tight.

"I can't breathe," I wheezed. "I need lung capacity to fight."

"Fashion requires sacrifice," the man muttered, tightening the laces until my ribs groaned.

Next came the pants. Tactical weave, high-waisted, tight enough to cut off circulation but flexible enough to kick someone in the head. Then the boots. Knee-high, polished black leather with steel caps on the toes.

I stomped my heel. Hollow. Good. I could transfer the picks later.

Finally, they strapped on the belt. It was wide, heavy, and fitted with holsters for daggers I didn't have yet.

"Done," the man said, stepping back.

He gestured to the full-length mirror.

I looked.

I didn't recognize the person staring back.

She was tall. Lethal. The outfit was black on black on black, hugging every curve, emphasizing lines I usually tried to hide under baggy canvas. The corset pushed my chest up. The pants highlighted the muscle in my thighs.

I looked like a fetishized version of an assassin. I looked like something a rich man bought to scare his friends and turn on his mistress.

"I look ridiculous," I said. "I look like a dominatrix for the infantry."

"You look like the Royal Guard," the man said, packing up his kit. "Hair."

One of the women attacked my head. She pulled my messy, grease-streaked hair back into a severe, tight braid that was pinned against my skull so it couldn't be grabbed in a fight.

They left as quickly as they had arrived, taking my old clothes—my history—with them in a sealed bag.

I stood alone in the silent room, feeling exposed. The leather creaked when I moved. The corset dug into my hips. I felt like a doll in shrink-wrap.

The door to the adjoining suite opened.

Dorian walked in.

He was dressed for the gala. Black formal military dress, high collar, silver epaulets. The metal arm was polished to a mirror sheen, gleaming against the dark fabric. He looked devastating. He looked like the Prince of a kingdom that crushed people like me for fuel.

He stopped dead when he saw me.

His eyes swept over me, starting at the boots, traveling up the legs, over the corset, and landing on my face. He didn't blink. His gaze felt physical, like a touch.

I crossed my arms over my chest, trying to hide. The leather squeaked.

"Say it," I snapped. "Get the joke out of your system."

Dorian walked a slow circle around me. He was inspecting me like he'd inspected the Hydra. Checking for flaws.

"Standard issue Shadow Guard uniform," he mused. "Modified for... aesthetic appeal, apparently."

"It's a straightjacket," I muttered. "If I have to bend over, I'm going to snap a rib."

He stopped in front of me. He tilted his head, his mismatched eyes narrowing.

"You clean up nice," he said, his voice dry. "For a piece of Slag."

I bristled. My hand went to the empty belt where a weapon should be. "Careful, Chrome. I can still break your nose, corset or not."

"I don't doubt it."

He stepped closer. He reached out. I flinched, expecting him to touch the corset, maybe test the leather.

He didn't. He reached past me, to the wardrobe.

He pulled out a heavy, charcoal-gray cloak. It was wool, lined with silk. Practical. Warm. And big.

He shook it out and swung it around my shoulders.

The weight of it settled on me, covering the ridiculous corset, hiding the curves, shielding me from the air and his eyes.

I blinked, surprised. I looked up at him. He was adjusting the clasp at my throat, his metal fingers deft and careful not to pinch my skin.

"I hired a bodyguard," Dorian said quietly, his eyes fixed on the clasp. "Not a showgirl."

He smoothed the shoulders of the cloak.

"Keep the cloak on," he ordered. "The court is full of sharks. No need to put blood in the water."

He stepped back, admiring his handiwork. I looked less like a sex object and more like a shadow. A dangerous, shapeless shadow.

"Better?" he asked.

I touched the wool. It smelled like him. Cedar and ozone.

"It's... heavy," I said. But I didn't take it off. I pulled it tighter.

"Good," Dorian said, turning toward the door. "Heavy reminds you it's there. Let's go, 412. Try not to stab any Dukes unless they touch you first."

"What happens if they touch me first?"

He glanced back, a wicked glint in his human eye.

"Then aim for the throat."

Chapter 12: The Ambush

Dorian

The State Dinner was, as expected, a torture device disguised as a meal.

The Grand Hall was suffocating. Five hundred candles floated near the ceiling, dripping magic wax that vanished before it hit the floor. The air smelled of roasted peacock, heavy wine, and the desperate ambition of minor dukes trying to secure a trade deal with the Crown.

I sat at the High Table, to the right of my father. The King wasn't eating. He was docked into a specialized chair that trickled a nutrient paste directly into his veins, but he went through the motions of cutting meat with a golden knife to make the guests feel less like they were dining with a necromancer's experiment.

I drank. It was the only way to blur the edges of the room.

"Lord Vane is looking at you," I murmured into my glass.

"He's looking at my neck," a voice whispered from the shadows behind my chair. "He's wondering if a garrote would slice through the leather collar."

Sara.

She stood three feet behind me, blending into the heavy velvet drapes. The cloak I'd given her swallowed her frame, making her look like a wraith. Only her eyes were visible, scanning the room with a restless, paranoid intensity that made the Royal Guards look like statues.

"He's a textile merchant, Sara. He's looking at the embroidery on your cloak. Relax."

"I don't relax," she whispered back. "Not when there are this many knives in one room."

I took a sip of wine, hiding a smile. She was right, of course. Everyone in this room had a knife; most were just metaphorical.

I watched her reflection in the polished silver of my goblet. She hadn't touched the food on the side table provided for the guard. She hadn't moved a muscle in two hours, except for her eyes. She was miserable, suffocated by the perfume and the pretension.

I felt a perverse kind of satisfaction. *Welcome to my world, Rat.*

"My loyal subjects," King Aric buzzed. He didn't stand—the cables prevented it—but his voice amplified, silencing the hall instantly. "Tonight we celebrate the anniversary of the Unification. The triumph of Order over Chaos."

Applause rippled through the room. Polite. Terrified.

"Order," Aric continued, his golden hand clenching on the table, "is the wall that keeps the rust at bay. It is the iron spine of our society."

I rolled my eyes. I'd heard this speech a thousand times. *Order. Iron. Compliance.*

"Hey," Sara whispered. The tone of her voice had changed. It wasn't snarky anymore. It was sharp.

I tilted my head back slightly. "What?"

"The waiters," she murmured. "The ones bringing the dessert course. Their boots."

"What about them?"

"They're heavy. Weighted. Those aren't service shoes. Those are combat boots."

I frowned, glancing at the line of servers marching in with silver platters. They moved with a synchronized, heavy cadence.

"Maybe the soufflé is heavy," I deadpanned.

"Dorian," she hissed, dropping the honorific. "Look at their hands. No tremors. No strain. But the veins in their necks are popping. They're adrenaline-dumping."

I set my glass down. I looked at the server nearest to the High Table. He was sweating. His eyes were fixed not on the table, but on the King.

My internal sensors spiked. *Threat Detected.*
"Father—" I started to say.

The server dropped the platter.

It didn't shatter. It exploded.

Sara
The world turned into noise and fire.

I didn't think. I didn't process the flash of magical energy that erupted from the silver platter. I just moved.

"Down!" I screamed.

I launched myself over the back of the Prince's chair.

I hit Dorian hard, tackling him out of his seat just as the shockwave hit. We went down in a tangle of limbs, chair legs, and expensive fabric.

BOOM.

The concussion wave slammed into us like a physical hammer. The heavy oak table splintered. The floating candles were extinguished instantly, plunging the room into a chaos of smoke and screaming darkness.

Debris rained down on us. Chunks of marble. Shards of glass. A piece of the ceiling the size of a coffin crashed into the floor inches from my head.

I covered his head with my arms, burying my face in his shoulder, shielding him with my body. The heavy wool cloak he'd given me took the brunt of the shrapnel, glass slicing into the fabric but not the skin.

The roaring stopped, replaced by the high-pitched ringing in my ears and the screams of the wounded.

For a second, I couldn't breathe. The dust was thick, tasting of pulverized stone and magic.

I checked my vitals. *Arms: working. Legs: working. Ribs: protesting.*

I checked the asset.

I pushed myself up on my elbows. I was straddling him. My knees were pinned on either side of his hips, my chest pressed against his.

Dorian was alive. His eyes were wide, staring up at me through the gloom.

"You're heavy," he wheezed.

"Shut up," I coughed, wiping blood from a cut on my cheek. "Are you hit?"

"I... don't think so."

I looked down. My hand was resting flat on the center of his chest, right over his heart.

And then I felt it.

It wasn't a heartbeat. It was a revving engine.

Beneath the silk of his ruined tunic, something *surged*. A spike of raw, kinetic energy shot from his chest into my palm. It was hot—burning hot—and it vibrated through my entire skeleton.

The *Torque*.

His eyes flashed. The mismatched irises glowed—the dark one turning obsidian, the fractured one blazing with blue light. His metal arm, pinned under my knee, whined loudly, the servos locking and unlocking in a spasm.

He gasped, his back arching off the floor, pressing him harder into me.

"Sara," he choked out. "Get off."

"Stay down," I ordered, ignoring the weird electricity arcing between us. "Whatever that was, it wasn't an assassin. That was a breach charge. There will be a second wave."

"Get. Off." He grabbed my hips with his human hand. His grip was bruising. He wasn't trying to push me away; he was holding on for dear life. "The Core... it's reacting."

"To what?"

"To *you*."

The air between us sizzled. I could feel the heat radiating off him, baking through my leather corset. My own pulse hammered in my throat, syncing with the mechanical thrumming of his chest. It was terrifying. It was intimate.

And for a split second, amidst the screams and the rubble, I didn't want to move. I wanted to press my hand harder against that heat.

"Rebels!" a voice shouted from the smoke. "Secure the King!"

The spell broke.

I scrambled off him, rolling into a crouch, dragging him up with me.

"Move," I barked, shoving him toward the service entrance. "We're leaving."

Dorian stumbled, clutching his chest. He looked dazed, like he was drunk on lightning. He looked at me—at the dust in my hair, the blood on my face—with an expression I couldn't read.

Fear? Hunger?

"The King," he muttered, looking back at the dais.

"The King is a golden statue," I said, grabbing his human arm and yanking him into the shadows. "He'll survive a rock falling on him. You won't."

A second explosion rocked the hall, closer this time. Gunfire erupted—primitive, black-powder cracks mixing with the hum of magic.

I kicked the service door open.

"Kitchens," I commanded. "Now."

Dorian didn't argue. He ran. But as we sprinted into the dark corridor, I could still feel the ghost of that vibration on my palm. The hum of a machine that had woken up the moment I touched it.

What the hell are you, Chrome? I thought.
But I pushed the question down. Survival first. Existential dread later.

Chapter 13: The Bathhouse

Sara

I smelled like a barbecue at a graveyard.

It was a specific, cloying scent: pulverized drywall, burnt hair, expensive roast peacock, and the copper tang of fear-sweat. It coated the inside of my nose. It sat heavy on my tongue.

"Secure the perimeter!" Voss's voice boomed down the corridor, bouncing off the marble walls. "I want a full sweep of the servant's quarters! Check the vents! If a mouse moves, I want to know about it!"

I pressed my back against the inside of my door, listening to the heavy thud of jackboots sprinting past. The Royal Wing wasn't just on lockdown; it was being dissected.

Dorian had been whisked away by his medical team the second we hit the secure zone, muttering about "stabilizing the core". In the confusion, I'd slipped away, becoming invisible again. Just a shadow in a cloak.

But I couldn't hide from the smell.

I looked at the bathroom in my suite. The tub was nice, sure. But the water pressure was polite. I needed to drown. I needed heat so intense it would boil the memory of the explosion out of my pores.

I remembered the map I'd stolen—the one Dorian had corrected with his own hand. He'd marked the laundry chute, but he'd also marked something else on the floor below.

A large, circular room fed by the geothermal lines running up the central spire. The Royal Bathhouse.

I grabbed a towel and a bar of the stolen lavender soap. I didn't take a weapon. If I got caught, a naked girl with a shiv was an assassin. A naked girl with a bar of soap was just lost and looking for a wash. Plausible deniability.

I slipped the latch on the service door behind the vanity—the one Dorian had shown me.

The air in the passage was stale, smelling of dust and old stone. I pulled the panel shut behind me, plunging the narrow shaft into darkness.

Thump.
Above me, a grate rattled.

"Clear sector four," a guard's voice echoed down the ventilation shaft. "Moving to the service ladders."

I froze. My heart hammered against the leather corset like a trapped bird. They weren't just checking the halls; they were sweeping the guts of the castle.

I moved down the maintenance ladder, counting the rungs in the dark, placing my boots silently on the iron. One floor.

A beam of light sliced through the darkness above, missing my head by inches.

"Anything?"

"Just rats," another voice grunted. "Place is full of them."

I held my breath, pressing my forehead against the cold metal of the ladder. *Just a rat,* I thought. *Make yourself small.*
I waited until the beam swept away and the footsteps faded before I dared to move again. Two floors.

I found the access hatch. It wasn't the simple mechanism I expected. The explosion must have triggered a secondary security seal; a red mag-light blinked angrily on the panel.

"Great," I mouthed.

I knelt on the narrow grating. My hands were shaking—the adrenaline crash mixing with the fine tremors of exhaustion. I pulled the tension wrench from my boot heel.

This wasn't a three-second job. This was a surgical procedure.

I slid the pick in. The pins were stiff, fighting the tension. I felt the vibration of heavy boots on the floor outside the hatch. A patrol was passing right in front of the door.

Click. One pin.
The boots stopped.

"Did you hear that?"

I froze, the pick still inside the lock. I didn't breathe. I didn't blink.

"Hear what?"

"Clicking. Like... metal on metal."

"Probably the pipes cooling down. Come on, Voss wants the report."

The boots moved on. I exhaled, the sound harsh in my own ears. I twisted the wrench.

Click-clunk.
The mag-light died. The hatch hissed open.

I slipped inside and pushed the hatch shut, engaging the manual lock before my knees finally gave out. I was hit by a wall of steam.

It was warm, wet, and smelled of eucalyptus and money.

I was in a cavern. The room was massive, domed with frosted glass that let in the moonlight. The floor was mosaic tile—gold and lapis lazuli.

And in the center was the pool.

It was vast, fed by a waterfall that cascaded from a lion's mouth carved into the wall. The water was a milky, opaque turquoise, churning gently with geothermal heat.

"Obscene," I whispered.

There was enough water here to hydrate the entirety of District 12 for a year. And the Chrome used it to soak their bunions.

I did a sweep of the room. Shadows danced in the corners, but the steam was thick, creating a heavy, white fog that hovered over the water. It was silent, save for the rush of the waterfall.

Empty.

I walked to the edge of the pool. My hands were still shaking as I undid the clasp of the cloak. It fell to the floor in a heavy heap.

Next, the corset.

I unlaced it with frantic fingers. When the last knot gave way, I sucked in a breath that hurt. My ribs expanded, aching where the leather had bruised them. I peeled the armor off and kicked it aside.

Then the tactical pants. The boots. The socks.

I stood naked on the cold tiles, shivering not from cold, but from the sheer exposure. I was covered in bruises. A purple welt on my hip where I'd hit the floor. Scrapes on my arms from the debris. And under the grime, the pale, roadmap scars of a life spent in the Scrapyard.

I stepped into the water.

It burned. It was glorious.

I hissed as the heat hit my scrapes, wading deeper until the water lapped at my chin. I pushed off the steps and floated, letting the current take me.

I closed my eyes and ducked my head under.

Silence. The muffled roar of the water. The heat soaking into my bones, loosening the knot of tension in my lower back.

I surfaced, slicking my hair back. I grabbed the soap and started to scrub. I scrubbed until my skin was red. I scrubbed until the smell of smoke was gone, replaced by lavender.

But I couldn't scrub off the feeling of Dorian's chest against my hand.

That hum. That *surge*.

When I had touched him, it hadn't felt like touching a machine. Machines were cold. Logical. Dorian felt like a storm trapped in a bottle. And for a second, when the torque spiked, I had felt... connected.

Like I was the ground wire for his lightning.

It terrified me.

I stopped scrubbing. I let the soap drift away. The adrenaline finally crashed. The anger faded, leaving behind a hollow, aching exhaustion.

I thought of Elara.

She was sleeping on a cot in a metal box, coughing up rust, while I was floating in a pool of liquid gold. I had steak for dinner. She probably had ration bars.

I was failing her. I was playing dress-up in the castle while she rotted.

The unfairness of it rose up in my throat like bile.

I pulled my knees to my chest, wrapping my arms around my legs. I buried my face in my wet knees.

I didn't sob. Sobbing was loud. Sobbing attracted attention.

I just let the tears leak out. Hot, angry tears that mixed with the bathwater. My shoulders shook, just a little. I bit my lip until I tasted blood, trying to keep the sound inside.

Just five minutes, I told myself. *Five minutes to be weak. Then I put the armor back on.*

I sat there in the steam, naked and small, letting the weight of the city crush me for just a moment.

I was so sure I was alone.

I was so sure the steam hid everything.

I was wrong.

Chapter 14: Steam

Dorian

I wasn't bathing. I was cooling down.

The explosion at the dinner had spiked the Torque in my chest to dangerous levels. My core temperature was pushing a hundred and four degrees. If I didn't dissipate the heat, the biological components of my body—the heart, the lungs, the brain—would start to cook inside the metal shell.

So I sat in the darkest corner of the Royal Bath, submerged to my neck in geothermal water that was hot enough to scald a normal man. To me, it felt like a lukewarm breeze.

I had my eyes closed, listening to the hum of my own internal fans, trying to force my pulse to slow down.

Inhale. Exhale. Don't explode.
Then I heard the lock pick.

It was a subtle sound—the *click-clack* of tumblers falling into place—echoing off the domed ceiling.
I didn't move. I didn't open my eyes. I just stopped breathing.

If it was an assassin, they were lazy. They hadn't checked the perimeter. If it was a guard, they were about to get fired.

The hatch opened. Light footsteps on tile. The sound of clothes dropping.

Heavy wool. Leather. Boots.
I opened my eyes then, just a slit. Through the thick, white curtain of steam, I saw a silhouette.

Sara.

She was standing at the edge of the pool, stripping. I should have looked away. I didn't. I watched as she peeled off the armor I'd forced her into. I watched the tension leave her shoulders as the corset hit the floor.

When she stepped into the light, I saw the map.

She wasn't smooth like the court ladies. Her skin was a history book of violence. There was a jagged white line running down her thigh. A burn scar on her shoulder. A constellation of small, circular scars on her back that looked suspiciously like buckshot.

She was beautiful. In a terrified, jagged, broken sort of way.

She slipped into the water on the opposite side of the pool. She didn't see me. The steam was too thick, and I was tucked into the shadow of the lion statue.

I prepared to speak. To make a snarky comment about breaking and entering. To scare her.

Then she curled into a ball and started to cry.

It wasn't a theatrical, sobbing cry. It was silent. Her shoulders shook, creating tiny ripples in the milky water. She buried her face in her knees and just... fell apart.

I froze.

I had seen men die. I had seen my father turn people into statues. I had killed a hydra four hours ago. None of that made me flinch.

But watching this girl—this feral, sarcastic, pipe-wielding maniac—break down? It felt like someone had reached into my chest and squeezed the biological heart.

She wasn't crying because she was scared. She was crying because she was tired. I knew that exhaustion. It was the weight of keeping everyone else alive while you slowly drowned.

I stayed silent. I gave her the only thing I could: time.

I waited. Five minutes. Ten.

The shaking stopped. She took a deep, shuddering breath and splashed water on her face. She slicked her hair back. The mask of the "Rat" slid back into place.

She thought she was alone.

"You missed a spot," I said.

Sara yelped—a genuine, high-pitched sound—and scrambled backward in the water, slipping on the smooth tiles. She went under, flailing, and surfaced sputtering, coughing up water.

"You!" she gasped, wiping her eyes. "Where—how long have you been there?"

"Since before you broke in," I said calmly. I didn't move from my corner. "The heat exchange on my arm was running hot. I needed to submerge."

"You watched me?" Her voice pitched up, panicked and furious. She sank lower in the water, until only her nose and eyes were visible. "You perv!"

"I didn't watch you," I lied. "The steam is thick. All I saw was a blurry shape that talks too much."

"You stayed silent! You let me—" She cut herself off. She didn't want to say *You let me cry.*

"I let you have your moment," I said, my voice dropping to a low rumble. "Because I figured if I interrupted, you'd try to drown me with a bar of soap."

She glared at me, treading water. The panic was fading, replaced by the defensive anger I was used to.

"Turn around," she ordered. "I'm getting out."

"No," I said.

She froze. "Excuse me?"

"You broke into my private bath, Sara. You don't get to give orders."

I stood up.

The water cascaded off my chest. I wasn't wearing a shirt. I wasn't wearing anything.

The water was opaque, thank god, hiding the lower half of my body, but from the waist up, I was on display. The metal of my left arm gleamed wet and dark in the moonlight. The gold circuitry embedded in my collarbone hummed with blue light. The scars where the metal met the flesh were angry and red from the heat.

Sara's eyes widened. She didn't look at my face. Her gaze dropped. It traveled down my chest, over the hard lines of my abdomen, and drifted lower, toward the waterline.

"Eyes up, Slag," I said sharply. "The royal jewels aren't for display."

Her gaze snapped back to mine. Her face flushed a deep, furious red that had nothing to do with the steam.

"I wasn't looking at your—" She sputtered. "I was looking at the scar. On your ribs."

I looked down. There was a long, pale line on my right side. Human. Vulnerable.

"Assassin," I said. "Three years ago. He used a glass dagger."

"He missed," she said.

"He didn't miss. I just didn't die."

I waded toward her. Slowly. The water swirled around my waist.

Sara backed up until her shoulders hit the tiled wall. She was cornered.

"Stay back," she warned. She raised a hand beneath the water, probably making a fist. "I'm naked, Dorian. If you come any closer, I scream."

"Scream all you want. The room is soundproofed."

I stopped three feet away from her. Close enough to feel the heat radiating off her skin. Close enough to see the individual lashes framing her terrified, defiant eyes.

"Why are you crying?" I asked.

It was the wrong question. Or maybe the right one.

Her face hardened. "I wasn't crying. I got soap in my eyes."

"Liar."

"It's the steam. It causes condensation."

"You're terrible at this," I said. "You can lie about your name, Sara. You can lie about your background. But don't lie about the weight."

"What weight?"

"The weight of the people you're trying to save. The ones who are rusting out while you play soldier in the castle."

She went still. The water lapped against her collarbone.

"You don't know anything about me," she whispered.

"I know you have scars on your back that look like buckshot," I said. "I know you steal silverware to pay for medicine. And I know that right now, you feel guilty because the water is warm and your bed is soft."

She looked away, biting her lip. I saw a tear leak out. Just one.

I felt a sudden, violent urge to wipe it away. To touch her face. My human hand twitched at my side.

"It's not fair," she said, her voice breaking. "You have all this... magic water. And we drink sludge."

"No," I agreed. "It's not fair."

"I hate you," she said. She looked back at me, her eyes fierce. "I hate everything you are. The Chrome. The Gilt. All of it."

"Good," I said. "Hold onto that. Hate is fuel. Use it."

I stepped back, giving her space. The tension in the air was so thick I could taste it—iron and lavender.

"Get dressed, Sara," I said, turning away. "The water is getting cold."

"Dorian?"

I paused, looking back over my shoulder.

She was hugging herself, the water swirling around her shoulders. She looked small again.

"You didn't... you didn't see anything? When I got in?"

I looked at her. At the curve of her neck. The shadow of her collarbone. The memory of her naked silhouette against the steam was burned into my retinas like a brand.

"Nothing worth seeing," I lied smoothly.

I walked toward the steps, feeling her eyes on my back.

"And Sara?"

"What?"

"Next time you break in," I said, grabbing a towel, "lock the hatch behind you. You're a terrible thief."

ACT II: HIGH TORQUE

Chapter 15: Sparring

Sara

"You're telegraphing."

"I'm breathing," I snapped, wiping sweat from my eyes with the back of my wrapped hand.

"You're breathing like a dying pug," Dorian corrected. He was leaning against the weapon rack, looking annoyingly fresh. "And you drop your left shoulder before you strike. Every time. If I were a Sterling knight, you'd be missing an arm by now."

"If you were a Sterling knight," I panted, circling the training mat, "I'd have thrown sand in your eyes five minutes ago."

"There is no sand here, Sara. Just mats. And me."

We were in the Royal Dojo, a high-ceilinged room with floor-to-ceiling windows overlooking the clouds. It smelled of conditioned leather and disinfectant. The floor was padded with shock-absorbent foam, which was lucky for me, because Dorian had spent the last hour throwing me onto it.

I was wearing standard sparring gear: tight leggings and a sleeveless compression top that showed off every bruise I'd acquired since moving into this gilded hellhole.

Dorian had ditched the tunic. He was wearing loose gray sweatpants and a black tank top that clung to his chest. It was unfair. The man was half-metal, yet he moved with a fluid, feline grace that made me want to punch him in his perfect, symmetrical face.

The metal arm gleamed under the magelights. The servos whirred softly as he flexed his fingers.

"Again," he ordered.

I didn't argue. I attacked.

I lunged forward, feinting a jab to his throat. He didn't blink. He swatted my hand away with his human wrist—casual, dismissive—and stepped inside my guard.

"Too slow," he murmured.

He swept my legs.

The world flipped. I hit the mat hard, the air leaving my lungs in a *whoosh*. Before I could scramble away, he was on me.

He didn't use his hands. He used his weight. He settled his hips over mine, pinning my legs, and leaned forward, trapping my wrists above my head with one hand—the human one.

I bucked my hips, trying to throw him off. It was like trying to bench press a boulder.

"Get off," I grunted, straining against his grip.

"Not until you admit you lost," he said, his face hovering inches from mine. A bead of sweat dripped from his temple and landed on my collarbone. It was hot.

"I tripped," I lied.

"You were outmaneuvered." He shifted, settling his weight more firmly. His knees bracketed my waist. "You fight like a scavenger, Sara. You look for the cheap shot. The easy exit."

"It's called survival."

"It's called luck. And luck runs out." His eyes were dark, intense. "In the Vault, there is no sand. There are no exits. There is just you and the constructs. You need to be faster. You need to be closer."

"I can't get much closer than this," I spat.

The air in the room seemed to thin. We were tangled together, chest to chest, hips to hips. I could feel the heat radiating off him. I could smell him—cedar, musk, and the sharp, electric tang of the Torque.

My struggle slowed. I looked up at him. His pupils were blown wide. His breath hitched, just once, a small, jagged sound in the quiet room.

He didn't move. He didn't let go of my wrists.

And then I felt it.

Pressed against my thigh, through the thin fabric of his sweatpants and my leggings, was a distinct, rigid hardness.

He was excited.

The Prince of the Chrome, the man who looked at me like I was a science experiment, was hard. And he was currently grinding against me.

My eyes widened. I went very still.

Dorian realized it a second later. His eyes widened too, panic flashing through the fractured blue iris. He started to pull back, his face flushing a dark, humiliating crimson.

Oh, no. I wasn't letting him retreat. Not after he spent an hour lecturing me on "control."

I smirked. I made it sharp and cruel.

"Careful, Your Highness," I drawled, looking him dead in the eye. "Is that a dagger in your pocket, or are you just happy to be winning?"

Dorian froze. The flush deepened, spreading down his neck to the metal collar.

He released my wrists like they were made of white-hot iron. He scrambled off me, rolling backward and springing to his feet in one fluid, frantic motion. He turned his back to me instantly, adjusting his sweatpants with a violent tug.

"Session over," he choked out. His voice was an octave higher than usual.

I sat up slowly, leaning back on my elbows. I felt triumphant. I felt powerful.

"What's the matter, Chrome?" I taunted to his back. "I thought we were working on close-quarters combat? I was just starting to learn the... thrust of it."

He whirled around. His face was a mask of furious embarrassment. "You are insufferable."

"And you," I said, standing up and wiping the mat dust off my legs, "are flushed. You might want to check your coolant levels. You're running hot."

"It is a biological reaction," he snapped, crossing his arms over his chest to hide the obvious evidence. "Adrenaline. Proximity. Friction. It means nothing."

"Sure," I said, walking toward the water bench. I took a long, slow drink, watching him over the rim of the bottle. "Just simple physics. Friction. Heat. Expansion."

"Get out," he growled.

"I'm not done stretching."

"Get. Out."

He pointed to the door with his metal arm. The servos whined loudly—a high-pitched keen that sounded suspiciously like frustration.

I set the bottle down. I walked past him, making sure to sway my hips just a little more than necessary. I was playing with fire, I knew that. But seeing the unshakeable Prince flustered? It was worth the burn.

I stopped at the door and looked back.

He was still standing in the center of the mat, hands clenched into fists, chest heaving. He looked like he wanted to murder me. Or devour me.

"Same time tomorrow?" I asked sweetly.

" wear looser pants," he warned.

I laughed. It was a real laugh, the first one I'd had in months.

"I'll try not to telegraph my moves," I said. "Wouldn't want to catch you off guard again."

I slipped out the door before he could throw a training dummy at my head.

As the heavy wood clicked shut, I leaned against it in the hallway. My own pulse was hammering in my throat. My skin tingled where his weight had pressed me into the floor.

I looked down at my hand. It was shaking.

"Physics," I whispered to myself. "Just physics."

But as I walked back to my room, I couldn't stop thinking about the way his eyes had looked right before I mocked him. Dark. Hungry. Human.

Physics was going to get me killed.

Chapter 16: The Snooping

Dorian

I couldn't sleep.

It wasn't just the insomnia, though that was a constant companion. It was the memory of the sparring mat. The phantom sensation of Sara's weight against my hips, the smell of her sweat, and the humiliating, biological betrayal of my own body.

Friction, I told myself, pacing the length of my bedroom. *Simple mechanics.*

But mechanics didn't explain why, three hours later, I was still thinking about the way her eyes had narrowed right before she mocked me.

I needed a distraction. I needed to work.

I pulled on a heavy silk robe, leaving it loose over my trousers, and stepped out into the hallway. The palace was asleep. The magical sconces were dimmed to a low, amber hum. The guards were at their posts at the far ends of the corridor, statues in gold armor.

I walked silently, the velvet carpet swallowing the sound of my boots. I was heading for the library, intending to review the schematics for the Vault again.

Then I heard it.

Scritch. Click. Mutters.

I stopped. The sound was coming from the alcove halfway down the hall. The entrance to the Royal Apothecary.

I moved into the shadows of a tapestry, blending into the dark. I watched.

Sara was there.

She was out of uniform. She was wearing the oversized gray sweatpants she slept in and a tight black tank top. She was crouched in front of the heavy oak door, her back to me. Her hair was loose, falling over her shoulders in a messy curtain of dark waves.

She was hunched over the lock. I saw the glint of metal in her hand—a tension wrench and a rake pick.

"Come on, you piece of junk," she whispered. "I've opened safes harder than you."

I leaned against the wall, crossing my arms. I should have been angry. She was breaking Rule Two, Rule Four, and probably half the penal code.

Instead, I felt a smirk tugging at my mouth.

She was good. Her hands were steady, her movements precise. She wasn't forcing the pins; she was massaging them. She was listening to the mechanism.

Click.
"Gotcha," she breathed.

She reached for the handle.

"You're using a standard rake on a pin-tumbler," I said, stepping out of the shadows. "It's effective, but noisy."

Sara jumped a solid foot in the air.

She spun around, dropping into a defensive crouch, the lockpicks disappearing into her waistband faster than the eye could follow. When she saw it was me, her shoulders didn't drop, but her expression shifted from *fight* to *flight*.

"I was sleepwalking," she said instantly.

"With lockpicks?"

"It's a condition."

I walked toward her. She backed up until she hit the door she'd just unlocked. She looked terrified. Not of me, I realized, but of the consequences. She thought I was going to call the guards. She thought she was going back to the cells.

"Step aside," I said.

She hesitated, then shuffled to the left, keeping her eyes on my hands.

I reached out and turned the handle. The door clicked open.

"After you," I said, gesturing into the dark room.

Sara stared at me. "What?"

"You wanted in. Go in."

"You're... you're not arresting me?"

"Not yet. I want to see what you steal."

I walked past her into the Apothecary. The room smelled of dried herbs, ethanol, and magic. Shelves lined the walls, filled with jars of rare ingredients and vials of glowing liquids.

I waved my hand, and the magelights flickered on, casting a soft glow over the room.

Sara lingered in the doorway, looking ready to bolt.

"Close the door," I ordered. "Unless you want the night patrol to join us."

She closed it. She walked into the room, her steps silent. She didn't look at the gold dust. She didn't look at the expensive poisons.

She went straight to the refrigeration unit in the back.

She opened it. The cold air hissed out. She scanned the racks of vials. She ignored the recreational narcotics. She ignored the enhancement serums.

She reached for a small, unassuming blue vial.

Suppressants. High-grade. The kind used to slow the spread of the Rust in the early stages.
She held it in her hand, looking at it like it was a diamond. Then she looked at me, waiting for me to take it away.

"For the sister," I said.

Sara's hand tightened around the vial. "Elara. Her name is Elara."

"And she's rusting out."

"Yes." She lifted her chin. "So go ahead. Take it back. Send me to the dungeon. I don't care."

I leaned against the counter, watching her.

"Keep it," I said.

Sara blinked. "What?"

"Keep it. Take two. Take the whole box." I gestured vaguely. "We have crates of the stuff downstairs. It's basically aspirin to us."

She stared at me, processing. "You're letting me steal from the Crown."

"I'm letting you take what you need," I said. "Because I need you focused. I can't have my bodyguard distracted by worrying about her sister's cough."

"This isn't charity," she said suspiciously. "You don't do charity."

"Correct. It's a transaction."

I pushed off the counter and walked toward her. She held her ground this time, though I saw her pulse fluttering in the hollow of her throat.

"You have good hands, Sara," I said softly. "I watched you on the lock. You have the touch. You feel the pins before they set."

"My father taught me," she murmured.

"He taught you well. But that lock was a level two security rating. It was child's play."

I stopped in front of her.

"Can you crack a level ten?"

Her brow furrowed. "There's no such thing as a level ten. The scale stops at seven."

"The City Vaults are level ten," I said. "Triple-warded. Blood-keyed. And protected by a mechanical tumbler system that rotates every sixty seconds."

Her eyes widened. "The King's Vault."

"Yes."

"You want me to... protect it?"

"I want you to break into it."

The silence in the room was heavy. Sara looked at the vial in her hand, then up at me. She was smart. She put the pieces together instantly.

"The Wish," she whispered. "You didn't pick me because I'm a fighter. You picked me because I'm a thief."

"I picked you because you're a rat," I corrected gently. "And rats can get into places lions can't."

"Why?" she asked. "You're the Prince. You live here. Why do you need to rob your own house?"

"Because what I want isn't given, Sara. It has to be taken." I stepped closer, lowering my voice. "There is something in that Vault. Something my father uses to keep the city choking on smog and rust. I'm going to steal it. And I'm going to shut this whole damn machine down."

She searched my face. She was looking for the lie. She wouldn't find one.

"You're insane," she decided. "It's treason. It's suicide."

"Probably."

"If we get caught, they won't just kill us. They'll smelt us."

"Then don't get caught."

The door behind us opened.

Sara spun around, the vial disappearing into her pocket, her body dropping into a combat stance.

Captain Voss stepped in. He was in full armor, helmet under his arm. He looked at me. He looked at Sara. He looked at the open refrigeration unit.

"Captain," I said, not moving.

"Your Highness," Voss grunted. He looked at Sara. His gaze was heavy, unimpressed, but not hostile. "She pick the lock?"

"Under ten seconds," I said.

Voss nodded, a slow, appreciative movement. "Not bad."

Sara looked between us, confused. "You... he's the Guard Captain. He's supposed to arrest me."

"Voss isn't Chrome," I said. "He's just plated."

Voss walked over to Sara. He towered over her. He reached into his belt pouch. Sara flinched, expecting handcuffs.

Voss pulled out a small, folded piece of parchment. He handed it to her.

"The patrol schedules for the lower vault level," Voss rumbled. "There's a three-minute gap at 0400 during the shift change. Don't waste it."

Sara took the paper, her mouth falling open slightly. "You're in on it?"

"The Prince saved my life in the Wars," Voss said simply. "I follow the Prince. Not the Crown."

He looked at me. "The King is asking for you, sir. He knows you're awake."

"Of course he does." I sighed. "Go, Voss. Keep the hallway clear."

Voss nodded to me, then gave Sara a short, sharp nod of respect. "Don't make him regret this, girl."

He turned and left, closing the door.

I looked back at Sara. She was staring at the patrol schedule, then at the vial of medicine, then at me. The fear was gone. Replaced by something sharper. Adrenaline. Ambition.

"So," I said, crossing my arms. "Are we doing this? Or should I call the guards back and report a theft?"

Sara looked at the vial. She tucked it deep into her pocket.

She looked up at me. A slow, dangerous smile spread across her face. It was the same smile she'd had in the arena right before she smashed the knight.

"A level ten," she mused. "I'm going to need better tools."

"I'll get you the tools," I promised. "You just get me the door."

"Deal," she said.

She held out her hand.

I looked at it. Small, scarred, calloused. A thief's hand.

I reached out and took it. My metal fingers wrapped around hers. Her skin was warm against the cold alloy. The connection hummed between us—not the violent surge of the Torque this time, but a steady, rhythmic thrum.

Partners.

"Get some sleep, Rat," I said, releasing her. "Training starts at dawn. And tomorrow, we're not doing mats. We're doing tumblers."

She walked to the door, pausing with her hand on the latch.

"Dorian?"

"Yeah?"

"Thanks for the aspirin."

"Don't mention it," I said. "Literally. If you mention it, I'll deny everything."

She laughed softly and slipped out into the night.

I stood alone in the Apothecary, surrounded by poisons and cures, and for the first time in years, the silence didn't feel empty.

It felt like the quiet before the storm.

Chapter 17: The Bargain

Sara

The tools were beautiful.

They were spread out on the velvet duvet of my bed like surgical instruments. Tension wrenches made of aerospace titanium. Rakes so fine they looked like needles. A decoder key that hummed with a low-level decryption spell.

"These are illegal," I said, picking up a diamond pick that weighed less than a feather. "Possession of these in the Lower Districts carries a mandatory sentence of hand amputation."

"Good thing we're in the Upper Districts," Dorian said.

He was standing by the window again, staring out at the city. He did that a lot. Standing just close enough to the glass to see the drop, like he was calculating the terminal velocity of a Prince.

"So," I said, sliding the pick into my boot heel. It fit perfectly. "We have the tools. We have the map. We have Voss on the perimeter. When do we hit the Vault?"

"Not tonight," Dorian said. He didn't turn around.

"Why not? The rotation is in two hours. We're ready."

"I'm not."

He turned then. He looked restless. Not the bored, arrogant restless I was used to, but something sharper. Like a wolf pacing a cage that had suddenly become too small. His human hand was flexing at his side, opening and closing in a rhythm that matched the whir of his metal arm.

"I need air, Sara."

"Open a window."

"Real air," he said. "Dirty air. I want to go down."

I froze, a tension wrench halfway to my pocket. "Down? To the city? You just gave me a lecture on how dangerous it is for you to be exposed."

"I don't want a parade," he snapped, walking toward me. "I don't want the carriage and the guards and the waving. I want to see it. The Slags. The clubs. The places where people don't bow when I walk in."

"You want to go slumming," I said, my voice cooling. "You want a safari. Look at the poor people, watch them fight for scraps, then come back up here and wash the grime off in your magic pool."

"No." He stopped at the foot of the bed. His eyes were dark, intense. "I want to know what I'm saving. Or what I'm destroying. I've spent my whole life in this tower, looking down. I want to look up."

"You'll get killed," I said flatly. "You have a price on your head the size of the national debt. If the Rust doesn't get you, the rebels will."

"I have a bodyguard," he said, a smirk touching his lips. "She's scrappy. Fights dirty. Hits people with pipes."

"She's also not paid enough for this." I crossed my arms. "No. It's stupid. We stick to the plan. We hit the Vault, get the power source, and end this."

Dorian went quiet. He looked at me, really looked at me, with that unnerving, fractured gaze. He calculated the leverage.

"I can get you a full vial of Elixir," he said softly.

My heart stuttered.

"I already have the suppressants," I said, patting my pocket.

"Suppressants buy time," Dorian said. "The Elixir buys life. One vial clears the blood for a year. Maybe two. It reverses the calcification."

He took a step closer.

"I have a personal stash in my safe. Not the Vault. Here. I can give it to you tonight."

I stared at him. A year. A whole year where Elara wouldn't cough up blood. A year where she could walk without pain.

"That's low," I whispered. "Bribing me with my sister's life."

"It's a trade," Dorian corrected. "You want the cure. I want one night of freedom. One night where I'm not the Prince. Where I'm just... a guy."

"You're never 'just a guy,' Dorian. You're half a toaster."

"Then dress me down," he challenged. "Disguise me. Hide the metal. Take me to the places you go. Show me the Rust, Sara."

I looked at the tools on the bed. I looked at the desperation in his eyes. It wasn't just boredom. It was hunger. He was starving for something real, even if that reality was ugly.

And I wanted that Elixir. God, I wanted it.

"One night," I said slowly. "We leave via the laundry chute. We stick to the shadows. If anyone asks, you're my mute, idiot cousin from the mines."

"Mute?"

"Your voice is too posh. If you open your mouth and start talking about 'structural efficiency,' we're dead."

He grinned. It transformed his face, cracking the marble mask into something startlingly human.

"Deal."

Dorian

She made me shake on it.

"Skin," she ordered, looking at my metal hand with distrust. "I don't shake with the machine. The machine does what it's programmed to do. I want the man."

I hesitated.

I didn't touch people with my right hand often. The metal hand was a shield—people expected it to be cold, hard, unfeeling. The flesh hand was intimate. It was warm. It had a pulse.

I extended my right hand.

Sara took it.

Her hand was rough. Calloused palms, a scar running along the thumb, nails bitten short. But her grip was firm. Strong.

When our skin touched, the air in the room seemed to contract.

It wasn't the electric surge of the Torque this time. It was something subtler. A warmth that traveled up my arm and settled in my chest, right next to the biological heart that was beating a little too fast.

She didn't let go immediately. She looked down at our joined hands.

"You have soft hands," she noted, her voice strangely quiet. "For a killer."

"I have lucky hands," I murmured. "For a prince."

She looked up, her dark eyes catching mine. For a second, the banter died. The sarcasm evaporated. We were just two people standing in a white room, holding on to a pact that was almost certainly going to get us both killed.

She squeezed my hand once—hard—then dropped it.

"Right," she said, turning away briskly, clapping her hands together. "If we're doing this, we need to do something about... all of this."

She gestured vaguely at my entire person.

"What's wrong with me?"

"You shine, Dorian. You literally gleam. In the Slags, shiny things get stolen or broken." She walked to my wardrobe and threw the doors open. "We need to make you look like you've had a hard life."

"I have had a hard life."

She snorted, pulling out a pair of black trousers and tossing them at my head. I caught them with my metal hand.

"You've had a *traumatic* life," she corrected. "There's a difference. Hard means you worry about where your next meal is coming from. Hard means dirt under your fingernails that won't scrub out. You?" She pointed a finger at my chest. "You look like you exfoliate with diamond dust."

She dove back into the wardrobe.

"Put those on. And lose the silk. Do you have anything that isn't made of spiderwebs and money?"

"I have... wool?"

"Wool works. And boots. Scuffed ones, if you have them."

I started to unbutton my tunic. Sara didn't turn around. She was rifling through my shirts, muttering about "impractical weaves."

I stripped off the tunic. The air was cool against my skin. I watched her back.

"Sara."

She paused, holding a gray knit sweater. "What?"

"The Elixir," I said. "It's in the wall safe behind the painting of my grandfather. The combination is the date of the Unification."

She turned around slowly, holding the sweater to her chest. She saw me shirtless again. This time, she didn't flush. Her gaze was clinical, assessing the metal plating on my shoulder, the way it locked into the clavicle.

"You're giving it to me now?" she asked. "Before we go?"

"I'm giving it to you now," I said. "Because if we die down there, I don't want to owe you a debt in the afterlife."

She stared at me. The suspicion in her eyes warred with something else. Gratitude? Surprise?

"You're weird, Chrome," she said softly.

"Put it in your pocket," I said, pulling on the trousers. "And find me a hat. If someone sees this face, the game is over."

She threw the sweater at me. It hit me in the chest.

"We're going to the Sinkhole," she said, a wicked grin spreading across her face. "If you want to see the Rust, Dorian, I'm going to show you the corrosion."

I pulled the sweater over my head. It was itchy. It was tight.

"Lead the way, Rat."

I felt a thrill zip through me—electric, terrifying, and entirely biological. I was sneaking out of my own castle. I was going into the belly of the beast. And I was following a girl who looked at me like I was a puzzle she couldn't wait to take apart.

For the first time in twenty-three years, I didn't feel like a weapon.

I felt like a runaway.

Chapter 18: The Night Out

Sara

"You have got to be kidding me."

Dorian stood looking into the open maw of the laundry chute. It was a dark, metal throat that smelled of bleach, wet cotton, and the distinct, sour funk of a thousand sweaty guard uniforms.

"It's gravity-fed," I said, adjusting the strap of my stolen satchel. "It dumps directly into the basement sorting facility. From there, it's a straight shot to the service elevators."

Dorian peered into the darkness. He was wearing the gray knit sweater, the black trousers, and a pair of boots I'd scuffed up with a cheese grater from the kitchenette. He looked... strangely normal. Like a rugged, handsome dockworker who happened to have a billion-credit bountiful on his head.

"Is it... sanitary?" he asked, wrinkling his nose.

"It's laundry, Dorian. It's where the dirt goes. You wanted the 'real' experience? This is it. The glamorous exit."

I didn't wait for him to debate the hygiene of the situation. I sat on the edge of the chute, crossed my arms over my chest, and pushed off.

The slide was fast, dark, and terrifying. I careened down the metal spiral, bouncing off the sides, picking up speed until—

Fwump.
I landed in a massive pile of towels. It was soft, damp, and smelled like lemon detergent.

Three seconds later—*Thud.*

Dorian landed next to me. He didn't flail. He hit the pile with a heavy, controlled impact, rolling instantly to his feet before sinking knee-deep into the linens.

"Elegant," he muttered, picking a stray sock off his shoulder.

"Effective," I corrected, climbing out of the bin. "We're in the basement. Keep your head down."

The sorting room was loud. Massive steam-powered tumblers roared against the walls, drowning out our footsteps. The air was hot and humid. Droids—low-level copper constructs with no vocal chips—were mindlessly folding sheets in the corner.

We moved through the shadows, dodging the patrol bots. Dorian moved well. He was quiet, mirroring my steps, checking the corners. Maybe he had been paying attention during our training sessions after all.

We reached the service elevator. I jammed the call button.

"Okay," I said, turning to him. "Inspection."

Dorian straightened up. "I'm wearing the itchy sweater. I'm wearing the scuffed boots. I look like a commoner."

"You look like a Prince in a costume," I sighed. "You're too... symmetrical. Your skin is too clear. You look like you've never missed a meal or a night's sleep."

I scanned the loading dock. My eyes landed on a bucket of axle grease sitting by the conveyor belt.

"Come here," I ordered.

Dorian stepped closer. "What are you—"

I dipped my fingers into the black grease. It was cold and thick.

"Hold still."

I reached up. He flinched slightly, then held his ground. I smeared the grease along his jawline, darkening the perfect stubble. I rubbed it into his hairline, dulling the shine of his dark hair. I took a smudge and pressed it under his eyes, giving him the hollow, tired look of a shift worker.

My hand lingered on his cheek. His skin was warm under my fingers. He was watching me, his mismatched eyes dilated in the dim light. He wasn't pulling away. He was leaning into my touch, just a fraction.

"You're enjoying this," he murmured, his voice vibrating against my fingertips.

"I'm enjoying ruining your complexion," I lied, my voice breathless. "There. Now you look like you work for a living."

I grabbed a roll of bandages from my bag—stolen from the infirmary supply closet—and pointed to his left arm.

"Wrap it," I said. "Tight. If anyone asks, it's a burn injury from the foundries. Nasty stuff. We don't talk about it."

Dorian obeyed, winding the gauze around the gleaming metal until the chrome was hidden. He pulled the sleeve of the sweater down, hiding the bulk.

"And the hat," I said, tossing him a woolen beanie I'd swiped from the laundry pile.

He pulled it on low, covering his ears and shadowing his eyes.

I stepped back.

Grease-stained. Bandaged. Slouching slightly in the heavy boots.

"Well?" he asked. "Do I pass?"

"You look like trouble," I said, suppressing the sudden flutter in my chest. He didn't look like a Prince anymore. He looked like the kind of guy you met in a dark alley and made a bad decision with. "Don't speak. Remember the cover. You're mute."

"Silent as the grave," he promised.

The elevator arrived with a rusted groan. We stepped in. I pulled the lever down to *Sub-Level 4: The Slags*.
The descent was long.

As we dropped, the air changed. The smell of lemon and steam faded, replaced by the heavy, metallic tang of the Lower City. Sulfur. Rust. Ozone. Fried food.

The elevator shuddered to a halt. The grate rattled open.

We stepped out into the noise.

It wasn't a street; it was a canyon. Buildings made of scrapped metal and retrofitted shipping containers stacked fifty stories high, leaning over the narrow alleyways like drunk giants. Neon signs flickered in pink and toxic green, advertising *Cheap Spirits*, *Parts for Cash*, and *Girls with Real Skin*.

Steam hissed from cracked pipes. Hover-skiffs zoomed overhead, blasting bass-heavy music that shook the pavement.

Dorian stopped. He looked up, his eyes wide, taking it all in. The chaos. The filth. The life.

"Keep moving," I hissed, grabbing his human arm. "You gawk, you get mugged."

I steered him into the crowd.

The Slags were alive tonight. It was shift change at the factories, so the streets were packed with workers—humans, cyborgs, and everything in between.

Dorian was a head taller than most people. He drew looks. Not because they recognized him, but because he moved with a predator's confidence. I tightened my grip on his arm.

"Where are we going?" he whispered, leaning down so his breath ghosted over my ear.

"The Sinkhole," I said. "It's a club. Neutral ground. If we're going to blend in, we need to be where the noise is loud enough to hide your accent."

We navigated the maze of alleys. I led him past the chop-shops where back-alley doctors installed second-hand cybernetics. I led him past the food stalls selling "meat" skewers of dubious origin.

Dorian stopped at a stall. He stared at a vat of bubbling blue liquid.

"What is that?" he asked, breaking character.

"Engine coolant mixed with gin," I said, yanking him forward. "Do not drink it. It will dissolve your stomach lining."

"Fascinating."

We reached the district known as the Rust Belt. The heart of the nightlife.

The Sinkhole was easy to find. You just followed the bass. It thumped in the ground, vibrating up through the soles of your boots. The entrance was a massive, rusted blast door guarded by a minotaur—a gene-spliced heavy with horns and a bad attitude.

"Cover charge," the minotaur grunted.

I flicked a silver coin—one of the ones I'd stolen from Dorian's room—at him. He caught it, bit it, and grunted approval.

"In."

I looked at Dorian. I adjusted his collar, checking the bandage on his arm.

"Stay close," I warned. "This isn't a ballroom. People here dance with knives."

Dorian looked at the flashing neon sign above the door. He looked at the crowd of punks, scavengers, and criminals pushing their way inside.

He grinned. A sharp, reckless, terrifyingly happy grin.

"After you, Rat."

We pushed through the heavy vinyl curtains and stepped into the dark.

The heat hit us first. Then the smell of sweat and synthesized adrenaline. Then the music—a wall of industrial noise that drowned out thought.

We were in.

And I had a terrible feeling that the Prince wasn't just going to watch the show. He was going to want to join the circus.

Chapter 19: The Club

Dorian

The bass didn't just vibrate the floor; it rearranged my internal organs.

The Sinkhole was a sensory assault. It was a cavernous, subterranean rotunda packed with bodies that writhed like maggots in a wound. The lighting was erratic—strobes of toxic green and arterial red that cut through the haze of smoke. The air tasted of recycled sweat, pheromones, and cheap synthetic alcohol.

It was disgusting.

It was perfect.

"Stick close," Sara shouted over the roar of the music. She grabbed the cuff of my itchy wool sweater and towed me through the crush.

I didn't need to be told. The crowd was a solid wall of flesh and metal. A cyborg with a hydraulic jaw slammed into my shoulder; a girl with neon circuitry tattooed on her face spilled her drink on my boot. Nobody apologized. Nobody bowed.

I was invisible.

For a man who had spent twenty-three years being the focal point of every room he entered, the anonymity was more intoxicating than the whiskey.

Sara shoved her way to the bar—a slab of corrugated steel welded to some piping.

"Two shots of Rot!" she yelled at the bartender, a massive man with four arms.

He slammed two dirty glasses on the counter and poured a viscous, amber liquid from an unmarked jug.

Sara handed one to me. "Drink it fast. If you taste it, you'll regret it."

I looked at the glass. It smelled like turpentine and burnt sugar. I downed it in one swallow.

It hit my stomach like molten lead. My vision blurred for a microsecond, and the HUD in my mechanical eye flashed a warning: *TOXIN DETECTED. INITIATE PURGE?*
I mentally swiped the notification away. *Override.*
"Another," I signed to Sara, holding up two fingers.

She looked at me, eyebrows raised. "Easy, big guy. That stuff creates holes in your memory."

"I want holes," I mouthed.

She rolled her eyes but slapped another coin on the bar.

Two shots later, the room started to swim in a pleasant, hazy way. The sharp edges of my existence—the constant hum of the arm, the weight of the Crown, the knowledge of the Vault—softened. The noise wasn't annoying anymore; it was a blanket.

The music shifted. The tempo dropped, becoming heavier, grinding. A beat that you felt in your groin.

"Come on," Sara said, grabbing my human hand. "We can't stand here. We're blocking the trough."

She pulled me onto the floor.

We didn't have a choice about dancing. The crowd pressed us together instantly. I felt the heat of her back against my chest. She was small, but solid. A compact package of muscle and tension wrapped in black leather and scavenged wool.

She tried to keep a professional distance, scanning the room for threats.

I didn't let her.

The alcohol had stripped away the Prince. The man left behind was hungry.

I stepped closer, eliminating the gap. I placed my hands on her hips.

Sara stiffened. She turned her head slightly, shouting over her shoulder. "Dorian. Space."

I shook my head. *No.*
I leaned down, my chest pressing against her back, my chin grazing the top of her head. I let the heavy, rhythmic thrum of the bass dictate the movement. I swayed, dragging her with me.

She resisted for a moment—a reflex of control—and then, she yielded.

She leaned back against me.

The sensation was electric. Through the thin wool of my sweater and the leather of her corset, I could feel the curve of her spine. I could feel her hips moving, grinding slowly against mine in time with the beat.

My metal arm was heavy, wrapped in bandages, resting on her hip bone. My human hand slid lower, spreading over her stomach.

She gasped, her hands coming up to cover mine. She didn't push me away. She laced her fingers through my human ones.

We moved together in the dark, surrounded by strangers. The world narrowed down to the points of contact. Her hair tickling my jaw. The smell of lavender soap cutting through the stench of the club. The way her ass brushed against me with every beat.

I buried my face in her neck, inhaling deeply. She tasted like salt and shadows.

Mine, the alcohol whispered. *She's mine.*

It was a dangerous thought. A possessive, irrational thought. But in the dark of the Sinkhole, it felt like the only truth that mattered.

Then, the spell broke.

A man—a scavenger with a jagged scar running down his neck and eyes that looked too glassy—stumbled into us.

He didn't apologize. He leered. His gaze dropped to Sara's chest, lingering on the curve of the corset. He reached out, his greasy hand grabbing her arm, pulling her away from me.

"Hey, sweet thing," he slurred. "Ditch the mute. Dance with a real man."

Sara reacted instantly, her body tensing to throw an elbow.

She didn't get the chance.

The world went red.

I didn't think. I didn't calculate the political ramifications. I didn't check for guards.

I moved.

I released Sara and stepped between them. I used my left hand—the metal one, wrapped in bandages. I didn't punch him. That would have killed him.

I grabbed his wrist.

The servos in my arm whined—a sound drowned out by the bass—as I applied four hundred pounds of pressure per square inch.

Crunch.
The man's eyes went wide. His mouth opened to scream, but the music swallowed the sound. He dropped to his knees, his face turning a sickly shade of gray.

I leaned down. I brought my face close to his ear.

"Touch her again," I whispered, forgetting I was supposed to be mute, "and I'll tear it off."

He couldn't hear me over the music, but he understood the pressure. He understood the look in my eyes.

I released him. He scrambled backward into the crowd, cradling his shattered wrist, vanishing like a rat in a sewer.

I stood there, breathing hard. My blood was singing. The Torque was spiking, feeding off the violence and the lust.

I felt a hand on my chest.

Sara.

She was staring at me. Her eyes were wide, reflecting the strobe lights. She had seen it. She had seen the violence. She had seen the possessiveness.

She should have been afraid.

She wasn't.

Her pupils were blown. Her lips were parted. Her hand slid up my chest, gripping the wool of my sweater. She pulled me down.

"You're insane," she shouted, her voice breathless.

"I'm dancing," I shouted back.

She looked at the crowd where the man had disappeared, then back at me. A flush crept up her neck.

"We have to go," she said, though she didn't let go of my shirt. "Before you break someone else."

"One more song," I pleaded, grabbing her waist again.

"No." She was firm, but her voice was shaky. "You're running hot, Dorian. I can feel the heat coming off you. If you overheat here, you'll cook inside that sweater."

She was right. My internal fans were spinning at maximum, trying to vent the excess thermal energy generated by the Torque spike. I was burning up.

"Alley," she commanded. "Now."

She grabbed my human hand and started to drag me toward the exit.

I let her lead me. But as we pushed through the sweating, grinding crowd, I didn't look at the exit. I looked at her.

I watched the way her hips moved. I watched the fierce set of her jaw.

And I knew, with the absolute certainty of a drunk man, that if we didn't get out of here soon, the heat wasn't going to be the thing that consumed me.

I wanted her. Not as a guard. Not as a thief.

I wanted her against a wall, in the dark, with the bass still thumping in our blood.

"Lead the way, Rat," I murmured to her back. "But run fast."

Chapter 20: The Alley

Sara

The cold air hit us like a slap in the face.

We burst out of the heavy vinyl curtains of the Sinkhole and stumbled into the street. The contrast was violent. Inside, it was a humid, screaming pressure cooker. Outside, the Slags were freezing, the air tasting of ozone and impending rain.

"Air," Dorian gasped, ripping the woolen beanie off his head. Steam—actual, literal steam—curled off his skin into the night.

"Keep the hat on!" I hissed, snatching it from his hand and shoving it back onto his head. "You are glowing, you idiot. If a patrol sees a man steaming like a radiator, they're going to scan you."

"Let them scan me," Dorian laughed. It was a dark, reckless sound. The 'Rot' had hit his system hard, stripping away the polish and leaving something raw and jagged underneath. "I'll break their scanners."

He stumbled, his heavy boot catching on a loose cobblestone. I caught him.

He was dead weight. Solid muscle and metal. And he was *burning.*

Through the thick wool of the sweater, heat radiated off him in waves. It wasn't a fever; it was a reactor meltdown. The Torque spike from the fight—and the dancing—had pushed his internal systems into the red.

"We need to cool you down," I muttered, hooking my arm around his waist to steer him. "You're going to cook your own organs."

"I feel fine," he mumbled, draping his heavy arm over my shoulders. He buried his face in the crook of my neck. His nose was cold, but his breath was hot. "You smell good. Like soap and violence."

"And you smell like paint thinner and bad decisions. Move your feet."

I dragged him away from the club entrance, aiming for the shadows. We needed to get back to the elevator. Back to the laundry chute. Back to the safety of the gilded cage.

Whoop-whoop.
The sound cut through the ambient noise of the street like a knife.

Blue lights flashed against the rusted corrugated metal of the buildings above us. A patrol skiff. Low altitude. Scanning the crowd.

"Shit," I swore.

The searchlight swept over the street, illuminating the faces of the scavengers and factory workers. It was moving toward us.

"Dorian, move."

I grabbed the front of his sweater and shoved him backward.

We crashed into the narrow gap between a noodle shop and a derelict warehouse. It wasn't a street; it was a scar in the architecture. Dark. Damp. Smelling of old rain and garbage.

I pushed him back until his shoulders hit the brick wall.

"Stay down," I whispered, pressing myself against him to shield his body from the street view.

The skiff roared overhead, the engines vibrating in my teeth. The blue light slashed across the mouth of the alley, lingering for a heart-stopping second before moving on.

I didn't breathe.

Dorian didn't breathe either. But he wasn't looking at the skiff.

He was looking at me.

We were pressed together in the dark, trapped in a space barely wide enough for one person, let alone two. My chest was heaving against his. My thigh was wedged between his legs.

The danger passed, but I didn't move away. I couldn't.

The heat coming off him was intoxicating. It wrapped around me, fighting the chill of the night.

"They're gone," I whispered, my voice shaky.

"I don't care," Dorian murmured.

He wasn't slumped against the wall anymore. He was standing straight, using the brick for leverage. His hands—one flesh, one bandaged metal—came up to grip my waist.

He pulled me in. Hard.

"Dorian—"

"You felt it," he said, his voice rough, stripped of all the royal cadence. "In the club. You felt it."

"I don't know what you're talking about."

"Liar."

His hands slid up my sides. They were heavy, possessive. His thumbs dug into the soft leather of the corset, finding the sensitive spot between my ribs and my hip bone.

"You were grinding against me," he accused softly. "You liked it when I broke that guy's wrist."

"I did not—"

"You did." He leaned down, his forehead resting against mine. His eyes were dark voids in the shadow, swallowing me whole. "You like the monster, Sara. You hate the Prince, but you like the monster."

My breath hitched.

He was right. God help me, he was right. The violence, the heat, the sheer overwhelming *force* of him... it terrified me, and it made my knees weak.

"You're drunk," I said weakly.

"I'm honest."

His hand—the human one—slid up my back, tangling in the loose hair at the nape of my neck. He tilted my head back.

"Tell me to stop," he whispered. His lips were inches from mine. I could taste the cheap Rot on his breath. "Tell me to stop, and I will."

I should have said it. *Stop. Rule One. Rule Two.*
I didn't say anything.

My hands, seemingly of their own volition, slid under the hem of his wool sweater.

His skin was scalding. I touched the hard planes of his stomach, my fingers tracing the ridges of muscle. I moved higher, finding the place where skin met metal. The transition was seamless, terrifyingly smooth.

Dorian groaned, a low, guttural sound that vibrated through his chest and straight into mine.

He pressed his hips forward.

Oh.
There was no mistaking that. He was hard. Painfully hard. And he was pressing that hardness right against the juncture of my thighs, grinding slow and deliberate.

The friction sent a jolt of electricity through me that had nothing to do with the Torque.

"Dorian," I gasped, my fingers digging into his back.

"Sara," he breathed.

His mouth ghosted over my jawline. He kissed the spot just below my ear. Shivers cascaded down my spine. He kissed the corner of my mouth.

I turned my head. I wanted him to kiss me. I wanted to taste the fire.

Our lips brushed. It was a tease. A promise.

"You make me want to burn this whole city down," he whispered against my mouth. "Just to see you smile."

My heart hammered a frantic rhythm. *Do it,* the reckless part of my brain screamed. *Kiss him. Ruin everything.*

His hand tightened in my hair. He started to close the distance, to crush his mouth against mine—

Then he stopped.

He froze.

The bandaged metal arm on my waist went rigid. The hand in my hair stilled.

He pulled back. Just an inch.

He looked at me. The fog in his eyes cleared, just for a second, replaced by a stark, brutal clarity. He looked at my face. He looked at my hands under his shirt.

He realized who he was. And who I was.

"We can't," he rasped.

He pulled his hands away from me like I was made of acid. He slumped back against the brick wall, closing his eyes, fighting for breath.

"We can't do this," he said, his voice sounding shattered.

I stood there, bereft of his heat, my skin tingling, my lips throbbing from a kiss that never happened.

The rejection stung. It stung worse than a slap.

"Right," I said, stepping back. My voice sounded hollow. I pulled my hands out from under his sweater, smoothing my clothes. "Right. Of course."

"Sara, it's not—"

"Don't," I snapped. I turned away, staring out at the empty street. "You're the Prince. I'm the hire. Rule One. I forgot."

"It's not about the rules," he said to my back.

"It's about survival," I said, forcing the mask back into place. The sarcasm. The armor. "And making out in an alley with a nuclear reactor in a sweater is bad for my health."

I turned back to him. I looked at him—disheveled, panting, beautiful, and utterly out of reach.

"Come on, Your Highness," I said, my voice flat. "Let's get you back to your tower before you rust."

I walked out of the alley without waiting for him.

I heard him push off the wall. I heard his heavy boots following me.

But the distance between us felt wider than the canyon of the street. We had walked up to the edge, looked down, and realized the fall wouldn't just kill us.

It would destroy everything.

Chapter 21: The Morning After

Dorian

My head felt like someone had taken a sledgehammer to the base of my skull and left it there.

I opened my eyes. The light filtering through the curtains was an assault. It stabbed directly into my retinas, bypassing the optic nerve and drilling straight into the pain receptors.

"Ugh," I groaned, rolling over.

The movement was a mistake. My stomach—which had been subjected to industrial-grade solvent disguised as alcohol the night before—revolted. I swallowed hard, fighting down the bile.

System Status: Critical Toxicity. Hydration Levels: 15%. Recommend immediate purge.

I mentally swiped the HUD warning away. I didn't want a purge. I deserved the pain. It was penance.

I sat up, swinging my legs over the edge of the bed. The room spun. I gripped the mattress with my metal hand, tearing a small hole in the expensive silk sheet.

Memory washed over me in a disjointed, technicolor wave.

The bass thumping in my chest. The smell of sweat and ozone. The alley.

Sara.
I froze.

I remembered the cold brick wall against my back. I remembered the heat of her body pressed against mine. I remembered her hands—rough, bold, perfect—sliding under my sweater.

You make me want to burn this whole city down.

I groaned again, burying my face in my hands. I had actually said that. I had looked a woman in the eye—my employee, my bodyguard, a girl I was actively putting in mortal danger—and quoted a bad romance novel.

"Pathetic," I whispered to the empty room.

But the shame wasn't the worst part. The worst part was that I meant it.

I stood up, stumbling slightly, and made my way to the bathroom. I needed cold water. I needed to scrub the grease paint off my face and the smell of lavender out of my nose.

I turned the shower on full blast. Cold.

I stood under the spray, letting it shock my system. The water ran black as the axle grease washed out of my hair. I watched it swirl down the drain, taking the illusion of the "dockworker" with it.

When I stepped out, toweling off my hair, I looked at myself in the mirror.

The circles under my eyes were real now. The scar where metal met flesh was angry, inflamed from the heat of the Torque spike. I looked like exactly what I was: a machine running on fumes.

I was obsessed with her.

It wasn't just lust. Lust I could handle. I had been propositioned by Duchesses and courtesans my entire adult life. I knew how to say no to a body.

But Sara? Sara was different. She was the only thing in this palace that felt *real*. She saw the monster and didn't flinch. She saw the Prince and rolled her eyes.

And last night, in that alley, I had wanted to claim her so badly it terrified me.

If I touched her—really touched her—I wouldn't stop. I would consume her. And when my father found out... and he *would* find out... he wouldn't just fire her. He would use her. He would hurt her to control me.

She was a weakness. A glowing, sarcastic, pipe-wielding weak point in my armor.

I had to close the breach.

Knock. Knock.

I stiffened. I knew that knock. It wasn't the polite rap of a servant. It was the impatient, heavy-handed thud of a Slag.

"Enter," I called out. My voice sounded like gravel.

The door opened. Sara walked in.

She looked tired. Her hair was messy, pulled back in a loose knot. She was back in the uniform—the corset, the tactical pants—but she hadn't put the cloak on yet.

She held a tray. Coffee. Black. And a bottle of water.

She stopped a few feet away. She looked at me, searching for the man she'd danced with in the club. The man who had almost kissed her.

"You look like hell," she said. It was an attempt at banter. A bridge.

I didn't cross it.

I walked over to the wardrobe, turning my back to her to pull on a fresh, stiff-collared shirt.

"Put it on the table," I said. My voice was cool. Detached. "And close the door. You're letting a draft in."

The silence behind me was deafening.

"Right," she said slowly. I heard the clink of the china on the table. "I figured you'd need the caffeine. That Rot is nasty stuff."

"It was a lapse in judgment," I said, buttoning the shirt with precise, mechanical movements. "I was intoxicated. It won't happen again."

"A lapse in judgment," she repeated. Her voice went flat. "Is that what we're calling it?"

I turned around. I forced my face into the mask of the Prince. Bored. Arrogant. Untouchable.

"What would you call it, Sara? A bonding exercise?" I scoffed, a short, cruel sound. "I was bored. I wanted to see the slums. You were a convenient tour guide. Don't read into it."

She flinched. Just a tiny movement, like I'd flicked her on the nose.

"Convenient," she said.

"Yes. You're here to do a job. Open the Vault. Keep me alive. Not to... fraternize." I walked past her to the table, picking up the coffee. I didn't look at her. "Speaking of the job, I need you to run a diagnostic on the tools. We hit the

Vault in three days. I want to make sure you didn't damage the picks trying to open a window last night."

She stood there, staring at me. Her hands were clenched into fists at her sides. I saw the hurt in her eyes, raw and open, before she slammed the shutters down.

The wall went up. Her chin lifted. The fire went out, replaced by ice.

"Understood, Your Highness," she said.

The title sounded like a slur.

"Good," I said, taking a sip of the coffee. It was bitter. It tasted like ash. "You can go. I have meetings. Send Voss in on your way out."

Sara looked at me for one long, agonizing second. She looked at the man who had begged her to stay close in the dark, and she realized he was gone.

"Yes, sir," she said.

She turned on her heel, military precision, and marched to the door.

"Sara," I said, before she could leave.

She paused, hand on the latch. She didn't look back.

"The sweater," I said, gesturing to the pile of clothes on the floor. "Burn it. It smells like the Sinkhole."

She went rigid.

"I'll take care of it," she said.

She opened the door and walked out, closing it with a soft, final click.

I stood alone in the silent room. I looked at the closed door. I looked at my reflection in the mirror—the perfect, polished Prince.

I picked up the coffee cup and hurled it across the room.

It shattered against the wall, spraying black liquid over the pristine white silk wallpaper.

"Damn it," I whispered, leaning my forehead against the cool glass of the window.

I had saved her. I had pushed her away so she wouldn't get burned by the fire inside me.

So why did it feel like I was the one who had just burned down?

Chapter 22: The Ball

Sara

If the leather corset was a straightjacket, the gown was a death trap.

It was liquid silver—a slip of silk so fine it felt like it would tear if I breathed too hard. It clung to me like a second skin, pooling at my feet in a puddle of mercury. The back was non-existent, plunging down to the base of my spine, leaving my scars exposed to the air conditioning.

"I hate it," I said to the mirror.

"It is the height of fashion," the stylist sniffed, pinning a diamond clasp into my hair. "House Vane calls this shade 'Bullet Casing'."

"House Vane can bite me," I muttered.

I looked at the reflection. The woman staring back wasn't Sara the Rat. She wasn't Sara the Bodyguard. She looked like a weapon wrapped in expensive wrapping paper.

"Where do I put my knife?" I asked.

The stylist sighed, the sound of a long-suffering artist dealing with a philistine. "There are no pockets in couture, darling."

"Then make one."

I lifted the skirt. It had a high slit up the left leg—high enough to make a priest blush. I grabbed the leather thigh holster I'd scavenged from my tactical gear and strapped it on. It bit into my skin, tight and reassuring.

I slid the obsidian dagger—a gift from Voss—into the sheath.

I dropped the silk. The knife vanished. But I could feel the weight of it against my thigh. A cold, hard secret.

"The mask," the stylist said, handing me a piece of metal filigree.

It wasn't a delicate lace mask like the ones the noblewomen wore. It was jagged. Sharp. Black iron worked into the shape of a hawk's skull, covering the upper half of my face. It looked predatory.

I tied it on.

"Perfect," the stylist said, stepping back. "You look terrifying."

"Good."

I walked out of the suite. I didn't check the adjoining door. I didn't want to see him.

Since he'd dismissed me yesterday morning—since he'd called our night out a "lapse in judgment"—Dorian had been a ghost. He gave orders through Voss. He ate in his study. He treated me like exactly what I was: a hired gun he regretted touching.

Convenient tour guide.
The words still burned in my chest like swallowed acid.

I took the elevator down to the Grand Ballroom. The doors opened, and the noise hit me.

It wasn't the thumping bass of the Sinkhole. It was a polite, murmuring roar. A thousand voices whispering lies over the sound of a string quartet.

I stepped inside.

The room was a kaleidoscope of gold, velvet, and jewels. Chandeliers the size of small houses hung from the ceiling, dripping magic light. The floor was polished marble, reflecting the swirling colors of the dancers.

Everyone was masked. Foxes. Lions. Swans. Dragons.

I scanned the room, my HUD—mental, not digital—highlighting threats.

Exits: North, South, East (Service). Security: Perimeter only. Threat Level: Moderate.
And then I saw him.

He was standing on the dais, next to the Golden Throne where his father was docked.

Dorian wasn't wearing the "dockworker" disguise tonight. He was the Prince in full glory. He wore a military dress uniform of white and gold, fitted perfectly to his broad shoulders. A cape of white velvet hung from one shoulder.

His mask was gold. It covered the right side of his face—the human side. The left side, the metal side, was left exposed. He had inverted the masquerade. He was hiding the man and showing the monster.

He looked cold. Remote. Beautiful.

He was scanning the crowd, looking bored. Then, his gaze snagged on me.

Even across the room, even through the crowd of peacocks, he found me. His eyes—the dark one hidden behind gold mesh, the fractured blue one exposed—locked onto mine.

He didn't smile. He didn't nod.

His gaze traveled down the silver dress, lingering on the slit in the skirt, then snapped back to my face. His jaw tightened. The servos in his neck flared.

He looked away, turning to whisper something to a Duke standing nearby.

Asshole, I thought.

I moved into the crowd. I wasn't here to dance. I was here to intercept.

"Champagne, mademoiselle?" A waiter offered a tray.

"Water," I said. "And keep it coming."

I skirted the edge of the dance floor, positioning myself near a pillar where I had a clear line of sight to the dais. I crossed my arms, then realized it ruined the line of the dress, and dropped them.

"My, my," a voice purred. "What a sharp little bird."

I turned. A man in a red velvet suit and a fox mask was standing too close. He smelled of brandy and entitlement.

"I'm working," I said flatly.

"Working?" He laughed, stepping closer. His hand reached out to touch the bare skin of my arm. "A creature like you shouldn't be working. You should be... displayed."

I didn't move away. I stepped *into* his space.

"Touch me," I whispered, leaning close so only he could hear, "and I will pin that hand to the wall with a shrimp fork."

The fox mask froze. He looked at my mouth, then at the jagged hawk mask, then down at the slit in my dress where the outline of the dagger was faintly visible against my thigh.

"Feisty," he muttered, backing away, his hands raised. "I like them feisty."

"Run along, Fox," I said. "Before I decide to hunt."

He scuttled away.

I let out a breath, leaning back against the pillar. I hated this. I hated the games. I hated the masks.

"You look like you're planning a murder," a voice said beside me.

I didn't jump. I knew that voice.

I turned slowly.

Dorian was standing there. He had come down from the dais. The crowd had parted for him like the Red Sea, leaving a respectful bubble of space around us.

Up close, the gold mask was unnerving. It made him look like his father.

"I'm always planning a murder," I said, keeping my voice cool. "It's in the job description."

"You're supposed to be blending in," he said. His voice was low, tight. "That dress is not blending in."

"Your staff picked it. Blame them."

"It's... effective." His human eye was hidden, but I could feel him looking at the exposed skin of my back. "You've terrified Lord Vane. He's currently hiding behind the punch bowl."

"He tried to touch me."

"He has a death wish."

Dorian stepped closer. He was radiating that same cold, controlled energy from the morning. The wall was up. But beneath it, I could feel the hum. The vibration of the machine.

"Why are you here, Dorian?" I asked. " shouldn't you be up there, looking down on us plebs?"

"I needed to check the perimeter," he lied.

"The perimeter is secure. I checked it."

"I wanted to double-check."

He stood next to me, shoulder to shoulder, both of us facing the crowd. We looked like a matched set. The Golden Prince and the Iron Hawk.

"The Vault," he whispered, barely moving his lips. "Voss signaled. The rotation has been shifted. We have a smaller window. Two minutes."

"I can do it in one," I whispered back.

"Good."

Silence stretched between us. The string quartet began a waltz. It was slow, haunting.

"You're standing too close," I murmured. "People are staring."

"Let them stare."

"I thought you didn't want to 'fraternize' with the help."

Dorian turned his head. The gold mask gleamed under the chandelier light.

"I lied," he said softly.

My heart did a traitorous little flip.

"About what?"

"About being bored," he said. "In the alley."

He reached out. His metal hand took mine. The cold alloy against my skin sent a shiver straight up my spine.

"Dance with me, Sara."

"I don't waltz," I panicked. "I brawl."

"It's the same thing," Dorian said, pulling me toward the floor. "Just with better music."

"Dorian, no. The King is watching."

"My father is watching a graph of his own heart rate," Dorian said, not stopping. "He won't notice."

He dragged me into the center of the floor. The other dancers cleared a space, staring. The Prince and the Slag. The Gold and the Iron.

He stopped. He turned me to face him.

He placed his human hand on my waist, right on the bare skin of my lower back. His fingers burned.

"Follow my lead," he ordered.

"If you step on my toes," I warned, placing my hand on his shoulder, "I'm tripping you."

"Deal."

The music swelled. And the Prince swept me into the spin.

Chapter 23: The Dance

Dorian

The waltz is a weapon.

Most people think it's a dance. They think it's about romance, or tradition, or showing off your expensive hemline. They are wrong.

The waltz is about control. It is about momentum, centrifugal force, and the ability to steer another human being exactly where you want them to go, all while making it look like they are floating.

I held Sara's waist with my human hand. Her skin was hot, damp with a sheen of nervous sweat, and utterly bare beneath my fingers. The silver silk of her dress was slippery, threatening to slide away, but I held on.

"Stop marching," I murmured, leaning down so my lips brushed the shell of her ear. "You're counting steps. Stop counting."

"I have to count," she hissed through a fixed, terrifyingly fake smile. "If I don't count, I'm going to kick you in the shin."

"Kick me, and we both fall. And if we fall, my father notices. And if he notices, he starts asking why the Slag is dancing with the Prince instead of guarding the door."

I spun her.

She gasped, gripping my shoulder. Her hand—the one usually holding a pipe or a knife—dug into my epaulet. She was light, surprisingly so. For all her talk of being grounded and heavy, she moved like smoke when she wasn't trying to fight the current.

"Relax," I ordered. "Let me drive."

"I hate not driving."

"I know."

I steered us through the sea of spinning couples. We were a shark moving through a school of tropical fish. The nobles parted for us, their eyes hungry, watching the spectacle. The Golden Prince and his dangerous pet.

I could feel their judgment. I could feel their jealousy.

But mostly, I could feel Sara.

Every time our thighs brushed, a jolt of static electricity snapped against my skin. My metal arm—resting on her shoulder to maintain the frame—hummed a low, harmonious note. The proximity sensors were screaming *Contact. Contact. Contact.*

I ignored them. I focused on the room.

"Three o'clock," I whispered against her hair. "Lord Silas. Fat man. Purple velvet. Mask that looks like a depressed walrus."

Sara didn't look. She kept her eyes on my throat, her chin tilted up. "I see him in my peripheral. What about him?"

"He's the High Steward. He holds the Master Key for the service elevators. The mechanical override."

"I thought we were using the laundry chute."

"We are. But if the chute is blocked, or if the alarm triggers, the elevators lock down. We need that key as a fail-safe."

I tightened my grip on her waist.

"We're going to intercept," I murmured. "I'm going to spin you into him. You're going to stumble. You're going to apologize. And you're going to lift the key from his sash."

Sara's eyes snapped to mine. The dark pupils widened behind the jagged iron mask.

"You want me to pickpocket a High Lord in the middle of a ballroom?"

"I want you to do what you're good at, Rat."

I pulled her closer, closing the gap until there was no air between us. The music swelled—a crescendo of violins.

"Ready?"

"Always," she breathed.

I changed the tempo. I drove us forward, cutting across the grain of the dance floor. One, two, three. Spin. One, two, three. Spin.

We gained speed. The room blurred into streaks of gold and candlelight. Sara moved with me, matching my stride, her body fluid and responsive.

We bore down on Lord Silas. He was dancing—badly— with a young Duchess who looked like she wanted to be anywhere else.

"Now," I commanded.

I spun Sara out.

It was a calculated error. I put too much force into the turn, sending her stumbling backward—right into Silas's path.

She played it perfectly. She gasped, flailing a hand out to catch her balance. She collided with Silas's ample stomach.

"Oh!" she cried, her voice pitched high and breathless. "My Lord! I am so clumsy!"

Silas grunted, steadying her with meaty hands. "Steady on, girl! Watch your—"

He stopped when he saw the iron mask. He stopped when he saw me looming behind her.

"My apologies, Lord Silas," I said, stepping in smoothly. "My partner is... unaccustomed to the finer points of the waltz. She has two left feet."

"Your Highness!" Silas bowed as best he could while holding Sara. "No harm done. A spirited dancer, indeed."

I looked at Sara. She was pressed against Silas, her hands resting on his chest, her face turned up in apology.

But I watched her right hand. It was sliding down.

"Apologize properly, Sara," I said, keeping my voice low, commanding.

I saw her fingers twitch.

"I am terribly sorry, my Lord," she purred, brushing imaginary dust from his purple sash. "I was just... overwhelmed by the music."

Her hand slipped inside the folds of the velvet sash. Fast. Invisible.

I saw the faint glint of brass.

Then, her hand was back at her side. The key was gone. Vanished into the secret slit of her dress, tucked against the obsidian dagger.

"Charming," Silas mumbled, looking flushed. He had no idea he'd just been robbed. He was too busy staring at Sara's neckline.

"Come along, darling," I said, grabbing Sara's hand and pulling her away. "Let's not bruise any more dignitaries."

I swept her back into the dance.

As soon as we were clear, the adrenaline hit. I felt it rolling off her in waves. Her skin was hotter now, her breath coming faster.

"Got it," she whispered. Her eyes were shining with the high of the theft. "Brass key. heavy. Old tech."

"Good girl," I murmured.

The words slipped out before I could check them.

Sara faltered. She missed a step. Her boot clipped mine.

She looked up at me, startled. The phrase hung in the air between us, charged and heavy. It wasn't a commendation for a soldier. It was something else. Something possessive. Something dark.

I didn't take it back.

I pulled her back into the rhythm, harder this time. I slid my hand from her waist down to the curve of her hip, pressing my fingers into the silk.

"Dorian," she warned, her voice shaky.

"You like the danger," I whispered, leaning close again. I wanted to rattle her. I wanted to see if the thief could handle the Prince. "I can feel your heart hammering against my chest. You're enjoying this."

"I'm enjoying the job," she lied.

"Liar."

I spun her again, a tight, fast rotation that forced her to cling to me. Her breasts pressed against my chest. Her thigh slotted between mine.

"You look like you want to bite me, Sara," I taunted softly. "Go ahead. I'm plated. You won't break skin."

Her eyes narrowed behind the mask. The predator woke up.

"Careful, Chrome," she whispered back, her voice dropping to a smoke-filled growl. "I don't need to break skin to hurt you. I know where your off switch is."

I laughed. It was a breathy, broken sound.

"Then hit it," I dared her. "Turn me off."

We stared at each other, spinning in the center of the golden room, locked in a stalemate of lust and violence.

The music ended with a final, dramatic chord.

We stopped. We were breathing hard, chest to chest, staring into each other's eyes. The applause of the crowd sounded distant, muffled by the roaring of the blood in my ears.

I didn't want to let go. I wanted to drag her off the floor, throw her over my shoulder, and carry her out of here.

But the King was watching.

I stepped back. I bowed, perfectly formal.

"Thank you for the dance," I said, my voice loud enough for the crowd.

Sara curtsied. It was stiff, reluctant, and sarcastic.

"The pleasure was all yours, Your Highness."

She turned and walked away, the silver dress rippling like liquid metal. She didn't look back.

I watched her go. I watched the way her hips moved. I watched the way the crowd parted for her, sensing the danger.

I touched my chest, right over the mechanical heart. It was racing.

Checkmate, I thought.
I had the key. I had the thief.

But I was starting to think she had stolen something much more dangerous than a piece of brass.

Chapter 24: The Balcony

Sara

I didn't walk off the dance floor. I marched.

The applause followed us, a polite, gloved thunder that made my teeth ache. I could feel Dorian's eyes on my back—heavy, burning, possessive.

Good girl.

The words echoed in my skull, bouncing around like a ricocheting bullet. It was patronizing. It was arrogant.

And god help me, it had sent a jolt of heat straight to my core that nearly made me trip over my own expensive hemline.

I needed air. I needed cold, dirty, smog-filled air to clear the perfume out of my lungs.

I shoved through the heavy velvet curtains of the nearest balcony door and stepped out into the night.

The noise of the party cut out instantly, replaced by the distant hum of the city below and the wind whipping around the spire. It was freezing. I didn't care. The silver dress offered zero protection, but my blood was running so hot I could have melted snow.

The curtain rustled behind me.

I didn't turn around. I knew who it was. I could hear the heavy, rhythmic tread of his boots. I could feel the static charge in the air.

"You're running away," Dorian said. His voice was low, stripped of the ballroom charm.

"I'm tactical retreating," I snapped, gripping the stone railing. "Before I stab a diplomat. Or you."

"You have the key," he said, stepping closer. "Mission accomplished. Why are you angry?"

"I'm not angry." I spun around to face him. "I'm... agitated."

He was standing three feet away, the golden mask still in place, the white cape fluttering in the wind. He looked like a statue of a god that had decided to walk off its pedestal just to ruin my life.

"Agitated," he repeated, testing the word. He took a step forward. "Is it the adrenaline? Or is it the fact that for three minutes out there, you forgot you hated me?"

"I didn't forget."

"Liar."

He stepped into my personal space. Again. Always pushing. Always testing the perimeter.

"You liked it," he whispered, looking down at me. The gold mesh over his eye caught the moonlight. "You liked the control. You liked being held."

Something inside me snapped.

Maybe it was the stress of the heist. Maybe it was the dress. Maybe it was the way he looked at me—like I was something wild he had caught but hadn't quite figured out how to cage yet.

"You think you were in control?" I hissed.

I lunged.

I didn't hit him. I grabbed the lapels of his pristine white uniform and shoved him backward.

It was a stupid move. He weighed three hundred pounds and was anchored to the floor by magnetic boots. But I caught him off guard. He stumbled back, his calves hitting the low stone bench, and he fell back against the railing.

I didn't let go. I followed him down, pressing my body against his, pinning him to the stone.

"Sara," he gasped, his hands coming up to hover over my waist, unsure whether to push me away or pull me closer.

"Shut up," I growled. "You talk too much."

I was furious. I was terrified. I was turned on.

I pushed my knee between his legs.

Dorian's breath hitched, a sharp, strangled sound. His head knocked back against the stone pillar, exposing his throat.

I pressed closer. The slit in my dress fell open, leaving nothing but a thin layer of silk and my own bare skin against the coarse wool of his trousers.

I felt him react instantly. He hardened against my thigh, a rigid line of heat that made my own breath catch.

"You want to play games, Chrome?" I whispered, bringing my face inches from his. "You want to see who breaks first?"

"Sara," he warned, his voice straining. "Don't."

"Don't what?"

I moved my hips. Just a fraction. A slow, deliberate grind against the erection straining against his pants.

Dorian's hands gripped the stone railing on either side of him. He gripped it so hard I heard the marble crack. The stone pulverized under his metal fingers, dust raining down onto the balcony floor.

He was using every ounce of his strength not to touch me. Because he knew—we both knew—that if he put his hands on me right now, the dress wouldn't survive.

"You are playing with fire," he rasped, his human eye blown wide, staring at my mouth.

"I was born in the fire," I murmured.

I dragged my hand up his chest, over the medals, over the gold braid. I reached up and grabbed the edge of his mask.

I ripped it off.

It clattered to the floor.

He looked wrecked. His hair was windblown, his mismatched eyes wild with hunger. The scar where the metal met his skin was glowing faint red—he was overheating again.

"Kiss me," I dared him. "Do it."

He leaned forward. He wanted to. I could see the war happening behind his eyes—the Prince vs. the Man. The logic vs. the biological imperative.

He groaned, a low, guttural sound of pure frustration. He bucked his hips upward, driving himself into my thigh.

The friction sent a shockwave through me that curled my toes. I gasped, my head falling back, exposing my neck.

"Sara, please," he begged. It wasn't a command. It was a plea. "Stop. I can't... I can't hold back much longer."

"Then don't."

"I will hurt you," he said, his voice raw. "I am five hundred pounds of torque and steel. If I lose control... I will break you."

The words hung in the cold air.

I will break you.
It wasn't a threat. It was a confession. He was terrified of his own strength. He was terrified of hurting the only thing that made him feel real.

The anger drained out of me, leaving me cold and shaking.

I realized what I was doing. I was teasing a bomb.

I stopped moving. I took a breath, inhaling the scent of him—ozone and desire.

I stepped back.

The loss of contact was physical pain. It felt like tearing a bandage off a fresh wound.

Dorian slumped against the railing, his chest heaving, his hands still white-knuckled on the stone. He looked destroyed. He looked beautiful.

I smoothed my dress. I adjusted the jagged iron mask on my face.

"You're right," I said, my voice trembling slightly. "We have a job to do."

Dorian didn't speak. He just looked at me, his eyes dark with unspent need.

"Consider that payback," I whispered. "For the 'good girl'."

I turned and walked back toward the curtain.

My legs were shaking. My core was throbbing. I felt like I was walking away from a warm hearth into a blizzard.

I paused at the door.

"Sara," he croaked.

I looked back.

He was still leaning against the railing, looking at the empty space where I had been.

"You have the key?" he asked. His voice was wrecked.

I patted the slit in my dress, feeling the cold brass against my skin.

"I have everything I need," I lied.

I slipped through the curtain, leaving the Prince alone in the dark, hard and aching and dangerously close to the edge.

Chapter 25: Blue Balls

Dorian

The water was freezing. It was pumped directly from the glacial melt reservoirs deep beneath the city, chilled to a temperature that would stop a normal human heart in three minutes.

I had been standing under it for twenty.

Steam was rising off my skin. Not the gentle, spa-like mist of the bathhouse, but angry, hissing clouds of vapor. My body was reacting to the cold like a forge dropped in a lake. The biological half was shivering, goosebumps rising on my human arm. The mechanical half was glowing, the cooling vents along my ribs wide open, trying to dump the excess thermal energy.

It wasn't working.

I leaned my forehead against the wet marble tiles and groaned. The sound echoed in the shower stall, low and pathetic.

"Stupid," I muttered. "Stupid, reckless, self-destructive..."

I let the insults roll over me, hoping they would drown out the other sensation. The throbbing, relentless ache in my groin.

Sara had played me. She had played me like a cheap fiddle. She had dragged me to the edge of the cliff, dangled me over the void, and then walked away, leaving me to deal with the fall.

I closed my eyes. Big mistake.

Instantly, I was back on the balcony. I felt the silk of her dress against my wool trousers. I felt the sharp point of her knee pressing between my legs. I felt the ghost of her breath against my mouth.

Kiss me. Do it.
My hands curled into fists. The metal one crunched a chunk of the expensive tile, turning it to powder.

"Dammit," I hissed.

I punched the wall. Just once. The impact shuddered through my shoulder, a dull, satisfying thud that momentarily distracted me from the frustration lower down.

It wasn't just sex. If it were just sex, I could handle it. I could go find a willing partner in the court—there were plenty of volunteers—and work it out of my system.

But I didn't want a volunteer. I wanted the Rat.

I wanted the girl who looked at my crown and saw a target. I wanted the girl who stole silverware and threatened to stab diplomats. I wanted the friction, the argument, the defiance.

I wanted to break her open and see if she burned as hot on the inside as she did on the outside.

But I couldn't.

I looked down at my metal hand. The water slicked off the chrome plating.

I will break you.
That wasn't a pickup line. It was a statistical probability. When the Torque spiked, my grip strength increased

exponentially. If I lost control in the heat of the moment... if I held her too tight...

I could snap her ribs like dry twigs. I could crush her spine.

I was a weapon. Weapons don't get to have soft things.

I turned the water off. The silence that rushed back into the room was deafening.

I stepped out, grabbing a towel. I dried off aggressively, avoiding the mirror. I didn't want to see the flush on my skin or the desperation in my eyes.

I walked into the bedroom. It was cold. The balcony door was still open, the curtain fluttering in the wind where she had left.

I slammed the door shut.

I pulled on a pair of loose linen pants, ignoring the shirt. My skin was still too sensitive, vibrating with unspent energy. I poured a drink. Whiskey. Neat.

I downed it. It didn't help.

The comms panel on my wall chimed.

"What," I barked.

"Your Highness," Voss's voice crackled through the speaker. "The King requests your presence in the War Room. Immediate priority."

"Tell him I'm indisposed," I snapped, pouring another drink. "Tell him I'm... having mechanical difficulties."

"He knows you're awake, sir. He's monitoring your biometrics. He says your heart rate is elevated."

"My heart rate is none of his business."

"He thinks you're having a panic attack."

"I am having," I said, staring at the empty space where Sara had stood, "a very different kind of attack, Voss."

"Sir?"

"Never mind. I'm coming."

I grabbed a tunic—black, high-collared, severe—and pulled it on. I fastened the buttons with trembling fingers. I needed to lock it down. I needed to be the Prince again.

I checked the internal HUD.

Core Temp: 101°F. Torque Output: Stabilizing. Adrenaline: Elevating.
It would have to do.

I walked out of the suite. I glanced at Sara's door. It was shut tight. I could hear the faint sound of movement inside—probably her hiding the stolen key or sharpening her knives.

I resisted the urge to kick the door down and finish what we started on the balcony.

Focus, I told myself. *The Mission.*
I marched down the hallway, my boots echoing on the marble. The guards snapped to attention as I passed. I ignored them.

I reached the War Room. The heavy iron doors groaned open.

My father was there, docked into the tactical table. A holographic map of the outer territories hovered in the air.

"You are late," the King buzzed.

"I was washing off the stench of the ball," I said, walking to the table. "What is the emergency? Did a Duke drop a monocle?"

"Insurrection," Aric said. The hologram zoomed in on a jagged mountain range to the north. "Sector 7. The Iron peaks. We have lost contact with the outpost."

"Rebels?"

"Likely. Or just incompetence. It is a remote listening post. Vital for the perimeter defense grid."

"So send a squad," I said, bored. "Send the Sterlings. They like marching."

"No," Aric said. His red lenses fixed on me. "I am sending you."

I paused. "Me?"

"You have been... erratic, Dorian. Distracted. The display on the dance floor tonight was unbecoming. Dancing with the help? Crushing railings?"

He knew. Of course he knew. He saw everything.

"I am sending you to re-establish contact," the King continued. "It is a diplomatic mission. Show the flag. Remind the outer districts of the Crown's power. If there are rebels, burn them. If it is incompetence, execute the commander."

"I have duties here," I argued. "The preparations for the festival—"

"Are secondary. You leave at dawn."

The King's mechanical hand tapped the table.

"Take the girl," he added.

I froze. "Excuse me?"

" The bodyguard. The Rat. Take her with you."

"Why?"

"Because if there are rebels, you will need a shield," Aric said coldly. "And if she dies in the line of duty... well, it solves the problem of your distraction, doesn't it?"

I stared at my father. He wasn't sending me on a mission. He was sending me on a test. He wanted to see if I would use her as a tool, or if I would bleed for her.

And he was hoping she wouldn't come back.

I felt a cold, sharp clarity settle over me. The frustration from the balcony evaporated, replaced by the icy calculation of the heist.

This wasn't a punishment. It was an opportunity.

If we were out of the city... if we were away from the surveillance, the guards, the eyes...

We could plan. We could prep.

And we would be alone.

"Fine," I said, keeping my face impassive. "I'll pack a bag."

"Dawn," Aric repeated. "Do not fail me, my son."

"I never do," I lied.

I turned and walked out. As the doors closed behind me, a slow, dangerous smile spread across my face.

Diplomatic mission. Remote outpost. Just me, the thief, and a carriage ride across the frozen wastelands.

My groin gave a phantom throb of anticipation.

I was definitely going to need more cold showers.

Chapter 26: The Mission

Sara

The Royal Carriage looked like a hearse designed by a paranoid jeweler.

It was black, armored, and trimmed with enough gold filigree to feed a Slag family for a decade. The windows were tinted obsidian glass, bulletproof and spell-sealed. The wheels were reinforced with runic iron treads meant for crushing bone and gravel alike.

"Subtle," I muttered, standing on the loading dock as the steam horses huffed clouds of vapor into the dawn air.

"It is built for security, not subtlety," Voss grunted. He was checking the harness of the lead mechanical stallion. He wasn't wearing his usual gold-plated armor. He was in heavy travel leathers, a scattergun strapped to his back.

"You're driving?" I asked.

"The Prince requested a driver who wouldn't panic if we hit a landmine," Voss said, patting the metal flank of the horse. "And I like the fresh air."

"Fresh air? Voss, we're going to the Iron Peaks. The air there is forty percent sulfur."

"Better than the perfume in the Palace," he countered.

I couldn't argue with that.

The heavy doors of the East Wing opened. Dorian emerged.

He looked... severe. He was wearing a heavy, fur-lined greatcoat over a black tactical uniform that mirrored mine— minus the corset, plus a lot of expensive tailoring. He wore gloves. He wore high boots. He wore a scowl that could curdle milk.

He walked straight to the carriage, ignoring the line of servants bowing to him. He stopped in front of me.

"You're late," he lied. I had been standing here for twenty minutes.

"And you're grumpy," I shot back. "Rough night?"

His eyes—dark and fractured blue—flickered to mine. There was a flash of heat, a memory of the balcony, before he slammed the shutters down.

"Get in," he ordered.

I climbed into the carriage.

The interior was crushed velvet. Red. The color of arterial blood. It was plush, soundproofed, and shockingly intimate. The seats faced each other, but the legroom was designed for normal humans, not a six-foot-two cyborg Prince and a woman wearing combat boots.

Dorian climbed in after me. The carriage dipped under his weight. He slammed the door shut, sealing us in.

"Move over," he grumbled, settling onto the bench opposite me.

"I'm against the wall," I said. "Unless you want me to climb out the window, this is as 'over' as I get."

He stretched his legs out. His heavy boots knocked against mine. He didn't pull back. He just sighed, leaned his head back against the velvet squabs, and closed his eyes.

"Wake me when we hit the perimeter," he said.

The carriage lurched forward. The steam horses engaged, their pistons firing with a rhythmic *chug-chug-chug*.

We rolled out of the Palace gates, leaving the Gilt behind.

I watched the city pass through the tinted glass. It was a lesson in geology.

First came the Upper Districts. White marble, manicured sky-gardens, and fountains pumping chemically treated blue water. The streets were clean. The people were soft, dressed in silks, oblivious to the machine that kept their lights on.

Then came the descent.

The carriage ramped down the massive spiraling causeways into the Mid-Levels. The marble turned to concrete. The silk turned to denim and synthetic wool. The air outside the window grew thicker, stained with the yellow haze of industry.

Then, the Slags.

My home. We rattled past the towering stacks of District 12, where the smelters burned twenty-four hours a day. I saw the smoke belching into the sky, thick and black, coating the washing lines in soot. I saw children playing in puddles of iridescent runoff.

It looked smaller from inside the velvet carriage. It looked fragile.

Finally, we hit the Wall. The massive blast-shield that separated the City from the world it had murdered.

The gates groaned open, and we passed into the Wastelands.

The smooth hum of the pavement vanished, replaced by the jarring rattle of gravel and bone.

I stared out the window. I had seen the Wastes before, but never like this. Never from the safety of a bubble.

It was a graveyard of the Before Times. Skeletal skyscrapers stripped of all metal stood like ribcages against the purple sky. Vast craters, left over from the Resource Wars, were filled with toxic, glowing sludge lakes.

But the worst part was the Rust.

It covered everything. A sea of red dust that stretched to the horizon. It coated the dead trees. It buried the ruins. It wasn't just oxidation; it was a cancer. The land had been sucked dry, drained of every drop of vitality to power the golden spire behind us.

The Chrome City was a parasite, and this was its host corpse.

"It's ugly, isn't it?"

I jumped. Dorian's eyes were open. He was watching me watch the world.

"It's honest," I said, my voice quiet. "It doesn't pretend to be pretty."

"Unlike the Palace."

"The Palace is just a shiny tomb," I said, gesturing to the desolation outside. "This... this is just a murder scene. And your father is holding the weapon."

Dorian sat up, shedding the lethargy. He didn't argue. He looked out at the red dust swirling against the glass, his expression unreadable.

He pulled a silver flask from his greatcoat.

"Breakfast?" he offered.

"It's 7 AM."

"It's coffee," he said. "Spiked with a little accelerant for the core."

He took a swig and handed it to me. I wiped the rim—mostly to annoy him—and took a drink. It was black coffee, hot and bitter, with a kick of cinnamon and something chemical.

"So," I said, handing it back. "Sector 7. The Iron Peaks. Why are we really here, Dorian?"

"Diplomatic outreach," he recited tonelessly.

"Bullshit. You don't send the Crown Prince to a listening post to shake hands. You send him to burn things."

Dorian capped the flask. He leaned forward, elbows on his knees. The cabin was too small. His knees pressed against the outside of my thighs. The contact was firm, unavoidable.

"We lost contact with the outpost forty-eight hours ago," he said quietly. "My father thinks it's a rebellion."

"And if it is?"

"Then I am authorized to liquidate the asset."

"Liquidate," I repeated. "You mean kill everyone."

"I mean level the mountain."

A chill went through me that had nothing to do with the drafty window.

"And why am I here?" I asked. "To hold your coat while you commit war crimes?"

Dorian looked at me. His gaze was heavy, searching.

"He sent you to die, Sara."

The air left my lungs. "What?"

"He thinks you're a distraction," Dorian said. His voice was devoid of emotion, which made it terrifying. "He saw us at the ball. He saw the balcony. He thinks I'm... compromised. So he sent you to the front lines, hoping a stray bullet or a rebel bomb would solve his problem."

My hand went to the dagger in my thigh holster. "That old golden bastard."

"Careful," Dorian smirked, though it didn't reach his eyes. "That's my father you're talking about."

"He wants me dead because I danced with you?"

"He wants you dead because I *wanted* to dance with you," Dorian corrected. "There is a difference."

The carriage hit a massive pothole—likely a crater from an old mortar shell. We were thrown upward. I slammed back into the seat, and Dorian lurched forward.

His hand shot out to brace himself, landing on the seat next to my hip.

For a second, we were tangled. My legs between his. His face inches from mine.

The flask rattled on the floor.

He didn't move back.

"But he made a mistake," Dorian whispered.

"What mistake?" I breathed, my heart hammering against my ribs.

"He sent us away," he said. "Together. Alone. No cameras. No guards. Just us and the road."

He reached out with his metal hand. He didn't touch me. He traced the outline of the hawk mask I wasn't wearing, hovering just above my skin.

"He thinks this is a punishment," Dorian murmured. "He doesn't realize he just gave me exactly what I wanted."

"And what is that?"

"Time," he said. "And privacy."

He sat back, breaking the spell. He picked up the flask and dusted it off.

"We have two days of travel, Sara," he said, his voice returning to that cool, arrogant drawl. "We can use it to plan the heist. Or we can use it to drive each other crazy. Your choice."

I looked at him. The challenge was there. The heat was there.

"We plan," I said firmly. "The heist comes first."

Dorian smiled. It was a slow, wicked thing.

"Of course," he said. "The heist."

He closed his eyes again.

"But just so you know," he added, keeping his eyes shut. "The road to the Peaks is rough. There's going to be a lot of... friction."

I glared at him. I kicked his boot.

"Go to sleep, Prince."

He chuckled.

I turned back to the window, watching the endless rust roll by. The world outside was dead, eaten alive by the city we had left behind.

But inside the carriage, looking at his reflection in the glass, things felt dangerously alive.

Two days in a box with a weapon who wanted to burn the world down.

The King wanted me dead? Fine.

But I had a feeling the real danger wasn't the rebels outside. It was the man sitting across from me.

Chapter 27: One Bed

Sara

The outpost wasn't a military base. It was a glorified tin can clinging to the side of a frozen mountain like a barnacle on a whale.

"Welcome to Black Ridge," Voss grunted, pulling the carriage to a halt. "Elevation: too damn high. Temperature: lethal."

I opened the door and was immediately slapped in the face by a gust of wind that felt like it was made of razor blades. Snow—gray and gritty with industrial fallout—swirled around us.

"Charming," I muttered, jumping down. My boots crunched on the permafrost. "I can see why the rebels want it. It's prime real estate for freezing to death."

Dorian stepped out behind me. He didn't shiver. His internal heating systems were likely cranked up to *tropical*. He looked around the desolate courtyard, his expression unimpressed.

"Where is the garrison?" he asked Voss.

"The main listening post is three miles up the ridge," Voss shouted over the wind. "But the pass is snowed in. We can't take the carriage further until the plows come through in the morning. We stay here tonight."

He pointed to a squat, bunker-like structure with a flickering neon sign that read **LODGING - HOT FOOD - OXYGEN**.

"A hotel," Dorian said dryly. "How luxurious."

"It's a waystation for miners," Voss corrected. "I'll secure the carriage and sleep with the horses. The heating coils in the stable are reliable."

"You're sleeping in a stable?" I asked.

"I've slept in worse," Voss said, unhitching the lead mechanical mare. "Go. Before you turn into a popsicle, girl."

We went.

The inside of the waystation smelled of wet wool, burnt grease, and unwashed bodies. It was packed. Miners, stranded travelers, and a few mercenaries were huddled around a central heating vent, drinking mugs of something that looked like engine oil.

The room went silent when we walked in.

It wasn't every day a woman in tactical leather and a man in a fur-lined greatcoat who looked like he owned the planet walked into a dive bar at the edge of the world.

Dorian lowered his scarf. He didn't cower. He didn't apologize. He walked to the counter like he was approaching a throne.

The innkeeper was a woman with a cybernetic eye and a shotgun on the wall behind her.

"Room," Dorian said.

"Full," she grunted, wiping a glass with a rag that was dirtier than the glass. "Storm closed the pass. Everyone's stuck."

Dorian placed a gold coin on the counter. It was solid, heavy, and stamped with his father's face. It was worth more than this entire building.

"A room," he repeated softly.

The innkeeper looked at the coin. Her cybernetic eye whirred, zooming in.

"I have the supply closet," she said. "Or the Honeymoon Suite."

"We'll take the suite," Dorian said.

"It's got a draft," she warned, snatching the coin. "Room 4. Upstairs. Don't break the furniture."

We walked up the creaking metal stairs. The silence of the common room followed us.

Dorian unlocked Room 4. He pushed the door open. We stepped inside.

I stopped. I stared.

"You have got to be kidding me."

The "Honeymoon Suite" was a box. A literal metal box, maybe ten feet by ten feet. There was a cracked window taped over with plastic sheeting. There was a single, flickering lightbulb.

And there was a bed.

One bed.

It was narrow, sagging in the middle, and covered with a quilt that looked like it had been made from recycled cargo pants.

"Well," Dorian said, closing the door behind us. The lock clicked with a sound of finality. "It's... intimate."

"It's a cot," I snapped. "It's a cot for a dwarf."

I dropped my pack on the floor and walked to the heating unit on the wall. I banged it with my fist. Nothing. Not even a spark.

"Heater's dead," I announced, my breath fogging in the air. "It's going to be below freezing in here tonight."

I turned to Dorian. He was taking off his greatcoat, shaking the snow from the fur. Underneath, he was wearing the black tactical gear. He looked calm. Annoyingly calm.

"So," I said, crossing my arms to keep the shivering at bay. "How are we doing this?"

"Doing what?"

"Sleeping. There is one bed. I am the bodyguard. Therefore, I need to be rested to protect you. I get the bed."

Dorian laughed. He threw his coat over the only chair in the room.

"I am the Prince," he said. "My back is worth more than the GDP of this sector. I get the bed."

"You have a metal spine! You wouldn't even feel the floor!"

"My spine is fused with alloy, Sara. It doesn't mean I enjoy sleeping on concrete."

He sat on the edge of the mattress. The springs groaned in protest.

"Besides, the floor is freezing. I run hot, but even I have limits."

"Fine," I said, grabbing a pillow. "I'll sleep in the bathtub."

"There is no bathroom," he pointed out. "Just a bucket in the corner."

I looked at the bucket. I looked at the freezing floor. I looked at the window, where ice was already forming on the inside of the plastic sheeting.

I was shivering violently now. The adrenaline of the arrival was fading, leaving just the bone-deep cold of the Wastelands.

Dorian watched me. He sighed—a long, suffering sound.

"Sara," he said. "Don't be a martyr. You'll freeze to death before midnight."

"I'd rather freeze than sleep with you."

"Liar." He patted the mattress beside him. "It's a bed. Not a marriage contract. Take off your boots and get in."

I hesitated. My teeth were starting to chatter.

"If you touch me," I warned, my voice shaking, "I will dismantle you. I will pull out your wires one by one."

"If I touch you," Dorian countered, kicking off his boots, "it will be because you're stealing the blankets. Get in."

I groaned, frustrated by biology and thermodynamics.

I sat on the edge of the bed. I unlaced my boots and kicked them off. I kept the tactical pants on. I kept the corset on. I even kept the dagger in my thigh holster.

Dorian lay down on the left side. He turned on his side, facing away from me.

"Lights," he said.

He snapped his fingers. A tiny spark of magic killed the bulb.

Pitch black.

I lay down on the right side. I stayed on the very edge, clinging to the frame like a barnacle, leaving a foot of cold air between us.

"Goodnight, Rat," he mumbled into the pillow.

"Night, Chrome."

Silence settled over the room, broken only by the howling of the wind outside and the rhythmic *thump-thump* of Dorian's mechanical heart.

It was freezing.

The quilt was thin and smelled of mildew. The cold seeped up from the mattress, gnawing at my bones. I curled into a tight ball, tucking my hands between my knees, trying to conserve heat.

It wasn't working.

I shivered, uncontrollably, my whole body shaking against the springs.

"You're vibrating," Dorian's voice came from the dark.

"I'm c-cold," I chattered. "Shut up."

"Come here," he said. "I'm running at a steady one hundred degrees. Don't be stupid."

"I'm f-fine."

"Suit yourself."

He didn't push it. He didn't pull me in. He just lay there, a massive, radiant furnace, while I stubbornly froze to death three inches away.

I drifted into a fitful, shallow sleep.

I woke up two hours later.

I couldn't feel my feet.

My body wasn't shivering anymore. That was bad. That was the stage before hypothermia set in. The air in the room was so cold it hurt to inhale. My joints ached with a dull, throbbing pain.

I rolled over, gasping.

Dorian was asleep. Or in standby mode. He was lying on his back, breathing deeply.

And he was *hot*.

I could feel the heat radiating off him from across the mattress. It was a physical presence, like a fire in a hearth.

I looked at the gap between us. It was a demilitarized zone. Crossing it meant surrender. Crossing it meant admitting he was right.

I looked at my blue fingernails.

"Screw pride," I whispered.

I moved.

I didn't drift. I didn't accidentally roll. I scooted backward, inch by inch, until my back hit his side.

The relief was instant. It was violent.

The heat soaked through my clothes, melting the ice in my veins. I gasped, pressing myself harder against him. I aligned my spine with his side, soaking it up.

It wasn't enough. My front was still freezing.

I turned over.

I curled into him. I pressed my chest against his side. I tucked my freezing nose against his shoulder.

Dorian stirred. He didn't wake up fully, but he reacted to the contact.

His arm—the human one—lifted and dropped heavily over my waist. It wasn't a romantic embrace; it was a reflex. He was anchoring himself.

His arm was heavy, solid, and gloriously warm.

I should have pushed it off. I should have moved back to my side.

Instead, I grabbed his wrist. I pulled his arm tighter around me. I tucked my knees between his, stealing the warmth from his legs.

"Just physics," I mumbled into his shirt, my teeth finally stopping their chattering. "Thermal transfer."

I rested my head on his chest, right over the mechanical heart. The rhythm was steady. *Thump-thump. Thump-thump.*

It lulled me.

I stopped fighting the cold. I stopped fighting the Prince.

I closed my eyes and let the enemy keep me alive.

I woke up to sunlight and silence.

For a second, I didn't know where I was. I was warm. Incredibly, perfectly warm. I was buried in a cocoon of heat and scent—cedar, ozone, and skin.

I nuzzled closer to the source of the warmth, throwing my leg over it to anchor myself.

Wait.

My eyes snapped open.

I wasn't just sleeping next to Dorian. I was draped over him like a starfish.

We had shifted in the night. I was lying half on top of him. My head was on his chest, rising and falling with his breath. My leg was hooked over his hips, my thigh resting intimately between his. My arm was thrown across his neck.

And he was awake.

Dorian was lying on his back, one arm behind his head, the other resting casually on my lower back, his fingers idly tracing the line of my spine through my shirt.

He was looking at the ceiling, but I could feel the smirk in his chest.

"Morning," he rumbled. His voice was rough with sleep.

I froze. I didn't move. Maybe if I played dead, he would vanish.

"You're a aggressive little spoon," he noted conversationally. "Who knew the Rat liked to snuggle?"

"I was freezing," I said into his shirt, refusing to look up. "You were a heat source. Don't flatter yourself."

"Mmm. Is that why your leg is currently pinning me to the mattress?"

I realized exactly where my thigh was. I realized exactly what I was feeling against my thigh.

Hard. Again.

I scrambled backward, nearly falling off the bed. I hit the cold floor with a thud, tangling in the quilt.

"Ow," I groaned.

Dorian sat up. His hair was a mess, sticking up in every direction. The grease paint was gone, rubbed off on the pillow, leaving him looking unfairly handsome and drowsy.

He looked down at me on the floor. His eyes were soft. Not mocking. Just... present.

"Did you sleep?" he asked.

I sat up, untangling my legs. "Yes."

"Good." He stretched, his shirt riding up to expose a strip of skin and metal. "Because the plows are here. We move out in twenty."

He stood up and walked to the bucket of water in the corner to wash his face.

I stayed on the floor for a second, clutching the mildewy quilt.

I had slept. For the first time in years, I hadn't woken up from a nightmare. I hadn't reached for a knife.

I had reached for him.

And that terrified me more than the freezing cold ever could.

Chapter 28: Nightmare

Dorian

The problem with being half-machine is that you don't truly sleep. You standby.

The biological parts of my brain—the parts that remembered the smell of lavender and the feel of a cold brick wall—shut down. But the diagnostic subroutines kept running. They hummed in the back of my skull, monitoring fuel levels, coolant pressure, and threat proximity.

It meant my dreams were never just dreams. They were system errors.

We were parked in a ravine about forty miles from the outpost. The storm had broken, but the temperature had dropped to something lethal. The carriage was insulated, but the cold still seeped through the floorboards, eager to find a weakness.

Sara was asleep on the opposite bench. She was curled into a tight ball, her head resting on her pack, one hand tucked near the dagger on her thigh. Even in sleep, she was ready to stab someone.

I watched her for a long time, listening to the soft whistle of her breath.

eventually, the fatigue won. My human eye drifted shut. The HUD in my mechanical eye dimmed.

System Standby Initiated.
I fell.

I wasn't in the carriage anymore.

I was back in the Throne Room. But it wasn't the room I knew. The marble floors were gone, replaced by a churning ocean of molten gold.

I was standing on a pedestal. I tried to step down, but I couldn't move.

I looked down.

My legs were gone. They were fused to the floor, solid columns of gold. The metal wasn't stopping there. It was rising.

It crawled up my thighs like living ivy. It was warm. Suffocatingly warm. It ate the fabric of my trousers, then the skin beneath. Where it touched, the nerves didn't just die; they calcified. I couldn't feel pain. I couldn't feel anything.

"Father!" I tried to shout.

My voice didn't work. My throat was already metal. The vocal cords were replaced by brass reeds that only produced a static hiss.

King Aric sat on the Golden Throne across the room. He wasn't connected to life support anymore. He was the room. His face was the size of the wall, a massive golden mask with red lenses for eyes.

"Efficiency," the wall-face buzzed. *"The flesh is weak, Dorian. Let it go."*
"No," I tried to say.

The gold reached my chest. It poured into my lungs. I tried to inhale, but there was no air, only the heavy, liquid weight of the Gilt. I was drowning on dry land.

I looked at my arms. My left arm—the machine arm—was fine. It belonged here. But my right arm... my human arm...

I watched the skin turn gray. I watched the veins turn to silver wire. The fingers stiffened, locking into a permanent claw.

I was disappearing. The Prince was dying, and the Statue was taking over.

I couldn't breathe. I couldn't scream. I was trapped inside a coffin made of my own body.

"Perfect," the King's voice boomed. *"Beautiful. Silent."*
The gold reached my eyes.

The world went dark.

"Dorian!"

The scream wasn't mine. I didn't have a mouth.

I lashed out.

My body reacted before my brain came online. *Threat. Containment. Breach.*
I swung my left arm—the weapon—blindly into the dark.

THUD.
My metal fist connected with something hard. Wood. The carriage wall. The impact shook the entire vehicle, splintering the paneling.

"Dorian, stop! It's me!"

Hands grabbed my shoulders. Small hands. Strong hands.

I fought them. I was still drowning. I needed air. I needed to break the gold shell.

"Get off!" I roared, my voice tearing at my throat. "Get it off me!"

"There's nothing on you! You're dreaming!"

A sharp pain exploded across my cheek.

Slap.
The shock of it cut through the panic loop.

I froze. My chest was heaving, the internal fans screaming like jet engines. My mechanical eye was cycling through combat modes—*Target Acquired. Target Friendly. Error.*
I blinked, the red overlay fading.

I was in the carriage. The magelight was dim.

Sara was straddling my lap.

She had pinned my human arm to my chest. Her other hand was gripping my tactical vest. Her hair was wild, her face inches from mine, pale and terrified.

"Dorian," she said, her voice firm but breathless. "Look at me. Look at the Rat."

I stared at her. I focused on the jagged scar on her chin. The brown of her eyes. The imperfection of her skin.

Real. Not gold. Real.

"Sara," I gasped.

The fight drained out of me instantly, leaving me hollow and shaking. My head fell back against the velvet seat.

"I... I thought..." I couldn't finish the sentence. My throat felt raw.

"I know," she said softly. She didn't get off me. "You were screaming. You punched a hole in the wall."

I glanced to the left. There was a fist-sized crater in the reinforced mahogany paneling, inches from where her head would have been if she were standing.

Nausea rolled over me.

"Did I hurt you?" I asked, trying to sit up. "Did I hit you?"

"No. You hit the wall. I'm fine."

She slowly released my arm. She sat back on her heels, still perched on my thighs, watching me carefully.

I looked down at my hands. They were shaking. Violently. The metal one was vibrating with residual torque; the human one was trembling with pure, unadulterated fear.

I couldn't stop it. I clenched them into fists, trying to hide the weakness, but it was useless.

"I hate sleeping," I whispered. It was a confession I had never made out loud.

Sara didn't mock me. She didn't tell me to man up. She didn't make a joke about my battery life.

She reached out and took my hands. Both of them. She uncurled my fingers.

"Your heat sink is overloaded," she said quietly. "You're burning up again."

"It's the nightmare. It spikes the cortisol. Triggers the defense systems."

I closed my eyes, trying to force my breathing to slow down. *Inhale. Exhale. You are not a statue.*
"Lie down," Sara said.

"There's no room."

"Lie down, Dorian."

She shifted. She moved off my lap and sat on the floor of the carriage, her back against the opposite bench. She patted the space on the bench beside her legs.

"Put your head here," she said, tapping her thigh.

I opened my eyes. "What?"

"You need to ground. You're spinning out. Put your head in my lap."

"I'm the Prince," I muttered weakly. "I don't—"

"Shut up and get on the floor."

I didn't have the energy to argue. And God help me, I didn't want to.

I slid off the bench. I lay down on the rug, curling my long frame into the narrow space between the seats. I rested my head on her legs.

Her thighs were warm. Solid. The tactical canvas of her pants was rough against my cheek.

It was the most comfortable pillow I had ever felt.

Sara hesitated for a second. Then, her hand landed on my hair.

She started to stroke it. Long, slow motions. Her fingers scratched lightly at my scalp.

"I used to do this for Elara," she said, her voice low and rhythmic. "When the coughing fits got bad. It tricks the nervous system. Reminds the body it's not alone."

I let out a breath I felt like I'd been holding for a decade.

The tension in my shoulders unspooled. The whir of the servos quieted. The shaking in my hands stopped.

"What was it?" she asked. "The dream."

I stared at the dark under the bench seat.

"Gold," I whispered. "It was eating me. Replacing the skin. Until I was just... him."

Her hand paused in my hair, then resumed.

"You're not him," she said fiercely. "He's cold. You're... well, you're annoying. And sarcastic. And you run too hot."

I managed a weak chuckle. "Thanks."

"I mean it, Chrome. You're messy. Statues aren't messy."

She traced the line of my jaw, her thumb brushing over the scar where the metal plate began.

"Does this hurt?" she asked.

"Sometimes. When it's cold. Or when the magic spikes."

"It looks... tight. Like the skin is pulling."

"It is."

We sat in silence for a long time. The storm outside had died down, leaving a heavy, suffocating quiet. But inside the carriage, with her hand in my hair and her scent filling my nose, the quiet didn't feel like a tomb.

"Sara?"

"Yeah?"

"If I turn," I said. "If the Gilt takes me. If I start talking like a machine."

I turned my head so I could look up at her. Her face was upside down, shadowed, but I could see the glint of her eyes.

"Don't let me live like that," I said. "Promise me."

She went still. Her hand rested heavy on my forehead.

"Dorian..."

"Promise me. Use the dagger. Aim for the organic heart. It's the only way to stop the process."

She stared down at me. I saw her jaw tighten. I saw the thief—the survivor—weighing the cost.

"Okay," she whispered. "I promise."

"Good."

I closed my eyes again.

"But," she added, her voice sharp, "if you make me kill you, I'm keeping the boots. They're expensive."

I smiled. "Deal."

She went back to stroking my hair.

I didn't go back into standby mode. I slept. Real, human sleep. Anchored to the earth by the girl who had promised to murder me.

Chapter 29: The Massage

Sara

The sound was driving me insane.

Grind. Click. Hiss.

Dorian was sitting on the opposite bench of the carriage, staring out at the twilight sweeping over the Wastelands. He hadn't spoken in two hours. He was holding his left shoulder—the metal one—with his human hand, digging his fingers into the seam where the alloy plate met the trapezius muscle.

Every time the carriage hit a bump, he flinched. A tiny, micro-movement of the jaw. A tightening of the eyes.

Grind. Click.
"Stop it," I snapped.

Dorian didn't look at me. "Stop what?"

"Stop trying to crush your own clavicle. You're making a noise. It sounds like a garbage disposal chewing on a spoon."

He dropped his hand, sighing. "It's just stiff. The cold causes the metal to contract. It pulls on the organic anchor points."

"It pulls on the skin," I translated. "And it hurts."

"It is manageable."

"You're sweating," I pointed out. "And you're pale. For a guy who claims to be a nuclear furnace, you look like you're about to pass out."

I didn't wait for his permission. I moved.

I slid off my bench and crossed the small space between us. I knelt between his spread legs. It was a submissive position, technically, but the way I glared at him made it clear who was in charge.

"Take off the coat," I ordered.

Dorian looked down at me. His eyes were heavy, glazed with pain he was too proud to admit.

"Sara, I'm fine."

"Coat. Off. Or I sedate you with the heavy stuff."

He hesitated, then groaned and shrugged out of the heavy fur-lined coat. Underneath, he was wearing the black tactical shirt.

"The shirt too," I said.

"You're enjoying this," he murmured, but his voice lacked its usual bite. He pulled the shirt over his head, wincing as he lifted his left arm.

I tossed the clothes aside.

I looked at his shoulder.

It was angry. The seam—the boundary where the golden-chrome plating fused with his human flesh—was inflamed. The skin was red, swollen, and tight. The metal looked like it was trying to swallow him whole.

"It's seizing," I murmured, my mechanic's brain taking over. "The muscle is spasmsing against the rigidity of the plate. You need to release the tension or you're going to tear a ligament."

I reached into my belt pouch. I didn't have massage oil, but I had a small tin of multi-purpose lubricant I used for my lockpicks. It was organic-based, unscented grease. It would do.

I scooped a bit onto my fingers.

"This is going to be cold," I warned.

I laid my hands on him.

Dorian sucked in a sharp breath through his teeth. His whole body went rigid, the muscles turning to stone under my palms.

"Relax," I commanded softly. "You're fighting it. Let the muscle go."

I started to work.

I ignored the Prince. I focused on the machine. I traced the line of the metal plate, using my thumbs to dig into the inflamed tissue right at the border. I pushed deep, finding the knots where the biology was fighting the technology.

"Ffff-ck," Dorian hissed, his head falling back against the velvet seat.

"Breathe," I said. "I know it hurts. But the knot is right... here."

I pressed harder.

Dorian's human hand shot out and gripped my thigh. His fingers dug in hard enough to bruise. He didn't push me away; he used me as an anchor.

I worked the grease into his skin, sliding my hands from the cold, hard metal to the fever-hot flesh of his neck and back. I kneaded the trapezius. I traced the heavy cables of muscle running down his spine.

Slowly, the tension began to break. The rock-hard knots dissolved. His breathing shifted from sharp gasps to deep, rhythmic exhales.

"Better?" I asked, my voice dropping to a whisper.

"Yes," he rasped. He opened his eyes. He wasn't looking at the ceiling anymore. He was looking down at me.

The air in the carriage changed.

It happened in a heartbeat. One second, I was a mechanic fixing a broken part. The next, I was a woman kneeling between a man's legs, my hands slick with oil, touching his bare skin.

My thumbs circled the sensitive hollow at the base of his throat. I felt his pulse there. It was hammering.

"You have magic hands, Rat," he murmured. His voice was a low rumble that vibrated through his chest and straight into my palms.

"I'm good with my hands," I said distractedly. I was watching the way his chest rose and fell. I was watching the way his nipples hardened in the cool air.

I slid my hands down his chest, over the pectorals, following the line of the metal plating where it encased his ribs.

Dorian's grip on my thigh tightened. He slid his hand upward, his thumb brushing the inseam of my tactical pants.

"Sara," he warned. It was a low, dangerous sound.

I didn't stop.

"Does this hurt?" I asked, ghosting my fingers over his abs.

"No."

"Does this?"

I moved lower. My hands rested on his stomach, just above the waistband of his trousers. The muscles jumped under my touch.

Dorian groaned. He sat up, breaking his passive pose. He grabbed my waist with both hands—the metal one cold, the human one hot—and hauled me closer.

I was pressed against the V of his legs. I could feel the heat of him through his pants. I could feel how hard he was.

"You are playing a dangerous game," he whispered, his face inches from mine.

"I'm checking the structural integrity," I breathed.

He captured my mouth.

It wasn't a gentle kiss. It was a collision. He kissed me like he'd been starving for a decade. He tasted of coffee and dark desire. His tongue swept into my mouth, demanding, taking.

I made a noise—a small, pathetic whimper—and melted into him. My hands slid up his chest, wrapping around his neck, tangling in his hair.

His hands were everywhere.

One hand slid up the back of my shirt. Skin on skin. His palm was rough, calloused, and scalding hot. He traced my spine, making me arch into him. He cupped my breast through the sheer tactical fabric, his thumb teasing the peak until I gasped against his mouth.

The other hand—the metal one—slid down.

It moved over my hip. It moved over my ass, squeezing possessively. Then it moved to the front.

His metal fingers, cold and precise, fumbled with the button of my pants.

"Dorian," I gasped, breaking the kiss.

He didn't stop. He kissed my jaw, my neck, the sensitive spot behind my ear.

"I want you," he growled against my skin. "Here. Now."

His hand slid inside my pants.

The shock of the cold metal against my heated skin was electric. He brushed against me, and my hips bucked involuntarily.

I wanted it. God, I wanted it. I wanted to straddle him right here in the carriage and ride out the storm.

But then the carriage lurched. A wheel hit a rut.

The reality of where we were crashed back in. We were on a mission. We were exposed. And more importantly...

He was using this. He was using the sex to numb the pain of the nightmare, of the metal, of his father.

I couldn't be his drug.

I caught his wrist.

His human hand was half-unbuttoned on his own trousers. My hand landed over his, stopping him just as he started to push the fabric down.

"Stop," I whispered.

Dorian froze. He looked at me, his eyes black with lust, his chest heaving.

"Why?" he rasped. "You want this. I can feel how wet you are."

I flushed, but I didn't let go of his wrist.

"I do want it," I admitted, keeping my voice steady. "But not like this. Not because you're hurting. And not because you're trying to forget who you are."

I pulled his hand away from his waistband. I pulled his metal hand out of my pants.

I smoothed his shirt. I smoothed my own hair.

"Not yet, Your Highness," I said softly.

Dorian stared at me. The hunger was still there, raging, but something else flickered behind it. Respect.

He let out a long, shuddering breath and let his head fall back against the seat.

"You," he said to the ceiling, "are going to be the death of me."

"Probably," I said, climbing off him and sitting back on my own bench. My body was throbbing. My hands were shaking. "But at least you'll die with a relaxed shoulder."

Dorian looked at me. He cracked a smile. It was crooked and pained and devastatingly handsome.

"Small mercies," he said.

He reached for his shirt.

Then the world exploded.

There was no warning. No sound of an incoming shell. Just a blinding flash of light and a force that lifted the heavy, armored carriage into the air like a toy.

We were weightless for a second.

Then we slammed into the frozen earth, rolling, metal screaming as the world turned upside down.

Chapter 30: The Attack

Sara

The world smelled like burning velvet and ozone.

I woke up on the ceiling.

Gravity was wrong. My tactical belt was digging into my ribs, and my left arm was pinned under something heavy and hot.

"Dorian?" I croaked. My voice sounded like it was coming from underwater.

"Here."

The heavy weight shifted. Dorian groaned—a sound of grinding metal and pained flesh—and rolled off my arm.

I blinked, trying to clear the static from my vision. The carriage was upside down. The roof had caved in, turning the plush red interior into a claustrophobic, splintered coffin. The tinted window to my right was shattered, letting in a howling wind and stinging snow.

"Status?" Dorian asked. He was crouching in the debris, wiping blood from his forehead. His shirt was half-buttoned, exposing the metal plating of his chest.

"Alive," I wheezed, testing my limbs. "Nothing broken. Just... rattled."

"We need to move," he said, his voice turning cold and mechanical. "That was a shaped charge. It was designed to flip armor, not penetrate it. Which means..."

"Which means they want us alive," I finished, the mechanic's brain kicking in. "Or they want the loot inside."

Crack.

A bullet pinged off the outer hull of the carriage, inches from my head.

"Sniper!" I yelled, scrambling for cover behind a crushed seat cushion.

"Not a sniper," Dorian corrected, his mechanical eye glowing red in the gloom. "Suppression fire. They're closing in."

He grabbed his heavy coat from the wreckage and threw it at me.

"Put it on," he ordered.

"But you—"

"I have armor plating. You have skin. Put it on, Sara. We're going out."

I pulled the coat on. It smelled of him and the massage oil I'd just used. The memory of his hands on my skin flashed through my mind—hot, desperate, intimate—and was instantly vaporized by the adrenaline of combat.

Dorian kicked the carriage door.

It was jammed, warped by the crash.

He didn't kick it again. He placed his metal palm against the center of the door. I heard the whine of his servos spiking to maximum torque.

SCREECH.

With a sound like a banshee dying, he ripped the armored door off its hinges and hurled it into the snow.

"Go," he commanded.

I rolled out into the snow, staying low.

The cold was a physical blow. The wind howled through the pass, blinding white and deadly.

I scanned the ridge.

Three targets. Nine o'clock. Ridge line.
They weren't ragtag rebels. They were wearing white winter camo, advanced thermal goggles, and carrying kinetic rifles.

"Pros," I hissed, pulling my dagger. It felt woefully small against rifles.

"Voss!" Dorian shouted.

"Here!"

Voss was twenty yards back, pinned behind the carcass of the lead mechanical horse. He was firing his scattergun blindly over the flank of the dead machine.

"Engine block is cracked!" Voss roared. "We're grounded!"

Another volley of fire chewed up the snow around us.

"Get to the rocks!" Dorian shouted, grabbing the collar of the coat and dragging me toward a cluster of boulders near the ravine edge.

We dove behind the granite just as a grenade exploded where we had been standing.

Dorian
Threat Assessment: High.

Enemy Count: 12 detected signatures.

Ammo: 0.

Core Temp: 98% (Running Hot).

I pressed my back against the cold stone, checking the HUD. My left arm was functioning at 85%—the crash had misaligned a servo in the wrist. My human arm was bleeding from a cut on the forearm.

And I was furious.

Ten minutes ago, I had Sara in my arms. I was unraveling. I was happy.

Now, I was freezing, half-dressed, and being shot at by professionals.

"They're flanking," Sara said. She was crouched beside me, peeking through a crack in the rocks. She looked feral—hair wild, coat too big, obsidian dagger in hand.

"I see them," I said.

"Give me a weapon," she demanded.

"I don't have a weapon. I am the weapon."

"Then give me something to throw!"

I looked around. The ground was just ice and rock.

"Stay here," I ordered.

"Don't you dare—"

I broke cover.

I didn't run away; I ran *at* them.

I activated the magnetic clamps in my boots, giving me traction on the ice. I sprinted toward the nearest soldier, a massive figure in white armor.

He saw me. He raised his rifle.

He fired.

I raised my metal arm.

Ping. Ping. Ping.

The bullets sparked off the chrome plating. I felt the impacts—dull thuds that rattled my teeth—but the alloy held.

I closed the distance in three seconds.

I didn't punch him. I grabbed the barrel of his rifle with my metal hand. I twisted. The steel snapped like a dry twig.

The soldier gasped behind his mask.

I grabbed him by the throat—my human hand this time—and slammed him into the ground.

"Stay down," I growled.

I didn't kill him. I knocked him unconscious with a swift blow to the helmet.

I grabbed his sidearm—a heavy kinetic pistol—and tossed it behind me, blindly.

"Sara!"

I heard the slap of leather as she caught it.

Bang. Bang.
Two shots rang out from behind me. Two soldiers on the ridge dropped, screaming.

"Nice aim!" I shouted, dodging a knife thrust from a second attacker.

"I aim for the knees!" she yelled back. "It's harder to walk!"

I ducked under a swinging rifle butt and drove my metal shoulder into the attacker's solar plexus. He folded.

We were in the thick of it now. It was a brawl. The snow blinded us, turning the fight into a chaotic dance of shadows and violence.

I spun, backhanding a soldier who tried to flank me. My metal fist connected with his helmet, denting the reinforced plastic. He went flying.

Then, I felt a back press against mine.

Sara.

She was warm. Solid.

We rotated together, a perfect, deadly circle.

"Three on your left," she called out, firing the pistol. *Crack. Crack.*

"Got them," I grunted.

I channeled the excess heat from my core into my arm. The metal glowed red hot. I grabbed the sword of an attacker who swung at me. The blade melted under my grip.

He stared at his ruined weapon in horror. I headbutted him.

"Voss!" I shouted over the wind. "Status!"

"Clear on the right!" Voss bellowed, racking his scattergun. "But we have a heavy incoming!"

I looked up.

Coming down the ridge was a Power Loader—a retrofitted mining exo-suit. It was ten feet tall, painted yellow and rust, with a hydraulic claw that could crush a tank.

"Oh, that's not fair," Sara panted, reloading the pistol.

The Loader roared, its engine spewing black smoke. It charged.

"Sara, move!" I shoved her toward Voss.

I stood my ground.

The Loader swung its massive claw.

I caught it.

My boots dug furrows into the frozen earth. My metal arm screamed as the servos fought the hydraulics of the massive machine. I was holding back two tons of pressure with one arm.

"You're... very... heavy," I grunted through gritted teeth.

The Loader pilot laughed—a metallic, amplified sound. He pushed harder. My knees buckled.

"Dorian!" Sara screamed.

She didn't run. She sprinted toward the Loader.

She didn't attack the pilot. She attacked the machine.

She slid under the massive legs of the exo-suit. She jammed her obsidian dagger into the hydraulic line behind the knee joint.

HISS.
Fluid sprayed out—hot, purple oil.

The leg buckled. The Loader listed to the side, losing its balance.

I took the opening.

I let go of the claw and drove my fist into the cockpit glass.

SMASH.
I grabbed the pilot by his harness and ripped him out of the seat, throwing him into a snowbank.

The massive machine groaned, tipped over, and crashed into the earth with a sound that shook the mountain.

Silence fell.

The remaining rebels, seeing their heavy support destroyed, turned and fled into the whiteout.

I stood there, chest heaving, steam rising from my shoulders. My shirt was torn. My human arm was bleeding.

Sara crawled out from under the wreckage of the Loader. She was covered in hydraulic fluid and snow.

She looked at me. I looked at her.

The lust from the carriage was gone. Replaced by something colder. Sharper.

Survival.

"You okay?" she asked, wiping oil from her cheek.

"I'm functional," I said. I offered her my hand—the human one.

She took it. I pulled her up.

She stumbled, adrenaline crashing, and fell against my chest. I wrapped my arms around her, holding her tight. Not romantic. Protective.

"You fought well," I whispered into her hair.

"I hate the cold," she mumbled into my torn shirt.

Voss limped over, clutching his side. He looked at the wrecked carriage, the dead horses, and the unconscious bodies scattered in the snow.

"Well," Voss grunted, spitting a glob of blood onto the ice. "The carriage is totaled. The horses are scrap. And we're ten miles from the outpost in a blizzard."

He looked at me.

"Diplomatic mission accomplished, sir?"

I looked at the burning wreckage. I looked at the frozen horizon.

"The mission hasn't started yet," I said, my voice grim. "This wasn't a rebellion, Voss. These men were wearing House Vane winter gear underneath the camo."

Sara pulled back, looking up at me. "House Vane? The guy I pickpocketed?"

"The same."

I looked north, toward the Black Ridge.

"My father didn't just send us to die," I said. "He sent us into a trap. And someone else tripped it."

I squeezed Sara's shoulder.

"Grab the supplies," I ordered. "We walk from here."

ACT III: RUST AND RUIN

Chapter 31: The Revelation

Dorian

The Black Ridge Outpost was a tomb.

We arrived just as the sun was bleeding out behind the mountains, casting long, bruised shadows across the snow. The wind had died down, leaving a silence that felt heavy, expectant, and wrong.

"Gate's open," Voss grunted, raising his scattergun. He was limping, his left leg dragging in the snow, but he refused to let me carry his pack.

I scanned the perimeter with my thermal eye.

Heat Signatures: 0.

Electrical Activity: Low.

Status: Ghost Town.

"Stay close," I ordered Sara. She was shivering, her lips a pale shade of blue, huddled deep inside my greatcoat. She held the kinetic pistol with a white-knuckled grip.

We walked through the main gates.

There were no bodies in the courtyard. That was the first bad sign. In a raid, bodies are left where they fall. In a cleanup operation, bodies are moved.

"Where is everyone?" Sara whispered, the sound swallowed by the vast, empty concrete of the compound.

"Processing," I said grimly.

We moved toward the command center—a squat, reinforced bunker in the center of the complex. The door had been breached, the mag-lock melted by high-yield thermite. House Vane tech.

We stepped inside.

The air here was stale, smelling of ozone and copper. The emergency lights flickered red, pulsing like a dying heart.

"Voss, secure the door," I said. "Sara, watch the vents."

I walked to the central console. It was a massive bank of monitors, most of them smashed. But the central terminal— the direct link to the Capital grid—was intact. It was humming.

I didn't type. I pulled the data cable from my wrist port. The metal casing on my forearm slid back, revealing the interface jack.

"Dorian, don't," Sara said, stepping forward. "You don't know what's in that system. It could be trapped."

"I have to know," I said. "I have to know why my father sent a kill squad to a weather station."

I plugged in.

CONNECTION ESTABLISHED.
The world dissolved.

I wasn't in the room anymore. I was in the stream. Data flooded my neural pathways—a torrent of binary, encryption keys, and corrupted logs.

I fought the current, pushing past the firewalls. My internal fans spun up, whining in the quiet room.

Accessing Local Logs...

Log 454: Energy spike detected in Sector 12.

Log 455: Spike confirmed. Source: The Palace.

Log 456: Pattern analysis suggests...

The logs cut off. Deleted.

I dug deeper. I went into the ghost data—the shadow files that lingered on the drive after a wipe.

And then I saw it.

It wasn't a rebellion. It wasn't a diplomatic crisis.

The outpost hadn't gone silent because they were attacked. They had gone silent because they had *seen* something.
They had been monitoring the city's energy consumption. They had noticed that the power wasn't going to the grid. It wasn't going to the lights, or the heating coils, or the factories.

It was being diverted. All of it. To the Throne Room.

I pulled up the schematic labeled *PROJECT MIDAS*.
My breath hitched in the real world. My heart—the mechanical one—stuttered.

"Oh god," I whispered in the digital void.

The schematic showed the King. But not as he was now. It showed him fully integrated. No flesh. No blood. Just a consciousness suspended in a lattice of living gold.

But gold doesn't generate power. It consumes it.

To maintain that state—to achieve true immortality, to stop the Rust forever—he needed a fuel source denser than coal. Denser than steam.

He needed bio-lumens.

Life force.
I accessed the file marked *THE PURGE*.
It wasn't a plan to clear out the criminals. It was a harvest schedule.

Phase 1: Isolate the Slags (District 12-14).

Phase 2: Release the aerosol catalyst (The Rust).

Phase 3: Collection.

The Rust wasn't a disease.

It was a tag.

The metal infection was designed to make the victims conductive. It turned their bodies into batteries. And when the "Purge" happened, the King wasn't going to cure them. He was going to activate the city's grid and drain them dry.

Every man, woman, and child in the Slags who had the silver patches on their skin... they were walking fuel cells.

And Elara.

I ripped the cable out of my arm.

DISCONNECT.

I gasped, stumbling back from the console as reality crashed back in. I hit the desk, knocking a monitor to the floor.

"Dorian!" Sara was there instantly, grabbing my shoulders. "What happened? Your eyes... they went completely white."

I stared at her. I looked at the concern in her face. I looked at the collar of the coat she was wearing—my coat.

I looked at her wrist, where a faint, silver patch of Rust was just starting to form under her sleeve.

"We have to go," I said, my voice shaking. "We have to go back. Now."

"What did you see?" Voss asked from the doorway.

"Everything," I rasped. "The outpost wasn't attacked by rebels. It was liquidated by Vane because the Commander figured it out. He saw the power draw."

"Figured what out?" Sara demanded, shaking me. "Dorian, talk to me!"

I looked at her. How could I tell her? How could I tell her that her sister wasn't sick—she was being prepped for consumption?

"The Purge," I said, forcing the words out. "It's not a crackdown on crime, Sara. It's a ritual."

"A ritual?"

"My father... he's trying to become pure metal. Eternal. But he needs power to make the transition permanent."

I grabbed her hands. They were warm. So fragile.

"He's not going to cure the Slags," I whispered. "He's going to harvest them. The Rust... it makes you conductive. When he flips the switch, everyone with the infection... they won't just die. They'll be drained. Their life force will be funneled into the Throne to keep him alive."

Sara went still. Her face drained of color, leaving her looking like a ghost in the red emergency light.

"Elara," she breathed. "She has it. It's in her lungs."

"I know."

"When?" she asked. Her voice was deadly quiet. "When does he flip the switch?"

I looked at the countdown timer I had seen on the last file.

"The Festival of Unification," I said. "Three days."

Sara released my hands. She stepped back.

She didn't scream. She didn't cry. She turned into something terrifyingly cold.

"We have to get back," she said. "We have to steal the Elixir. If I cure her... if I get the metal out of her... she won't be conductive. She'll be safe."

"Sara," I said gently. "The Elixir... I saw the formula. It doesn't remove the metal. It just puts it to sleep. It won't stop the drain."

She looked at me. "Then what stops it?"

"Destroying the machine," I said. "We have to destroy the Core. The Heart of the City. If we shut down the grid, he can't drain anyone."

"But if we shut down the grid," Voss rumbled, "the city freezes. The shields fall. We'll be vulnerable."

"Better vulnerable than dead," I said.

I stood up straight. The exhaustion was gone. The pain in my shoulder was gone.

I had a mission now. Not a heist. A war.

"We are going back," I commanded. "We are taking the carriage remnants. We are walking if we have to. But we are getting back to the Palace."

I looked at Sara.

"And then," I said, "we are going to kill the King."

Sara looked at me. She reached into her pocket and pulled out the vial of suppressants I'd given her. She stared at it for a second, then crushed it in her hand. Glass tinkled to the floor.

"Lead the way, Chrome," she said.

And for the first time, she didn't say it like an insult. She said it like a rank.

Chapter 32: The Ultimatum

Sara

We smelled like ozone, dried blood, and two days of forced marching through a frozen hellscape.

When we finally slipped back into the Palace—using a forgotten sewage maintenance hatch that dumped us into the sub-basement—I thought the hard part was over.

I thought we were on the same side.

I was an idiot.

"The timeline has shifted," Voss said.

We were in Dorian's suite. The curtains were drawn. The door was bolted.

I was sitting on the floor, stripping off my ruined boots, while Dorian paced like a caged tiger, his metal arm humming with agitation.

Voss stood by the door, looking grim. He had just come from the Guard briefing, and he looked like he'd swallowed a lemon.

"What do you mean, shifted?" Dorian demanded. He was shirtless again, checking the field dressings on his human arm. The cut was angry, but closing.

"The King moved the Festival up," Voss said. "He claims the 'stars have aligned.' The Unification Ceremony is tomorrow night."

"Tomorrow?" I stood up, ignoring the ache in my feet. "That's impossible. The logistics alone..."

"He's bypassing the logistics," Dorian said, stopping his pacing. His face was pale, his eyes hard. "He knows, Voss. He knows the outpost went dark. He suspects I know. He's accelerating the Purge."

"He wants to drain the city before you can stop him," I realized. My stomach dropped. "Dorian, if he starts the ritual tomorrow..."

"Then we have twenty-four hours," Dorian said. He walked to his desk, sweeping a pile of unread correspondence onto the floor to spread out the blueprints of the Core. "We hit the Heart tomorrow night. During the opening speech. When the grid is distracted."

"There's a complication," Voss interrupted. His voice was heavy.

Dorian looked up. "What complication?"

"To prep the Throne Room for the ritual, the King ordered a high-security transfer. Shipment 99-Alpha. It's moving through the sub-levels right now."

I froze.

99-Alpha. That was the code for Class A Biologics. I knew it because I'd seen the manifests in the trash heaps of Sector 12 for years—empty crates that used to hold the things rich people used to stay pretty.

"The Elixir reserve," Dorian said, his voice dropping.

"Yes," Voss confirmed. "They're moving the entire supply to the King's personal vault in the Throne Room.

Once it's in there, it's sealed until the Unification is complete."

My heart hammered against my ribs.

"Wait," I said, stepping forward. "They're moving it *now*? As in, tonight?"

"Transit completes at 0300," Voss checked his watch. "We have two hours before it's locked down."

I looked at Dorian. He didn't look at me. He was staring at the map of the Core, calculating blast radiuses.

"Dorian," I said.

"Ignore it," he said.

The words hit me like a slap.

"Excuse me?"

"It's a transfer," Dorian said, his voice turning mechanical. "It means the sub-level corridors will be swarming with Golden Guard. We can't risk exposure. We stick to the plan. We hit the Core tomorrow."

"If we wait until tomorrow," I said, my voice rising, "the Elixir will be in the King's vault. It will be untouchable."

"I know."

"You know?" I walked over to the desk. I slammed my hand down on the blueprints. "You know, and you don't care? That crate has the cure in it! It has the only thing that can save Elara!"

Dorian finally looked at me. His eyes were tired. Fractured. But there was no yielding in them.

"Sara, listen to me. We have one shot at the Core. One. If we divert to intercept a shipment, we lose the element of surprise. We lose the window."

"We have two hours!" I argued. "We can take the shipment, hide it, and *then* hit the Core. We can do both!"

"We can't," he snapped. "The shipment is guarded by a full platoon. If we engage them, the alarm goes up. The King locks down the Core. The shields go up. And then everyone dies."

He stepped closer, his metal hand gripping the edge of the desk until the wood groaned.

"If we trigger a lockdown tonight, the King starts the harvest early. He drains the city. He drains your sister. Is a vial of blue liquid worth three million lives?"

"It is to me!" I shouted.

The silence that followed was deafening.

Voss looked at his boots. Dorian just stared at me, his face hardening into the mask of the Prince.

"That is why you are a bodyguard," Dorian said softly, "and I am a ruler. You save the person. I save the people."

"You're trading her," I whispered. "You're trading her life for your victory."

"I am trading *possibility* for *certainty*," he corrected. "If we destroy the Core, the drain stops. She might survive."

"Might," I spat. "She has the Rust in her lungs, Dorian. Even if you stop the drain, the metal keeps growing. She needs the Elixir. She needs it now."

I grabbed his arm—the human one. I squeezed it, desperate.

"Please. We can do this. You and me. We took down a Power Loader. We can take a transport team."

He looked at my hand on his arm. For a second, I saw the conflict. I saw the memory of the carriage, of the massage, of the heat.

Then he pulled his arm away.

"No," he said.

The word was a wall. Cold. Immovable.

"Voss," Dorian commanded, turning his back on me. "Secure the explosives. Sara, go to your room. Prep the tools for the thermal shielding. We move at sunset tomorrow."

"Dorian—"

"That is an order, 412."

I stood there, staring at his back.

He wasn't the man who had held me in the dark. He was the Chrome Prince. He was the machine.

He had calculated the odds, weighed the variables, and decided that my sister was an acceptable casualty.

"Understood, sir," I said. My voice was hollow.

Dorian flinched, just slightly, at the tone. But he didn't turn around.

"Get some rest," he said to the map.

I walked into my room. I closed the adjoining door.

I didn't scream. I didn't throw things. I went cold.

I looked at the clock on the wall. 01:15 AM.

I had an hour and forty-five minutes before the shipment was locked away forever.

If I waited for Dorian's plan—if I trusted him to save the world—Elara died.

I looked at the closed door to Dorian's room. I could hear his voice, low and intense, planning the revolution.

He was trying to be a hero.

I wasn't a hero. I was a sister.

And I was done following orders.

I moved fast.

I stripped off the ruined tactical gear. I pulled on a fresh set—black cargo pants, a tight long-sleeved shirt, the heavy boots.

I strapped the obsidian dagger to my thigh. I loaded my pockets with every pick, tension wrench, and pry bar I owned.

I grabbed the brass key I'd stolen from Lord Silas—the one that opened the service elevators.

I walked to the adjoining door. I rested my hand on the wood.

"Greater good," I whispered, tasting the bitterness of the lie.

I didn't leave a note. Notes were for people who expected to be forgiven.

I turned and slipped out the service hatch behind the vanity.

Dorian wanted to save the city? Fine. Let him save the city.

I was going to save my world.

Chapter 33: The Betrayal

Dorian

The Halon gas tasted like bitter almonds.

It filled the corridor, a thick, white fog designed to choke out fire. It also choked out humans. It burned the eyes, filled the lungs, and induced panic.

I didn't panic. I broke.

My internal systems switched to closed-cycle respiration instantly. My optical sensors shifted spectrum, cutting through the opaque white cloud.

I saw the heat trail.

Footsteps glowing bright orange on the cold concrete floor. A smear of thermal residue where her hand had touched the wall.

She was running.

Target: Sara. Status: Hostile.

The words flashed on my HUD. I swiped them away, overriding the designation with a violent mental command.

She wasn't hostile. She was desperate.

I had pushed her. I had forced her to choose between her blood and my city, and I had been arrogant enough to think she would choose me.

I walked through the fog. I didn't run. I reached out with my mind—via the neural interface in my spine—and pinged the building's security grid.

Sector 3. Sub-Level B. Seal Bulkhead 4.

A hundred yards ahead, heavy blast doors slammed shut with a thunderous *boom*.

The heat trail stopped.

I kept walking. My boots rang on the concrete, a steady, rhythmic beat of doom.

I reached the blast door. It was sealed tight. On the other side, I could hear the frantic *clack-clack-clack* of titanium on steel. She was trying to pick a magnetic lock.

"It's a mag-seal, Sara," I said. My voice was amplified by the helmet's vox-caster, sounding deep and distorted. "You can't pick it."

The scratching stopped.

"Open the door, Dorian," her voice came through the steel, muffled and shaking. "Please. Just let me go."

"I can't."

I placed my metal palm on the interface panel. I didn't unlock the door ahead of her. I unlocked the door *behind* her—the one I was standing at.

The blast door hissed and groaned, sliding open.

I stepped into the airlock.

It was a small, reinforced chamber, designed to withstand a containment breach. Sara was backed against the far wall.

The heavy steel case—Shipment 99-Alpha—was at her feet. She had strapped the unconscious Lieutenant's heavy gold gauntlet to her belt—her key to opening the bio-lock later.

She held the obsidian dagger in her right hand. Her chest was heaving. Her eyes were wild, rimmed with red from the gas.

She looked like a cornered animal. But when she saw me, she didn't attack. She just looked... shattered.

"Stay back," she warned, raising the knife. But her hand was shaking so badly the blade vibrated.

I didn't draw a weapon. I didn't raise my fists.

I took a step toward her, my hands open, palms up.

"Sara," I said, my voice cracking, stripping away the mechanical distortion. "Don't do this. Put it down. We can figure this out."

"There's nothing to figure out!" she screamed, tears cutting tracks through the soot on her face. "You made the call, Dorian! You chose the mission! I chose *her*!"

"I was trying to save you!" I stepped closer, ignoring the knife. "If you take that case, there is no coming back. You become a fugitive. The King will hunt you to the ends of the earth. I can't protect you if you run."

"I never asked you to protect me!"

"I know!" I shouted back, the heartbreak finally bleeding through the composure. "I know you didn't ask! But I wanted to! I wanted to save all of it, Sara. The city. The girl. You."

I stopped three feet from the blade.

"Please," I whispered. "Put the case down. Come back to the room. We hit the Core tomorrow. We save her the right way."

She looked at me. She looked at the scars on my chest where the metal met the skin.

For a second, I thought I had her. I saw the hesitation in her eyes. I saw the memory of the carriage, of the turbine, of the promise we made.

Then she looked down at the steel case.

"I can't take the chance," she whispered. "I'm sorry, Dorian. I can't bet her life on your plan."

CLANG. CLANG. CLANG.

Heavy boots pounded on the metal grating outside. Shouting echoed down the corridor.

"Secure the perimeter! Breach in Airlock 4! Subjects armed and dangerous!"

The Golden Guard.

The spell broke.

I looked at the door. I looked at Sara.

"They're here," I said.

"I'm not going back to the cell," she said, her voice hardening. She grabbed the handle of the heavy case. "I'm leaving, Dorian. Move."

"You can't outrun them carrying that," I said. "It weighs fifty pounds."

"I'll drag it if I have to."

The airlock door behind me hissed. Red lights flashed.

"Open fire on sight!" a voice commanded from the hallway.

I made a choice.

I didn't arrest her. I didn't stop her.

I turned my back on her and faced the opening door.

"Run," I ordered.

"What?"

"I said run!" I roared.

I drew the kinetic pistol from my holster. As the first Golden Guard stepped through the breach, I fired.

The round hit him in the chest plate, staggering him back into the hallway.

"Go to the vents!" I shouted over my shoulder, firing again to suppress the squad. "Leave the case! It's too heavy! Just run!"

Sara didn't leave the case.

I heard the scrape of metal on metal. I glanced back. She was dragging it. She was hauling the massive steel box toward the ventilation hatch in the corner of the airlock.

"Sara, leave it!" I screamed, taking a plasma bolt to the shoulder. My armor absorbed it, but the heat seared my skin.

"No!" she yelled back, straining against the weight.

I turned back to the fight. I charged the door.

I hit the squad of guards like a battering ram. I used my metal arm to smash a rifle aside, drove my shoulder into a chest, kicked a knee.

I was buying her seconds. I was trading my own safety for her exit.

"Get to the vents!" I bellowed, grabbing a guard by the throat and throwing him into his squadmates.

I looked back.

She was at the hatch. She had it open.

But she couldn't lift the case.

She was trying to heave the reinforced steel box up into the shaft, but it was too bulky, too heavy. She was struggling, sobbing with frustration, refusing to let go.

"Leave it!" I begged her.

"I can't!"

A guard slipped past me. He didn't aim for me. He aimed for her.

He didn't shoot. He tackled her.

"No!" I turned, abandoning the door.

The guard slammed into Sara. She went down hard, her head cracking against the floor. The case skidded away.

I lunged for them.

I grabbed the guard by his belt and ripped him off her, hurling him across the room.

I reached for Sara. "Get up!"

But three more guards swarmed in. They didn't go for me—they knew better than to engage a Prince in close quarters.

They went for the asset.

Two of them pinned Sara to the ground. One pressed a shock-baton to her spine.

"Surrender!" the squad leader screamed, aiming a rifle at her head. "Surrender, Prince Dorian, or we execute the prisoner!"

I froze.

My metal fist was raised, ready to crush the skull of the guard nearest me. My chest was heaving.

Sara was pinned under them. Her face was pressed against the grate. She was reaching out... not for me.

She was reaching for the case.

"Don't," she whispered, her fingers brushing the steel handle. "I almost had it."

I looked at the rifle pointed at her skull. I looked at the dozen guards pouring into the room, weapons raised.

I lowered my hand.

"Stand down," I said, my voice dead.

"Dorian, don't," Sara choked out. "Fight them."

"I can't," I said. "I can't lose you."

The guards moved instantly. They kicked Sara's legs apart, snapping heavy runic cuffs onto her wrists and ankles. They dragged her away from the case.

"Secure the asset!" the leader barked. "The King has ordered immediate transfer to the Black Cells."

I watched them haul her up. She was bruised, bleeding, and covered in soot.

She looked at me.

She didn't look angry anymore. She looked defeated.

"You should have let me go," she whispered as they dragged her past me.

"I tried," I said, looking at the heavy steel case that sat on the floor—the anchor that had sunk us both. "You wouldn't let go."

They dragged her out of the airlock.

I stood alone in the wreckage, surrounded by the King's guard.

I looked down at my hands. One metal. One flesh. Both useless.

I had fought for her. I had bled for her.

But in the end, the weight of her love for her sister was heavier than my power to save her.

"Your Highness," the squad leader said, stepping forward cautiously. "The King is waiting."

I didn't look at him. I looked at the dark ventilation shaft—the exit she could have taken if she had just trusted me.

"Take me to him," I said.

Chapter 34: The Arrest

Sara

The handcuffs were made of runic iron.

That was the first thing I noticed as they dragged me down the corridor. Not the bruises forming on my arms, not the blood in my mouth, but the cold, biting burn of the metal against my wrists. Runic iron didn't just restrain the body; it dampened the nervous system. It made my fingers numb and my thoughts sluggish, like wading through molasses.

"Move, Slag," the Lieutenant grunted, shoving me forward.

I stumbled, my boots catching on the polished concrete. I didn't fall. I refused to fall.

We weren't going to the Black Cells. Not yet.

We were in the Grand Foyer of the sub-level, a massive, echoing chamber where the security elevators met the transport grid.

"Hold," a voice boomed.

It wasn't a human voice. It was the sound of grinding tectonic plates.

The guards stopped instantly, snapping to attention. Their boots clicked in unison.

I looked up.

The air in the center of the foyer shimmered. Gold light coalesced, twisting and forming into a massive, ten-foot-tall projection.

King Aric.

He wasn't physically here—he was stuck in his throne upstairs—but his presence was heavy enough to crush the air out of the room. The hologram was perfect, terrifyingly detailed, down to the red lenses of his eyes and the condensation dripping from his golden chin.

"Report," the King buzzed.

The Lieutenant stepped forward, bowing low. "We intercepted the asset in Sector 3, Your Majesty. She attempted to steal Shipment 99-Alpha. She has been neutralized."

The King's red eyes swiveled to me. They didn't look angry. They looked bored.

"A thief," Aric said. "I predicted this."

"She is secure, sire. We are transferring her to—"

"Dispose of it," the King interrupted.

My heart slammed against my ribs.

"Sire?" the Lieutenant asked, hesitating.

"She is a failed experiment," the King stated. "She has seen the shipment. She is a security risk. Execute her. Here. Now."

The Lieutenant drew his sidearm. A kinetic pistol. He leveled it at my forehead.

I stared down the barrel. I didn't close my eyes. I thought of Elara. I thought of the empty vial in my pocket. *I failed you, bug.*
"Belay that order."

The voice cut through the room like a whip.

Dorian walked into the foyer.

He looked calm. Terrifyingly calm. He walked with a slow, predatory grace, his metal arm hanging loose at his side. He didn't look at me. He looked at the hologram of his father.

"She is my bodyguard," Dorian said smoothly. "She falls under my jurisdiction."

"She is a traitor," the King buzzed. "She attacked my guards."

"She fell for a trap," Dorian corrected.

I blinked. *Trap?*
Dorian walked up to the Lieutenant. He didn't ask for permission. He reached out with his metal hand and pushed the barrel of the gun down until it pointed at the floor.

"I set the bait," Dorian lied, his voice echoing in the silent room. "I wanted to see if she was loyal. I left the data pad unlocked. I left the key accessible. I wanted to know if the Rat would bite."

He turned to look at me then.

His face was a mask. The Prince was back. The arrogant, bored, untouchable Prince. The man who had slept with his head in my lap was gone, replaced by the Chrome statue.

"She bit," Dorian said coldly. "Disappointing. But instructive."

"She is useless," the King said. "Kill her."

"No," Dorian said.

The air crackled. To defy the King was treason.

"She has value," Dorian continued, circling me. He looked me up and down like I was a piece of livestock. "She bypassed a Level 10 security grid to get here. She neutralized two armored guards in under ten seconds with nothing but a knife and a flash-bang."

He stopped behind me. He leaned close, his breath ghosting over my ear.

"She is not just a thief, Father. She is a weapon. And I want to know who sharpened her."

"Interrogation?" the King mused.

"She has connections in the Slags," Dorian said. "She knows the resistance. If we kill her now, we lose the intel. I want to break her first."

The King was silent. The hologram flickered as he processed the logic. *Efficiency. Data. Value.*

"Very well," the King decided. "Transfer her to the Black Cells. Process her. But Dorian..."

"Yes, Father?"

"If she does not sing within twenty-four hours... smelt her."

The hologram vanished.

The pressure in the room lifted, leaving only the cold reality of my situation.

Dorian turned to the Lieutenant.

"I'll take it from here," he said.

"Sir, protocol dictates—"

"I said," Dorian snarled, his human eye flashing with sudden, violent heat, "I will take her. Get out of my sight."

The Lieutenant paled. He holstered his weapon, signaled his men, and they retreated toward the elevators.

We were alone in the foyer. Me, Dorian, and the silence.

He grabbed my arm.

He didn't be gentle. He gripped my bicep with his metal hand, hard enough to bruise, and yanked me toward the service lift.

"Walk," he ordered.

I stumbled after him. "Dorian—"

"Shut up," he hissed. He didn't look at me. He stared straight ahead, his jaw clenched so tight a muscle feathered in his cheek.

He dragged me into the elevator. He punched the button for the Detention Level.

The doors closed.

As soon as we were moving, he released me. He shoved me—not hard, but firmly—against the back wall of the elevator.

"You are an idiot," he whispered venomously. "A reckless, selfish, suicidal idiot."

"I had the case," I argued, rubbing my arm. "I was *right there*."

"And now you're here," he snapped. "Heading to a cell where they use sonic probes to peel your mind apart like an onion. Was it worth it?"

"If I had gotten it open—"

"You couldn't open it!" He slammed his hand against the metal wall next to my head. "That case is a coffin, Sara! I told you!"

We stared at each other. He was furious. I was heartbroken.

"You lied to him," I said quietly. "About the trap."

"I saved your life," he corrected. "Again. I am getting very tired of saving your life, Sara."

"Then stop doing it."

"I can't!"

The words hung in the air. He looked shocked that he'd said them.

He stepped back, running his human hand through his hair. He looked wrecked. The mask slipped, just for a second, revealing the panic underneath.

"I bought you twenty-four hours," he said, his voice hollow. "That's it. That's all I can do. The King expects a confession. If I don't give him one by tomorrow night..."

"He smelts me."

"Yes."

The elevator chimed. *Detention Level.*

Dorian straightened up. The mask slammed back into place.

"Listen to me," he said, leaning in close, speaking fast and low. "The Black Cells are automated. No guards inside. Just droids. They feed you, they water you, they watch you."

He grabbed my chin, forcing me to look at him.

"Do not fight the droids. Do not try to pick the locks. The walls are electrified. If you touch them, you fry."

"So I just sit there?"

"You sit there," he said. "And you wait."

"For what?"

"For the heist."

My eyes widened. "You're still doing it?"

"I have to," he said grimly. "It's the only play left. I destroy the Core tomorrow night during the ceremony. When the power goes out... the containment fields on the cells will fail."

He looked at me, his eyes intense.

"When the lights go out, Sara... you run. You don't look for me. You don't look for the Elixir. You run for the surface."

"Dorian—"

The doors opened.

Two massive detention droids—skeletal chrome nightmares with shock-batons—were waiting.

Dorian shoved me toward them.

"Process the prisoner," he commanded loudly. "Level 5 containment."

The droids grabbed me. Their grip was cold, mechanical, unyielding.

I looked back at Dorian. He stood in the elevator, bathed in the harsh white light. He looked like the Prince again. Cold. Distant.

"I'll expect a full report on her contacts by morning," he said to the droids.

Then he looked at me. He didn't wink. He didn't smile.

But his left hand—the metal one—tapped twice against his thigh.

Tap. Tap.
Our code. *Wait for the signal.*
The droids dragged me away into the dark.

I didn't fight. I didn't scream. I walked into the dark, holding onto that sound.

Tap. Tap.
He hadn't given up on me.

Which meant I couldn't give up on him. Even if I had to sit in the dark for twenty-four hours while my sister died, I would wait.

Because when the lights went out, I wasn't just going to run.

I was going to finish the job.

Chapter 35: The Dungeon

Sara

The Black Cells didn't have bars. Bars were primitive. Bars implied that you were a physical threat.

The Black Cells were designed for something else entirely: erasure.

I was suspended in the center of a cylindrical room, my wrists and ankles shackled into magnetic cuffs that hovered in the air. I couldn't touch the floor. I couldn't touch the walls. I was just... floating.

Total darkness. Total silence.

The air was sterile, scrubbed of all scent. The runic iron of the cuffs had done its job; my body felt heavy, numb, like I was wrapped in lead wool. The magic dampeners in the walls were humming at a frequency I could feel in my teeth, suppressing any spark of adrenaline or thought.

I didn't know how long I'd been there. An hour? A day?

Time didn't exist in the dark.

My mind started to eat itself.

I thought about Elara. I pictured her lying on the cot in the shipping container. Was she coughing? Was she looking at the door, waiting for me? Did she know I wasn't coming back with the strawberries?

I had it, the voice in my head screamed. *I had the case.*
If I had been faster. If I hadn't hesitated. If I had thrown the knife at Dorian instead of the floor.

Guilt is a cold companion. It sat on my chest, heavier than the gravity field holding me in place.

Tap. Tap.

I replayed the sound of Dorian's metal fingers against his thigh. The signal. *Wait.*

But in the suffocating dark, the doubt started to creep in. Roots of paranoia took hold.

Did he signal me to save me? Or did he signal me to keep me quiet?

He was the Prince. He was the machine. He had talked about the "Greater Good." Maybe I was just a loose end he needed to tie up neatly before he blew the reactor. Maybe I was the sacrifice.

"Damn you, Chrome," I whispered. My voice sounded dead, absorbed instantly by the sound-dampening walls.

A hiss cut through the silence.

A panel in the wall slid open. Light—blinding, painful white light—flooded the cylinder.

I squinted, turning my head away, my eyes watering.

A walkway extended from the door toward me. Heavy boots rang against the metal.

I knew the stride.

Dorian stopped a few feet away.

He was backlit, a silhouette of broad shoulders and rigid posture. He wasn't wearing the tactical gear. He was back in the pristine white uniform, the gold braid gleaming, the medals chest-heavy. The Prince.

He held a data pad in his human hand. His metal arm hung at his side, the fingers twitching in a rhythmic sequence.

"Prisoner 412," he said. His voice was amplified, cold, devoid of any humanity. "State your name for the record."

I glared at him through the glare. "Go to hell."

"Non-compliant," Dorian noted, tapping the pad. "The King is watching, Sara. This feed goes directly to the Throne. I suggest you cooperate."

"Cooperate?" I laughed, a ragged, broken sound. "You locked me in a sensory deprivation tank. What do you want me to do? Thank you for the accommodation?"

"I want names," he said, stepping closer. He walked to the edge of the platform, within arm's reach. "Who is your contact in the resistance? How did you know the transfer schedule for the Elixir?"

"I don't have a contact."

"Liar."

"I hacked it!" I shouted, straining against the magnetic cuffs. The field buzzed, zapping my wrists with a jolt of pain. I gritted my teeth. "I stole a key from Lord Silas. I used a datapad I swiped from the outpost. I did it alone, Dorian. Me. Just me."

"Impossible," he said smoothly. "A Slag mechanic bypassing Level 10 security? You had help. Who gave you the codes?"

He was doing it on purpose. He was feeding the narrative. *The dangerous rebel. The mastermind.* He was making me valuable so his father wouldn't smelt me.

But I didn't care about the strategy. I was tired. I was heartbroken. And I was looking at the man who had stopped me from saving my sister.

"You want the truth?" I hissed. "Fine. Here's the truth."

I leaned forward as far as the field would allow.

"I trusted you," I said. "I thought you were different. I thought the metal was just a shell. But you're hollow, Dorian. You're just like your father. You trade lives like currency."

Dorian's jaw tightened. He stepped closer, entering the magnetic field's perimeter. The air around us crackled.

"I did what was necessary," he said, his voice dropping lower.

"Necessary?" I spat. "She's dying! Right now! And you let them take the cure away because you were afraid of getting caught!"

"I was afraid of you dying!" he snapped, the mask slipping for a fraction of a second.

"I would rather die trying to save her than live in this box!"

I pulled against the chains, screaming at him.

"I should have killed you," I wept, the anger dissolving into grief. "In the alley. In the carriage. I should have let the assassin take the shot. I should have let you rust."

The words hung in the white room. Brutal. Final.

Dorian went very still. His human eye looked shattered. The fractured blue eye whirred, the aperture closing and opening.

He reached out.

I flinched, expecting a strike.

He didn't hit me. He reached past me to the control panel on the suspension rig.

He tapped a sequence of buttons.

Hummmmm.
The magnetic field whined. A high-pitched frequency filled the room—audio distortion. It would sound like static on the King's feed.

Dorian leaned in. His face was inches from mine. He didn't look angry. He looked desperate.

"Keep hating me," he whispered, his voice barely audible over the static. "Hate is fuel, Sara. Use it. Stay angry. Stay warm."

He grabbed my chin with his human hand, forcing me to look at him.

"Tomorrow night," he said. "When the lights die... you run. You go to the sub-basement. Ventilator shaft 4."

"Why?" I choked out.

"Because I hid a fallback stash there," he whispered. "Money. Fake IDs. And a weapon."

"No Elixir?"

His eyes closed briefly. "No. I couldn't get it."

He opened his eyes. They were hard again.

"Survive, Rat," he commanded. "That's an order."

He pulled his hand away. He hit the panel again, killing the static.

"Interrogation paused," he announced loudly for the recording. "Subject is hostile. Further conditioning required."

He turned on his heel.

"Dorian!" I shouted after him.

He didn't stop. He walked down the gangway, the white cape swirling around his boots.

The door hissed shut. The lights died.

I was back in the dark.

I hung there in the silence, my heart pounding against my ribs. I replayed his words. *Keep hating me.*
He wanted me to hate him. Because if I hated him, I wouldn't mourn him when he destroyed the Core.

He wasn't planning to make it out.

"Idiot," I whispered into the blackness. "Stupid, noble, chrome-plated idiot."

I tested the cuffs. They were tight. The field was strong.

But he had touched the control panel. He had been close.

I closed my eyes. I focused on the anger. I focused on the heat.

I wasn't going to run to the sub-basement. I wasn't going to take the money and the fake IDs.

If the lights went out tomorrow, I wasn't going anywhere but up.

To the Throne Room.

Because I still had a spoon in my pocket that I hadn't returned. And I was going to gouge the King's eyes out with it.

Chapter 36: The Rescue Plan

Dorian

I walked out of the Detention Level and stripped off the white gloves. They were stained with the invisible residue of my own cowardice.

I dropped them in a trash receptacle.

"Status?" Voss asked. He was waiting for me by the service elevator, leaning against the wall, cleaning his fingernails with a trench knife.

"She hates me," I said, staring at the numbers counting up on the elevator display. "Which means she's focused. She'll survive."

"And the King?"

"He thinks I'm a loyal son who just locked up his favorite toy."

The elevator arrived. We stepped in.

"Barracks," I ordered.

Voss hit the button for the sub-level below the glamorous guard quarters. The Wolf's Den. It was where the "problem" soldiers went. The veterans who had too much PTSD to stand pretty at a gala. The cyborgs whose plating was scratched. The men who asked too many questions.

"They're ready?" I asked, watching the floor indicator blur.

"They're restless," Voss corrected. "They know something is coming. The King's Elites—the Golden Guard—have been taking up positions at all the primary vents. They're sealing the exits, Dorian."

"He's preparing the kill box," I murmured. "He wants the population trapped inside the shield grid when he flips the switch."

The elevator dinged.

The Wolf's Den smelled of stale beer, gun oil, and unwashed armor. It was a concrete bunker filled with cots and weapon lockers.

Ten men were waiting.

They stood up when I walked in. They didn't salute. They weren't the shiny toy soldiers upstairs. They were scarred, battered, and dangerous.

I knew every one of them.

Jax, the sniper who lost an eye in the Border Wars—I'd paid for his cybernetic replacement off the books when the Crown denied his pension.

Kael, the heavy infantryman—I'd pulled him out of a smelting pit myself when his squad left him for dead.

Rook, the demo expert—I'd pardoned him from a hanging after he punched a noble who spat on him.

They were the broken toys. And they were the only ones I trusted.

"At ease," I said.

"We hearing rumors, Prince," Jax said, his mechanical eye whirring. "Word is the Unification Ceremony has been moved up. And the King is recalling all leave."

"It's not a ceremony," I said, stepping into the center of the room. "It's a harvest."

I told them.

I didn't sugarcoat it. I told them about the Rust. I told them about the batteries. I told them that the people they were sworn to protect—the Slags, the workers, their own families in the Lower Districts—were going to be drained to feed a golden vampire.

Silence settled over the room. Heavy. Suffocating.

"So," Rook said, hefting a detonator pack. "We're killing the King."

"We're killing the machine," I corrected. "We hit the Core. We cut the power. The shields fall. The city goes dark."

"And then?" Voss asked.

"And then we fight."

The door to the barracks hissed open.

The conversation died instantly.

Three men walked in. They were tall, encased in gleaming, seamless gold armor. No faces. Just smooth, blank helms.

The Golden Guard. My father's personal executioners.

"Prince Dorian," the lead guard synthesized. His voice was flat, metallic. "By order of the King, you are to be escorted to your quarters. You are relieved of command until the Ceremony concludes."

I stood my ground. "I am the Crown Prince. I am not relieved until I say I am."

"Your command codes have been revoked," the Gold Guard stated. He raised a kinetic pulse rifle. "Please surrender your sidearm and the prosthetic interface. For your own safety."

My own safety.

Right. He wasn't securing me. He was decommissioning me. My father knew I had seen the files. He was locking me in a box until the harvest was done, and then he would probably scrap me for parts.

I looked at the Gold Guard. I looked at the rifle leveled at my chest.

I looked at Voss.

Voss gave a microscopic nod.

"I'm afraid I can't do that," I said softly.

"Resistance is treason," the Guard droned. "Compliance is mandatory."

"Compliance," I said, stepping forward, "is boring."

I moved.

I didn't go for a weapon. I went for the Guard.

I slapped the barrel of the rifle aside with my metal hand—*CLANG*—and drove my human fist into the unarmored joint at his neck.

At the same instant, Voss threw his trench knife. It sank into the throat of the second guard with a wet thud.

The room exploded into violence.

Jax and Rook were moving before the third guard could raise his weapon. Jax tackled him, dragging him to the concrete. Rook slammed a heavy boot onto the guard's helmet, shattering the lens.

It was over in six seconds.

Three Golden Guards lay dead or dying on the floor of the Wolf's Den.

I stood over the leader, breathing hard. The Torque in my chest was spiking, singing with the violence.

I looked at the rifle in his hand. I picked it up.

"Well," I said, turning to the stunned room. "I guess we just committed treason."

Voss wiped his knife on his trousers. "About time."

I looked at the ten men. They weren't looking at me with fear. They were looking at me with hunger. They had been waiting for this order for years.

"The plan has changed," I said, my voice hard.

"We're not just hitting the Core," I continued. "Voss, take Rook and Kael. You hit the armory. I want every kinetic rifle and EMP grenade you can carry. Distribute them to the resistance cells in the Lower City."

"The resistance?" Voss asked. "You want to arm the Slags?"

"If the lights go out, the Chrome Guard will panic. I want the Slags ready to riot. Chaos is our cover."

I turned to Jax.

"You and the rest of the squad... you're with me."

"Where are we going?" Jax asked, checking the charge on his sniper rifle.

I looked at the dead Golden Guard. I looked at the ceiling, toward the Throne Room, and the Black Cells beneath it.

"We're going to break the grid," I said. "But first... we have a delivery to make."

"Delivery?"

I smiled. It was the smile Sara had given me in the alley. Sharp. Dangerous.

"The King wants a show for the Unification," I said. "Let's give him a fireworks display."

I checked the charge on my metal arm. 98%.

I checked the time.

20 hours to the Ceremony.
"Get your gear," I ordered. "We hunt at sundown."

The men moved.

I stood in the center of the room, the stolen rifle heavy in my hand. I thought of Sara in the dark.

Wait for the signal.
I tapped my metal fingers against the rifle stock.

Tap. Tap.
"Hold on, Rat," I whispered. "The cavalry is coming. And we're bringing the fire."

Chapter 37: The Breakout

Sara

The first sign that the world was ending was the sound.

In the sensory deprivation tank, silence was absolute. But then, a low thrum started in the walls. It wasn't the magnetic hum of the dampeners. It was a physical vibration.

Boom. Boom. Boom.
Explosions. Distant, but getting closer.

Then, the gravity failed.

The magnetic field holding me suspended in mid-air flickered and died.

I fell.

I hit the metal grating of the floor hard, landing on my shoulder. The breath left my lungs in a pained whoosh. The mag-cuffs on my wrists and ankles deactivated with a *clack*, releasing me.
I scrambled to my feet, ignoring the spinning in my head.

The blinding white light of the cell cut out, replaced by the strobing red pulse of emergency klaxons.

ALERT. SECURITY BREACH. LEVEL 5.
"Finally," I hissed, rubbing my bruised wrists.

The door to my cell didn't open. The electronic lock was dead, but the physical bolts were still engaged. I was trapped in a red-lit can while the building burned down around me.

I looked for a weapon. Nothing. Just smooth walls.

I backed into the corner, waiting. If the droids came in to secure me, I'd have to dismantle one with my bare hands.

I'd done it before. Aim for the optical sensor, rip out the wiring.

THUD.

Something heavy slammed into the door from the outside. Metal groaned.

THUD.

A dent appeared in the center of the steel.

SCREECH.

The door was ripped off its tracks. It wasn't unlocked; it was peeled open like a tin can.

Smoke billowed into the cell. Through the haze, a figure stepped in.

He was covered in soot. He held a kinetic rifle in his human hand, and his metal arm was glowing cherry-red from heat stress.

Dorian.

He looked like a demon. His hair was wild, his uniform torn, and his eyes were blazing.

"Get up," he barked, extending his human hand.

I didn't take it. I stared at him, adrenaline warring with the lingering betrayal.

"You're early," I said. "You said tomorrow night."

"I got impatient," he growled. "We're leaving. Now."

He grabbed my arm and hauled me out of the cell.

The corridor was a war zone. Two detention droids lay in sparking heaps of scrap metal. Jax—the sniper from the Wolf's Den—was crouched by the elevator, covering the hall. Rook was planting charges on the structural pillars.

"Clear!" Jax shouted, firing a round down the hall.

Dorian dragged me toward the Evidence Lockup across the hall. The door was already blasted open.

He walked inside, holstered his rifle, and picked something up from the counter.

He turned to me. He held it out.

The steel case. Shipment 99-Alpha.

I froze. I looked at the bio-hazard symbol. I looked at Dorian.

"You got it," I whispered.

"It was logged into evidence," he said, shoving it into my chest. "I took a detour."

I wrapped my arms around the cold steel, clutching it like a lifeline. "But... you said it was impossible. You said I couldn't open it."

"You can't," Dorian said. He reached into his pocket.

He pulled out a jagged, bloody object. It looked like a piece of wet meat.

My stomach lurched.

It was a finger. A human finger, encased in a gold gauntlet.

"The Lieutenant," Dorian explained grimly, tossing the severed digit onto the case. "His biometrics are authorized for transit containers. Use it to open the lock. Then burn it."

I stared at the grisly key. Then I looked up at him.

He hadn't just broken me out. He had mutilated an officer to get me the cure. He had crossed a line he could never uncross.

"Dorian..."

"Don't," he cut me off. "We don't have time for feelings, Sara. We have time for running."

He grabbed my shoulder and steered me out of the room.

"Rook! Blow the pillars!" he shouted.

"Fire in the hole!"

Dorian threw me to the floor, covering my body with his own.

BOOM.
The detention block shook violently. Dust and concrete rained down. The lights flickered and died completely, leaving us in pitch blackness.

Dorian pulled me up. He activated the tactical light on his rifle.

"Vents," he ordered, pointing his beam at a service hatch that had been blown open by the blast. "That shaft leads to the sub-basement. From there, it's a straight shot to the sewers. You can be in the Slags in an hour."

He pushed me toward it.

I dug my heels in.

"No," I said.

Dorian spun around. "What?"

"I'm not leaving you," I said, clutching the case with one hand and grabbing his tactical vest with the other. "We have the Elixir. We have the explosives. Let's finish it. Let's go up to the Core."

"Sara, listen to me—"

"No! You listen! We're partners! You said hate was fuel? Well, I'm full of it. Let's burn him down together!"

Dorian grabbed my face. His hands were shaking.

"You can't go up," he said, his voice cracking. "The Core is unstable. When I breach the containment field... the radiation spike will be lethal to anyone without shielding."

He tapped his metal chest.

"I'm shielded, Sara. You're not. If you come with me, you die before we even reach the throne."

I stared at him. "You're going to die too."

"I'm a machine," he whispered. "I can take the heat."

"You're a liar," I choked out. "You're not planning on coming back."

"I never was."

He looked at me with such devastating intensity that my knees went weak. He leaned down and pressed his forehead against mine.

"Go," he breathed. "Save your sister. Save Elara. That was the deal."

"To hell with the deal! I want you!"

The confession hung between us, raw and bleeding in the smoke-filled corridor.

Dorian closed his eyes. He let out a shuddering breath.

"And I want you to live," he said.

He pulled back. He looked at the open vent.

"Go. Don't come back."

"Come with me," I pleaded. "Please. We can find another way."

"I have to buy you time," he said, stepping back. He raised his rifle, aiming it down the hallway where new alarms were blaring. "The Golden Guard is coming. If they breach this level before you're clear, they'll lock down the sewers."

He looked at me one last time.

"Run, Rat," he said. A ghost of a smile touched his lips. "Run like you stole something."

I looked at him. Standing in the wreckage. The Golden Prince, covered in soot, holding the line so I could escape.

I gripped the handle of the case until my knuckles turned white.

"I'm keeping the boots," I sobbed, my voice breaking.

"Keep them," he said. "Now go!"

I turned. I scrambled into the vent.

I crawled ten feet, dragging the heavy case. The metal was cold against my stomach.

I stopped. I looked back through the grate.

Dorian was standing in the center of the corridor. The blast doors at the far end were glowing orange—someone was cutting through.

He racked the slide of his rifle. His metal arm hummed, the blue light flaring bright in the dark.

"Come and get it," he growled at the door.

Then he turned his head slightly, looking toward the vent. He couldn't see me, but he knew I was there.

He tapped his metal fingers against his thigh. Two taps.

I'm with you.
I bit my lip to stifle a scream, turned around, and crawled into the dark.

I didn't run because I was afraid. I ran because he asked me to. And because I had a promise to keep.

But as I slid down the chute into the bowels of the city, I made a new promise.

If he died... I would tear this city apart brick by brick until I found his ashes. And then I would make the King eat them.

Chapter 38: The Sacrifice

Dorian

The blast door didn't open. It evaporated.

Thermite is a nasty way to make an entrance. It burns at four thousand degrees, turning reinforced steel into liquid slag in seconds. I watched the metal drip onto the concrete floor, glowing like forbidden honey.

I checked my rifle. Ammo: 12 rounds.

I checked my arm. Charge: 40%.

I checked the clock.

Sara had been gone for ninety seconds.

It wasn't enough.

The ventilation shafts in the sub-basement were a maze. She needed at least five minutes to clear the perimeter of the Palace. If they got past me now, they would flood the tunnels with gas. They would catch her before she even saw daylight.

"Come on, you shiny bastards," I muttered, raising the rifle. "Let's dance."

The smoke cleared.

They surged through the breach. The Golden Guard.

There were six of them. They moved like liquid gold, silent and terrifyingly fast. They didn't shout commands. They didn't hesitate. They were the King's will made manifest.

I fired.

Crack. Crack. Crack.

My aim was true. Two rounds took the point man in the visor. The kinetic force snapped his head back, but he didn't fall. The gold alloy of their armor was self-repairing. The dents smoothed out instantly.

"Target acquired," the lead Guard droned. "Prince Dorian. Lethal force authorized."

They opened fire.

The air filled with blue streaks of plasma.

I rolled behind a concrete pillar. Chips of stone rained down on me as the plasma bolts chewed through the cover. My heat sensors screamed a warning.

Armor Integrity: Critical.

I popped out, firing blindly. I caught one Guard in the unarmored joint of his knee. He went down. I put two more rounds into his neck before his squadmates suppressed me.

Click. Empty.

I threw the rifle at them. It bounced harmlessly off a golden chest plate.

"Out of ammo," I said to myself. "Perfect."

I stepped out from behind the pillar.

I didn't have a gun. I had a left arm that weighed sixty pounds and could crush a tank.

I charged.

The Guards hesitated for a fraction of a second—they weren't used to people running *at* plasma fire.

I closed the distance. I ducked under a swing of a shock-baton and drove my metal fist into the gut of the nearest Guard.

CRUNCH.

The impact was satisfying. Metal sheared. The Guard doubled over, wheezing. I grabbed him by the helmet and used him as a shield against the others. Plasma bolts slammed into his back, cooking him inside his own suit.

I threw the corpse at the squad leader.

It was a brawl now. Dirty. Close. Just the way Sara liked it.

A baton struck my human shoulder, shattering the clavicle.

I roared, the pain blinding white, and spun around. I backhanded the attacker with my metal arm. His helmet flew off. His head hit the wall with a wet thud.

Four down. Two to go.

But I was slowing down. My vision was tunneling. The Torque was spiking so high my blood felt like it was boiling.

One of the remaining Guards tackled me. We hit the floor. He was heavy, stronger than a human should be. He pinned my metal arm to the ground. The other Guard aimed his rifle at my head.

Game over, the logic center of my brain whispered.
Not yet, the biological heart screamed.
I headbutted the Guard on top of me. He reeled back. I kicked him off, scrambling to my feet.

I looked down the hall.

More were coming. I could hear the tramp of boots. Dozens of them. The King was emptying the barracks.

Sara needed time.

I looked at the narrow corridor behind me—the one leading to the vents. If I retreated, they would follow. If I fought here, they would overwhelm me.

I needed to block the path. Permanently.

I looked at the heavy support arches on either side of the hallway. Steel beams encased in concrete.

I remembered the nightmare. The gold rising. The metal eating the flesh.

I looked at my left arm. The blue light of the power core was pulsing rapidly.

Safety Protocols: Engaged.
I reached into the access panel on my forearm. I ripped the safety inhibitor out.

WARNING. CORE OVERLOAD IMMINENT. MELTDOWN SEQUENCE INITIATED.
"Shut up," I grunted.

The pain was instant. It felt like I had injected lava into my veins. The blue light turned a blinding, searing white. The metal plating on my arm began to expand, glowing hot.

I stepped into the center of the archway. I spread my arms.

I placed my metal hand on the left wall. I placed my human hand on the right wall.

"Channel it," I hissed through clenched teeth.

I pushed the energy outward.

It wasn't magic. It was alchemy. It was the Gilt.

The metal from my arm surged. It didn't just glow; it *grew*. It shot out like jagged vines, piercing the steel of the walls. It ate the concrete. It fused with the building's skeleton.
But it didn't stop at the walls.

It flowed back into me.

I screamed as the metal crossed my chest. It consumed the tactical vest. It consumed the skin. It wrapped around my broken clavicle, knitting the bone together with alloy.

My human arm—the right arm—began to turn gray. Then silver. Then chrome.

"Prince Dorian!" the Guard shouted, stopping ten feet away. "Stand down!"

They raised their weapons.

They fired.

The plasma bolts hit me. But they didn't burn flesh. They splashed against the wall of living metal I was becoming.

I was no longer a man standing in a hallway. I was the hallway.

The metal raced up my neck. It filled my throat, choking off the scream. It felt heavy. Cold. Eternal.

My vision began to fracture. Red threat assessments overlaying blue structural data overlaying the terrified faces of the Golden Guard.

Structure Integrity: 400%.

Biological Status: Failing.

I could feel the ventilation shaft behind me. I could feel the vibration of Sara crawling away.

Run, Rat, I thought. The words didn't reach my lips. My lips were steel.
The metal reached my eyes.

The world went dark. But not the empty dark of the void. It was the solid, heavy dark of the earth.

I couldn't move. I couldn't breathe. I couldn't feel the pain anymore.

I was a statue. I was a door.

And I was locked.

The Guards fired again. I felt the impacts as dull vibrations. They were pounding on the gate.

Let them pound.

I held.

I was fifty tons of rust and iron, anchored by a single, human thought.

She got away.

And for the first time in my life, the silence inside my head was peaceful.

Chapter 39: The Cure

Sara

I didn't run. I scrambled.

I was a creature of mud and panic, clawing my way out of the storm drain in District 14. I smelled like sewage and burnt ozone. The steel case dragged behind me like a dead body, banging against the rusted grate.

My lungs were burning. My legs were lead. But I didn't stop.

Tap. Tap.
The sound of Dorian's fingers against his thigh echoed in my head, a metronome keeping me moving. *I'm with you.*
"Liar," I wheezed, stumbling onto the cracked pavement of the Scrapyard. "You're not with me. You're back there."

I refused to think about what "back there" meant. I refused to picture the blast doors. I refused to imagine the silence.

I focused on the destination.

The stack of shipping containers loomed ahead, swaying slightly in the toxic wind. Home. It looked small. Dirty. Insignificant.

I climbed the ladder one-handed, hauling the heavy case up rung by rung. My muscles screamed. The bruises from the magnetic cuffs throbbed in time with my heart.

I reached the top. I kicked the door.

"Elara!"

I burst inside.

The air in the container was thick, smelling of sickness and metallic dust. It was freezing—the heater had died days ago.

"Elara?"

I dropped the case and rushed to the cot in the corner.

She was there. But she barely looked human.

The Rust had consumed her. The silver patches had joined together, forming a solid sheen of metal across her chest and neck. Her skin was gray, translucent. Her breathing was a shallow, rattling sound—*clack, wheeze, clack*—like gears grinding together without oil.

"No, no, no," I whispered, falling to my knees beside her. "Don't you dare check out on me. Not now."

I touched her face. It was cold. Hard. The metal was calcifying the soft tissue.

"Sara?" Her voice was a ghost. Her eyes fluttered open, but the whites were turning silver. She couldn't focus. "You... came back."

"I promised," I said, my voice breaking. "I brought the strawberries. Remember? The expensive ones."

I turned to the case.

My hands were shaking so bad I could barely grip the handle. I pulled the case onto my lap.

ACCESS DENIED. BIOMETRIC SCAN REQUIRED.
The red light blinked at me. Mocking me.

"Right," I muttered. "Biometrics."

I reached into my pocket. My fingers brushed the cold, wet flesh of the severed finger.

I pulled it out.

It was gruesome. The gold gauntlet was still attached to the knuckle, jagged bone sticking out the end. It was the stuff of nightmares. It was the price of admission.

I didn't vomit. I didn't have time to be squeamish.

I grabbed the dead Lieutenant's finger and pressed it against the scanner.

BEEP.

ACCESS GRANTED.

The latches hissed. The lid popped open.

Cold white mist poured out of the case.

Inside, nestled in shock-absorbent foam, was a single vial. It wasn't glass; it was diamond-reinforced polymer. The liquid inside was a swirling, luminescent blue. It looked like captured starlight. It looked like magic.

The Elixir.

I snatched it up. There was an auto-injector mechanism attached to the base.

"Elara," I said, turning back to her. "I need you to stay with me. This is going to hurt."

"Sara..." She coughed, a dry, metallic hack that brought up flecks of rust. "It's too late..."

"Shut up," I ordered, tears blurring my vision. "It's never too late."

I ripped the collar of her shirt down, exposing her neck. The metal was thick there, choking the jugular. I hunted for a patch of soft skin. A vein. Anything.

I found a small spot near her collarbone that was still pink.

"One wish," I whispered.

I pressed the injector against her skin. I hit the button.

HISS.
The blue liquid shot into her.

For a second, nothing happened.

Then, Elara screamed.

It wasn't a human scream. It was the sound of metal tearing.

Her body arched off the cot, her spine bowing violently. Her eyes rolled back in her head. The veins in her neck bulged, turning bright blue as the Elixir raced through her system.

"Elara!" I pinned her shoulders down, terrified I had killed her. "Breathe! Just breathe!"

She convulsed. Heat radiated off her—intense, feverish heat that burned my hands. Steam curled off her skin.

The silver metal on her chest began to hiss. It didn't disappear. It didn't melt away. But the color changed. The dull, corroded gray of the Rust shifted, darkening to a polished, inert gunmetal.

The rattling in her chest stopped.

She gasped—a huge, deep, desperate inhale of air.

Then she collapsed back onto the mattress, limp.

"El?"

I put my hand over her mouth. I waited.

Inhale. Exhale.
Warm air. Steady. Clear.

She was breathing. The grinding sound was gone.

I checked her pulse. It was strong. Fast, but strong.

I slumped back against the wall of the container, the empty auto-injector clattering to the floor. I pulled my knees to my chest, burying my face in my hands.

I sobbed.

It was ugly. It was violent. It was the crash after three days of running on pure terror and adrenaline.

She was alive. I had done it. I had beaten the King. I had beaten the Odds.

I stayed there for a long time, listening to my sister breathe, while the toxic wind howled outside.

"Sara?"

I looked up.

Elara was watching me. Her eyes were clear. The silver in the whites was gone, receding back to normal.

She looked at her arm. The metal was still there—a solid sleeve of dark iron covering her forearm. She tapped it against the bed frame. *Clink.*
"It's still there," she whispered.

"It's inert," I said, wiping my face with my sleeve. "The Elixir... Dorian said it stops the spread. It puts the metal to sleep. You won't rust out, El. You just... you have armor now."

She looked at me. She saw the bruises on my face. The soot in my hair. The blood on my collar that wasn't mine.

She saw the expensive tactical boots on my feet— Dorian's boots.

"Where did you get it?" she asked quietly. "The cure. Who gave it to you?"

"I stole it."

"From who?"

"From the King."

Elara sat up slowly. She looked at the empty case on the floor. She looked at the severed finger lying next to it. She didn't flinch. She was a Slag, too. She knew what survival looked like.

"And the Prince?" she asked. "The one on the flyer? The one you went to protect?"

I looked at the boots. I remembered the way he stood in the hallway. The way he looked at me.

Run, Rat.

A fresh wave of grief hit me, so sharp it felt like a physical stab wound.

"He stayed behind," I whispered.

"Why?"

"To hold the door."

I stood up. I walked to the dirty window of the container. I looked out toward the Upper City.

The Palace floated above the smog, a glittering jewel in the sky. It looked peaceful. Perfect.

But down here, I knew the truth.

Somewhere in the bowels of that golden tower, there was a hallway fused with metal. There was a statue made of a man who had saved my life.

"He's gone," I said.

I touched the glass.

"And I left him there."

Chapter 40: The Guilt

Sara

The silence in the container was different now.

Before, it was the silence of waiting for death. It was heavy, punctuated by the rattle of fluid in lungs and the grinding of rust.

Now, it was the silence of life.

Elara was sleeping. Deep, rhythmic, terrifyingly normal sleep. Her chest rose and fell without a hitch. The dark iron that now encased her left arm and part of her neck didn't move like skin, but it didn't encroach either. It was just there. Armor.

I sat on the floor, my back against the cold metal wall, hugging my knees.

I should have been celebrating. I should have been dancing on the table. I had done the impossible. I had broken into the heart of the Chrome empire, stolen the holy grail, and walked out alive. I had beaten the King.

So why did I feel like I was the one who had died?

I looked down at my feet.

I was still wearing his boots.

They were scuffed now, covered in sewer muck and scratches, but beneath the filth, the leather was still high-quality. The magnetic clamps in the soles—the ones that had saved us on the ice—were dormant.

They were too big for me. I had stuffed the toes with rags to make them fit.

Keep them, he had said.
I squeezed my eyes shut.

Instantly, I was back in the hallway. I saw the blue light of his core flare white. I saw the metal vines shooting out of his arm, eating the concrete. I saw the way he looked at me— not with fear, but with a terrifying, peaceful resolve.

He knew.

He knew he wasn't coming out. He knew the overload would fuse him to the building.

"Stupid," I whispered, hitting the back of my head against the wall. "Stupid, noble, battery-powered idiot."

I had left him.

I had crawled into a vent like a rat and left him to face six Golden Guards alone. I had traded his life for a vial of blue liquid.

It was the deal, my brain argued. *He makes the sacrifice. You save the girl.*
Screw the deal, my heart screamed.
"You're loud," a voice croaked.

I opened my eyes. Elara was watching me from the cot. She looked exhausted, pale, and metal-plated, but her eyes were sharp. She was my sister, after all. She saw everything.

"I didn't say anything," I said.

"You're thinking loudly. It's annoying." She pushed herself up to a sitting position, wincing as the new metal plating shifted against her collarbone. She tapped the iron skin with a fingernail. *Clink.* "So. I'm a cyborg."

"You're alive," I corrected. "The metal is inert. It won't spread."

"It's heavy," she noted. She looked at me. "And so is your conscience."

I looked away. "I'm fine, El."

"You're wearing a Prince's boots, Sara. You're covered in blast dust. And you haven't stopped staring at the door since you got here."

Elara swung her legs over the edge of the cot. She stood up. She was shaky, but she stood.

"Where is he?" she asked.

"I told you. He stayed behind."

"Is he dead?"

I flinched. "I... I don't know."

"Did you see him die?"

"I saw him turning," I whispered. "I saw the metal taking over. He overloaded his core to block the hallway. He turned himself into a wall, Elara."

"So he's a statue," she said. "Like the King."

"Yes."

"But is he *dead*?"

I stared at her. "What difference does it make? If he's fully integrated, he's gone. The metal eats the mind. He made me promise..."

My voice caught.

If I turn... use the dagger. Aim for the organic heart.
I touched the empty sheath on my thigh. I had lost the dagger in the airlock. I hadn't killed him. I hadn't saved him. I had just run away.

"He made you promise what?" Elara pressed.

"To kill him," I choked out. "If the Gilt took him. He didn't want to be a monster."

"And you didn't do it."

"I couldn't! I had to get the cure to you!"

"So he's trapped," Elara said. Her voice wasn't accusatory; it was just factual. Brutally factual. "He's trapped inside a metal shell, probably screaming, in the middle of a hallway filled with guards who want to scrap him."

I stood up. The guilt was a physical weight now, crushing my lungs.

"Stop it," I snapped. "I saved you. Isn't that enough?"

"Is it?" Elara looked at me. "You love him, don't you?"

"I don't love him," I shouted. "He's Chrome! He's the enemy! He's arrogant, and he talks too much, and he thinks he can save the world by blowing it up!"

"You love him," Elara repeated calmly. "I can see it. You look like you lost a limb."

I paced the small length of the container. Three steps. Turn. Three steps. Turn.

"It doesn't matter," I said. "He's gone. The Palace is on lockdown. The King has probably melted him down by now."

"Probably," Elara agreed. "But you don't know."

She walked over to the table where our meager food stash was kept. She picked up the severed finger I had used to open the case. She looked at it with disgust, then tossed it into the waste bin.

"You're the Rat," she said, turning back to me. "You don't leave things behind. You scavenge. You recover."

"He's not a spare part, El."

"No. He's the guy who gave you the Elixir. He's the guy who saved my life." She crossed her arms, the metal clinking against her ribs. "If I owe him my life, Sara, then *we* owe him a rescue."

"A rescue?" I laughed bitterly. "Elara, look at me. I have no weapons. I have no tools. I have a pair of stolen boots and a sister who is half-iron. How are we supposed to rescue a statue from the most secure building on the planet?"

"You said he has a plan," she said. "To destroy the Core. Tonight."

"He *had* a plan. He can't execute it if he's fused to a doorframe."

"Then who executes it?"

I stopped pacing.

I looked at her. I looked at the fierceness in her eyes. She wasn't the sick little girl coughing up blood anymore. She was a survivor.

"If the Core goes," I said slowly, "the power grid fails. The shields drop. The locks open."

"And if the locks open," Elara finished, "then the statue isn't trapped anymore."

My heart started to hammer.

It was suicide. It was madness. It was exactly the kind of plan Dorian would have come up with.

I checked the time on the wall clock.

14:00 Hours.

The Unification Ceremony—the Harvest—started at sundown. Six hours.

"I can't go back up there," I whispered. "They'll be waiting."

"They're waiting for a thief," Elara said. "They're waiting for someone trying to steal a box."

She walked over to me. She grabbed my hands. Her metal fingers were cold, but her human ones were warm.

"They aren't waiting for a revolution, Sara."

She was right.

The King thought he had won. He thought the thief was gone, the Prince was neutralized, and the city was ready for the slaughter. He was arrogant. Just like his son.

And arrogance creates blind spots.

I looked down at the boots again.

Run, Rat.
I had run. I had saved my sister.

But I wasn't done running.

"I need a weapon," I said, my voice hardening.

Elara smiled. It was a sharp, dangerous smile. A family trait.

"Jinx found a stash of mining charges in Sector 9," she said. "And I know where Old Man Rictus keeps his welding torch."

I grabbed my coat. It was torn, bloody, and smelled of smoke. I put it on. It felt like armor.

"Stay here," I ordered. "Lock the door."

"Where are you going?"

I opened the door of the container. The smog of the Scrapyard hit me—dirty, honest, and cold.

I looked back at her.

"I'm going to finish the job," I said. "And I'm going to get my damn spoon back."

Chapter 41: The Execution Decree

Dorian

Dying would have been quieter.

I woke up to the sound of a drill. It was a high-pitched, dental whine that vibrated inside my skull, rattling my teeth in their sockets.

I tried to move my right arm—my human arm—to swat the sound away.

I couldn't.

My arm was heavy. Immovable. And it was burning.

It felt like someone had stripped the skin off my forearm and dipped the raw muscle into boiling oil.

"Stabilize the graft," a voice buzzed. "The nerve endings are rejecting the interface."

"Force it," a deeper voice commanded.

I gasped, my eyes snapping open. The light was blinding gold.

I was on my knees. I was in the Throne Room.

I looked down.

My chest was bare, slick with sweat and blood. The left side was charred black from the overload in the hallway.

But the right side...

I stared at my shoulder. The flesh was gone. The clavicle had been exposed, drilled, and fitted with a golden anchor port. And extending from it, gleaming under the harsh lights, was a new arm.

It was chrome. Sleek. Perfect.

It mirrored my left arm exactly.

"No," I wheezed.

I tried to clench my fist. I expected the familiar delay of flesh and bone. Instead, I heard the instant, hydraulic *whir-click* of servos.

The metal fingers snapped shut with enough force to crush stone.

The pain hit me a second later—a jagged, white-hot spike traveling up the new wiring and slamming into my brain. It wasn't just pain; it was violation. My body was screaming that the limb didn't belong, that it was an invader.

"The integration is complete," King Aric said.

I looked up.

My father sat on the Golden Throne, towering over me. He looked younger. The tarnish I had seen on him days ago was gone, replaced by a lustrous sheen. He had fed on the energy I released in the hallway.

"You... you cut it off," I rasped. My voice sounded wrong—metallic, distorted. My vocal cords had been reinforced.

"It was damaged," Aric said, dismissing the loss of my humanity with a wave of his massive hand. "The flesh failed. It broke under the strain. The metal held."

He leaned forward, the red lenses of his eyes narrowing.

"You tried to destroy yourself, Dorian. You tried to become a wall. It was... inefficient. But instructive."

"I wanted to die," I spat. "I chose to die."

"Assets do not choose," Aric rumbled. "Assets function."

He signaled the guards. Two Golden Elites stepped forward. They didn't grab me; they grabbed the heavy chains attached to the floor.

They dragged me toward the pedestal at the foot of the throne.

"What are you doing?" I struggled, digging my new metal heels into the obsidian.

"The Unification is beginning," Aric said. "The city is waiting for the light."

They slammed me onto the pedestal. Magnetic clamps snapped around my wrists—both metal now—locking me in place.

"I won't do it," I snarled, pulling against the mag-locks until the new plating groaned. "I won't feed you. I'm empty. I gave you everything in the hall."

"You are not the source, my son," Aric said softly. "You are the straw."

A heavy, golden cable snaked up from the floor. It looked like an intestine made of brass.

A guard grabbed the back of my neck. He forced my head down.

I felt the port at the base of my spine open.

"Don't," I begged, panic flaring hot and bright. "Father, don't."

"Connect," Aric ordered.

The cable slammed into my spine.

There was no pain this time. There was only noise.

DATA UPLINK ESTABLISHED.

The world vanished.

I wasn't in the room. I was everywhere.

I was the grid.

I felt the city like a physical body. I felt the pulse of the streetlights in the Upper Districts. I felt the thrum of the ventilation fans in the sewers.

And then, I felt the *others*.

It started as a low hum in the back of my mind—a million tiny sparks of bio-electricity.

I felt them in the Slags. In the factories. In the tenements.

People.

But they didn't feel like people to the machine. They felt like capacitors.

I saw the map in my mind's eye. District 12. District 14. The Scrapyard.

Every person infected with the Rust lit up on the grid. The metal in their blood acted as a receiver. A tag.

"Do you see them?" Aric's voice boomed inside my skull, overriding my own thoughts. "Do you feel the potential?"

I gagged. The sensation was nauseating. I could feel their heartbeats. I could feel the warmth of their blood.

And I felt the *pull*.

The Throne wasn't generating power. It was a vacuum. And I was the nozzle.

"You're... you're harvesting them," I choked out, the realization hitting me harder than any physical blow.

I didn't just know it; I *felt* it. I felt the system preparing to reverse the flow. To suck the bio-lumens out of every infected man, woman, and child.

"They aren't citizens," I whispered, horror cold in my chest. "They're batteries. You infected them so you could plug them in."

"Efficiency," Aric murmured. "The Rust makes them conductive. It bridges the gap between flesh and current."

He engaged the first stage of the sequence.

Testing Connection.

I screamed.

It felt like fire rushing through me—but it wasn't my fire. It was theirs.

I felt a thousand people in District 12 gasp in unison as their energy was tapped. Just a sip. A taste.

I felt an old man in a workshop drop his wrench. I felt a child in a crib start to cry.

Their life force flowed through the grid, into the cable, into *me*, and then into the King.

I was the filter. I was the murder weapon.

"Stop it!" I roared, trashing against the chains. "Disconnect me! Let them go!"

"I cannot," Aric said. "The connection is vital. You regulate the flow. Without you, the surge would kill me. With you... I can drink them dry."

He sat back, satisfied. The golden light of his armor pulsed in time with the stolen heartbeats echoing in my head.

"The ceremony begins in one hour," Aric announced. "When the sun sets, we open the floodgates. You will feel them die, Dorian. You will feel every spark wink out. And you will know that it is your symmetry that makes it possible."

He gestured to the guards.

"Clean him up. Polish the new arm. The people need to see a hero."

The guards moved in with buffers and rags.

I stopped fighting. I couldn't fight. The data stream was overwhelming, pinning me down with the weight of a million lives.

I hung my head.

I looked at my new right hand. The chrome fingers were twitching, reacting to the screams of the city that only I could hear.

I closed my eyes, trying to find a quiet place in the static.

I thought of Sara.

I searched for her signature on the grid. I looked for the spark of the Rat.

I couldn't find her.

Either she was dead... or she had escaped the net.

Run, I thought, projecting the thought into the screaming void. *Run far. Run fast.*

Because when the sun went down, I wasn't just going to die.

I was going to kill everyone she had ever tried to save.

Chapter 42: The Rally

Sara

The sky above the Slags wasn't black. It was the color of a bruised peach, lit from above by the glow of the Upper City.

I stood on the roof of a derelict factory in District 14, watching the massive holographic screens that floated around the Palace spire like halos. Usually, they played propaganda—footage of grain shipments that never arrived or guards helping old ladies across the street.

Tonight, they were playing a funeral.

"Citizens of the Chrome," the King's voice boomed, rolling over the city like thunder. *"Tonight, we mourn. Tonight, we celebrate sacrifice."*

The image on the screen shifted. It showed the Throne Room.

My breath caught in my throat.

There he was.

Dorian was on his knees, chained to a pedestal at the foot of the Golden Throne. He was stripped to the waist. His skin was pale, bruised, and slick with oil.

But it was his arms that made me grab the railing of the roof until the rusted metal cut my palm.

They were both metal.

The human arm—the one that had held me in the carriage, the one with the warm fingers and the pulse—was gone. Replaced by a cold, symmetrical limb of polished chrome.

"He's alive," Elara whispered beside me. She was wearing a heavy coat over her new armor, her eyes fixed on the screen.

"Barely," I choked out.

"Prince Dorian," the King narrated, *"gravely injured in a cowardly rebel attack, has volunteered to undergo the final transition. Tonight, at the lighting of the Eternal Flame, he will give the last of his biological energy to the City Core. He dies so that the Shield may live."*

"Liar!" I screamed at the screen. My voice was lost in the wind, a tiny, useless sound against the roar of the city. "He didn't volunteer! You're murdering him!"

Below us, in the muddy streets of the Scrapyard, people were watching. Scavengers, factory workers, the sick, and the dying. They looked up with dull, tired eyes. To them, it was just another show. Another royal dying in a golden tower while they starved in the mud.

"They don't care," Jinx said, stepping out of the shadows. He looked better—I'd given him a dose of the suppressants from the stash Dorian left. "Why should they? He's Chrome. One less oppressor."

I turned on him. "He's not an oppressor, Jinx. He's the only reason you're not being liquidated right now."

I looked at the crowd gathering in the market square below. They were resigned. They were waiting for the show to end so they could go back to surviving.

"We have to tell them," I said.

"Tell them what?" Elara asked. "That the Prince is nice?"

"No," I said, checking the load on the kinetic pistol I'd stolen from the detention guard. "That the Prince is the warning shot."

I didn't take the stairs. I jumped.

I slid down a drainpipe, landing in the mud of the square with a heavy splash. The crowd rippled, startled.

I climbed onto a stack of shipping crates in the center of the market. I stood tall. I was wearing the black tactical pants and the heavy boots. I still had the soot on my face.

"Listen to me!" I shouted.

A few heads turned. Most ignored me. Just another crazy Slag shouting at the sky.

"Turn it off!" I yelled, pointing at the public address speaker on the pole above me.

Jinx, who had followed me down, grinned. He picked up a rock and hurled it with surprising accuracy. *Crack.* The speaker sparked and died, cutting off the King's droning voice in our immediate vicinity.
The silence drew their attention.

"My name is Sara!" I bellowed. "I am from Sector 14! I am the one who stole the Elixir!"

That got them. A murmur went through the crowd. They had heard the rumors. The Rat who broke into the Palace.

"You see that man?" I pointed to the silent, flickering image of Dorian on the distant screen. "The King says he's a hero. The King says he's making a sacrifice."

I scanned the faces. Dirty. Hungry. Angry.

"The King is lying!"

I paced the crate, my voice rising, fueled by the rage I'd been bottling up for three days.

"Dorian didn't volunteer. He was harvested. And do you know why? Because the King is hungry."

I pulled up my sleeve. I didn't have the Rust, but I pointed to a man in the front row who did. His neck was silvered with it.

"You!" I shouted. "How long have you had the cough?"

"Two years," the man grunted.

"And you?" I pointed to a woman holding a child. "How long has your boy been turning silver?"

"Since the winter," she whispered.

"It's not a disease," I told them, letting the horror of the truth sink in. "It's a tag. The King didn't fail to cure us. He infected us. The Rust makes us conductive. It turns us into batteries."

The crowd shifted. The resignation was cracking, replaced by fear.

"Look at the Prince!" I screamed, gesturing back to the screen. "He is fully integrated now. He is plugged into the Throne. When the sun sets... when that flame is lit... the King is going to pull the switch. He's going to drain Dorian dry. And then? He's going to drain *us*."

"Bullshit!" a voice shouted from the back. A mine foreman. "The King protects the city!"

"The King *eats* the city!" I roared back. "He eats the gold! He eats the power! And tonight, he's going to eat the Slags to make himself a God!"

I jumped down from the crate. I walked into the crowd. They parted for me. They saw the boots. They saw the eyes.

"Dorian fought for us," I said, my voice dropping to a fierce growl. "He gave me the cure for my sister. He fought the Golden Guard alone so I could get it out. He lost his arm—his *human* arm—saving a Slag."

I stopped in front of the foreman.

"He bled for me," I said. "He bled for you. And right now, he is sitting in that chair, waiting to die, because he tried to stop the Harvest."

I looked around.

"We are not livestock!" I shouted. "We are the rust that eats the iron! We are the dirt in the gears!"

I pulled the stolen kinetic pistol and fired a shot into the air.

CRACK.

"The ceremony starts in two hours," I yelled. "The Palace guards are all on the perimeter, watching the parade. The sub-levels are exposed. The sewers are open."

I looked at Jinx. I looked at Elara, who was standing on the edge of the crowd, her metal arm gleaming.

"I am going back up there," I said. "I am going to break down the doors. I am going to smash the Core. And I am going to get our Prince back."

I paused.

"Who's with me?"

Silence.

For a long, agonizing second, nobody moved. They were afraid. They had been beaten down for so long they had forgotten how to stand.

Then, a metal clang rang out.

The man with the rusted neck stepped forward. He was holding a heavy pipe wrench. He smashed it against his palm.

"For the Prince," he growled.

Then the woman with the child. She handed the baby to a neighbor. She picked up a piece of rebar.

"For the cure," she said.

Then Jinx. Then the foreman.

The sound grew. Weapons were drawn—makeshift, rusted, ugly weapons. Hammers. Chains. Shivs. Old mining lasers.

A roar started low in the crowd and built until it shook the windows of the factory. It wasn't a cheer. It was a war cry.

I climbed back onto the crate.

I looked out at the sea of angry, desperate faces. My army. The Army of the Rust.

I looked up at the screen, at Dorian's pained, stoic face.

Hold on, Chrome, I thought. *I'm bringing the fire.*

"To the sewers!" I commanded, pointing toward the drainage tunnels. "Tonight, we don't just survive! Tonight, we rust the Crown!"

The mob surged forward.

I jumped down and joined the wave. I wasn't leading from the back. I was the tip of the spear.

And I was aiming for the King's heart.

ACT IV: HEAVY METAL

Chapter 43: Siege

Dorian

The city was screaming.

I didn't hear it with my ears. I heard it with my blood.

The connection to the Throne was fully active now. The golden cable at the base of my spine was a highway of data and energy, bypassing my nervous system and dumping the sensory input of three million people directly into my brain.

I felt the pulse of the generators in the industrial district. I felt the hum of the neon signs in the Red Light sector. I felt the cold, terrified heartbeat of the crowd gathered in the plaza below.

And then, the King flipped the switch.

It started as a tickle at the base of my skull. Then it became a pull. Then a tear.

INITIATE HARVEST.

My back arched off the pedestal, the chains rattling violently. The new metal arm—the right one—clenched, digging furrows into the obsidian.

It felt like being flayed from the inside out. The Throne was drinking me. It was pulling the bio-electricity from my cells, the heat from my core, the very will to exist from my soul.

"Beautiful," King Aric murmured.

He loomed above me, bathed in the golden light of the transfer. The red lenses of his eyes were bright, hungry. He looked younger already. The tarnish on his gold plating was receding, replaced by a lustrous, oily sheen.

"Do you feel it, my son?" his voice boomed in my head. "The unity? The purpose?"

"I feel..." I gritted out, blood leaking from my nose, "...a parasite."

The drain intensified. My vision grayed. The HUD in my mechanical eye flickered with critical warnings.

System Failure Imminent.

Biological Integrity: 15%.

Estimated Time to Termination: 12 Minutes.

I looked at the countdown. Twelve minutes.

In twelve minutes, I would be a husk. A hollow metal shell. And once I was empty, the King would widen the aperture. He would reach past me, through the grid, into the city. He would start draining the Rust-infected citizens.

Elara. The workers. The children.

I tried to fight it. I tried to push back against the current. But I was just a conduit. A wire cannot fight the electricity flowing through it.

"Give in," Aric commanded. "Let go."

I closed my eyes. The darkness beckoned. It was soft. It was quiet.

Then, I felt a tremor.

It wasn't part of the drain. It didn't come from the Throne. It came from the floor.

A vibration. Low. Rhythmic.

Thump. Thump. Thump.
It felt like a heartbeat. A massive, angry, subterranean heartbeat.

The King frowned. The golden cables shifted uneasily.

"What is that?"

I opened my eyes. I focused on the grid map overlaying my vision.

Down in the sub-levels. In the waste processing sectors. In the foundations.

Sensors were winking out. Not fading—*vanishing*.
Security cameras were going dark. Pressure plates were triggering en masse.

I smiled. My metal lips cracked, but I smiled.

"That," I rasped, lifting my head to look at the monster on the throne, "is the plumbing backing up."

Sara
"Fire in the hole!"

I didn't wait for cover. I kicked the door.

The mining charge taped to the service hatch detonated with a dull *WHUMP*. The reinforced steel buckled, glowing orange, then blasted inward.

I surged through the smoke before the shrapnel settled.

"Go! Go! Go!"

I wasn't alone. Behind me, pouring out of the sewer tunnels like black water, was the Army of the Rust.

They were filthy. They were angry. And they were loud.

We spilled into the pristine white hallway of the Lower Palace. The contrast was violent. Muddy boots on marble floors. Rusted pipes smashing against gilded statues. The smell of sewage warring with the smell of lavender.

"Secure the stairwell!" I shouted, pointing with my kinetic pistol.

Jinx sprinted forward, swinging a heavy length of chain. A Palace guard—shiny, polished, terrified—stepped out of a patrol alcove. He raised his rifle.

He never got a shot off.

Jinx whipped the chain around the guard's ankles and yanked. The guard went down hard. Before he could scramble up, three factory workers were on him. They didn't have training. They had hammers.

It was brutal. It was messy. It was war.

"Up!" I commanded, stepping over the fallen guard. "We have to get to the Throne Room!"

We hit the main concourse. This was where the resistance met reality.

A squad of Chrome Infantry—heavy troopers in exo-suits—was blocking the grand staircase. They had riot shields and stun cannons.

"Halt!" the squad leader amplified. "Disperse immediately or be neutralized!"

The Slags hesitated. They looked at the massive, gleaming machines. They looked at their own rusted shivs.

Fear rippled through the line.

"They're big!" someone shouted.

"So what?" I roared, jumping onto a marble bench. "They're just cans! Open them up!"

I raised my stolen pistol. I didn't aim for the armor. I aimed for the ceiling.

Specifically, the massive crystal chandelier hanging directly above the squad.

Crack.
The bullet shattered the chain.

Gravity did the rest.

Two tons of crystal and gold plummeted.

The crash shook the entire wing. Glass exploded like shrapnel. The heavy squad was buried under a mountain of expensive glitter.

"Charge!" Elara screamed.

She led the rush. My little sister, the one I used to swaddle in blankets, sprinted toward the wreckage. Her metal arm caught the light. She vaulted over a stunned trooper, punched him in the faceplate with her iron fist, and kept running.

The mob followed her. They swarmed the remaining troopers, overwhelming them with sheer numbers. They jammed pipes into joints. They poured grease on visors. They fought like rats in a corner.

I jumped down from the bench and joined the fray.

I moved like water. I dodged a baton swing, slid under a shield, and drove my knife into the unarmored armpit of a trooper. He screamed. I kicked him away and kept moving.

"Sara!"

I turned. Voss was standing on the landing above us. He was holding a massive rotary cannon he must have ripped off a turret. He looked glorious.

"The elevators are locked down!" Voss shouted over the chaos. "The King has sealed the upper spire!"

"Then we climb!" I yelled back.

"Climb what?"

I pointed to the center of the concourse. The ventilation shaft. The main air intake for the Throne Room. It was a vertical tube, fifty feet wide, running straight up the spine of the building.

"The lungs," I said. "If we can't take the stairs, we crawl up his throat."

"That shaft is guarded by fans," Voss warned. "Industrial blades. They'll mince you."

"Not if we cut the power," I said.

I tapped the comms bead in my ear—Dorian's gear.

"Rook? Are you there?"

Static crackled. Then, a grunt. *"I'm here, boss. I'm at the substation."*
"Blow it," I ordered. "Blow it all."

"With pleasure."
A second later, the lights died.

The entire Palace groaned. The magelights flickered and went out. The hum of the air conditioning stopped.

The massive fans in the central shaft spun down, screeching into silence.

"Emergency lighting only," I shouted to my army. "Let's go!"

I ran to the maintenance hatch of the shaft. I pried it open with my knife.

Inside, it was dark, smelling of cold air and impending violence. The blades of the fan above were still, massive steel scythes waiting for us.

I holstered my gun. I grabbed the ladder rungs.

"Don't look down," I whispered to myself.

I started to climb.

Below me, hundreds of people followed. Above me, the Golden King was waiting.

And somewhere in the dark, Dorian was dying.

Hang on, Chrome, I thought, driving my boots into the rungs. *I'm coming to unplug you.*

Chapter 44: The Throne Room

Dorian

I was dissolving.

It wasn't painful anymore. Pain requires nerves, and my nerves were currently being repurposed as fiber-optic cables for my father's ego.

I was cold. Absolute zero. The kind of cold that stops atoms from vibrating.

Battery Level: 8%.

Core Temp: Critical Low.

System Status: Fading.

I stared at the floor. The polished obsidian reflected my face. It looked wrong. The human side—the left side of my face—was gray, sunken, the skin pulled tight over the bone. The new chrome right side was gleaming, unaffected by the biological collapse.

I was becoming the statue I had feared. Not by magic, but by simple subtraction. The King was subtracting the man and leaving the metal.

"More," King Aric demanded.

The demand vibrated through the cable in my spine. It wasn't a voice; it was a command code rewriting my autonomic functions. *Stop heart. Conserve energy. Divert to Throne.*

My mechanical heart stuttered. *Thump... pause... thump.*

"I'm empty," I whispered. My voice was a static hiss.

"You are holding back," Aric boomed. "There is a reserve in the limbic system. The emotional core. Release it."

"Go to hell."

Aric twitched a finger.

The drain spiked.

I screamed. It felt like he had reached into my chest and ripped the memories out of my brain. I saw my mother's face—*flash*—gone. I saw the first time I held a sword—*flash*—gone.
I saw Sara in the bathhouse. The steam. The curve of her neck.

No.
I clamped down on that memory. I built a firewall around it. I wrapped it in every encryption algorithm I knew.

You don't get her, I snarled silently. *She's not for you.*
The Throne Room shuddered.

At first, I thought it was my own body failing. Then the lights died.

The massive chandeliers went black. The magelights on the walls winked out. The hum of the air filtration system died, leaving a sudden, ringing silence.

For a second, there was only darkness.

Then, the emergency lights kicked in—dull, pulsing amber strips along the floor. And the King.

Aric glowed in the dark. The gold of his body was luminescent, powered by *my* life. His red eyes were twin lasers cutting through the gloom.

"What is this?" Aric roared. The sound shook the dais. "The grid! I have lost the grid!"

I laughed. It sounded like grinding gears.

"Blackout," I wheezed, my head hanging low. "Looks like someone... didn't pay the bill."

Aric swiveled his massive head toward the tactical displays floating near the throne. They were all red.

SECTOR 12: OFFLINE.

SECTOR 14: OFFLINE.

MAIN CONDUIT: SEVERED.

"The substation," Aric realized. "They destroyed the substation."

He turned back to me. The hunger in his red eyes flared. It wasn't just greed anymore. It was panic.

Without the city grid, he couldn't harvest the population. He couldn't drain the Slags. He was cut off from his food supply.

Except for one source.

Me.

"You knew," Aric accused. "You planned this."

"I told you," I rasped, lifting my heavy chrome head to look him in the eye. "I'm not a battery. I'm a bomb."

"If the city cannot sustain me," Aric thundered, his voice dropping to a terrifying sub-bass rumble, "then I will consume the source directly."

He didn't just widen the aperture. He tore the floodgates off.

The cable in my spine heated up to white-hot.

He wasn't sipping anymore. He was gulping. He was draining me to power his own life support, his personal shields, and the weapons of the remaining Guard.

My vision tunneled.

Battery Level: 4%.
I couldn't feel my legs. I couldn't feel the cold floor. I was just a point of consciousness floating in a sea of static.

Hold on, I told myself. *Just a little longer.*
I had to buy them time. If he was eating me, he wasn't looking at the doors.

Then I heard it.

It was a faint sound, muffled by the thick walls, but audible in the silence of the blackout.

Clang. Clang. Clang.
It was coming from above. From the central ventilation shaft.

Aric heard it too. His head snapped up.

"The vents," he hissed. "Rats in the walls."

He raised his hand. The Golden Guards lining the room—statues of obedience—stepped forward, their plasma rifles humming to life.

"Seal the vents!" Aric ordered. "Purge the shaft with nerve gas!"

"No," I groaned.

I tried to move. I tried to break the connection.

If they gassed the shaft, Sara died. She was climbing up the throat of the beast, and he was about to choke her.

I needed to stop him. I needed to distract him.

I needed to overload the system.

I couldn't give him power. But I could give him *noise*.
I accessed the link. I didn't pull away; I pushed. I pushed every ounce of chaotic, messy, unencrypted data I had left into the stream.

I pushed the memory of the Sinkhole. The bass thumping. The smell of sweat. The taste of cheap whiskey.

I pushed the feeling of the cold wind in the Wastelands.

I pushed the rage. The grief. The sheer, unadulterated hatred I felt for the gold.

Aric flinched.

"What are you doing?" he buzzed, clutching his head. "The data... it is corrupted! It is impure!"

"It's human!" I screamed, pouring it into him. "Choke on it!"

The King convulsed on the throne. The connection destabilized. The red lights in his eyes flickered.

"Guards!" Aric shrieked. "Kill them! Kill them all!"

The Golden Guards turned their weapons toward the high vents.

They began to fire.

Plasma bolts struck the heavy grate covering the main intake high on the wall. The metal sizzled and melted.

Sara, I thought, my mind fracturing. *Hurry.*
I was empty. I was done.

Battery Level: 1%.

System Shutdown: 10... 9...

I looked at the vent one last time.

And then, the grate exploded.

Chapter 45: The Reunion

Sara

The vent grate was secured by four heavy bolts.

"Blow it," I shouted to Rook, who was clinging to the ladder beside me.

"It's too close!" Rook yelled over the roar of the fans below. "The shrapnel will shred us!"

"We're wearing armor!" I lied. I was wearing a coat and a stolen shirt. "Do it!"

Rook slapped a shaped charge on the grate. He primed it. We dropped down the ladder a few rungs, huddled under our coats.

BOOM.

The explosion was deafening in the confined shaft. The heavy steel grate blasted outward into the Throne Room.

Smoke poured out.

I didn't wait for the dust to settle. I didn't wait for a rope.

I jumped.

It was a twenty-foot drop. I hit the obsidian floor in a roll, momentum carrying me forward. I came up in a crouch, the kinetic pistol in one hand, my obsidian dagger in the other.

I took a split second to assess the battlefield.

The Throne Room was dim, lit only by the terrifying golden glow of the King. He sat on his massive chair like a bloated spider.

And at his feet...

Dorian.

He was on his knees, chained to a pedestal. He looked wrecked. His head was hanging low, his body limp.

And his arms...

Both of them were metal.

The sight of that symmetry—the cold, hard chrome where his warm hand used to be—ignited a rage in me that felt like swallowing a live grenade. It wasn't a tactical assessment. It was pure, blinding fury.

"GET AWAY FROM HIM!" I screamed.

The voice didn't sound like mine. It sounded like something tearing.

The room froze. The Golden Guards turned. The King looked down.

I must have looked like a nightmare. I was covered in sewer muck, grease, and blood. My hair was matted. My eyes were wild behind the war paint Jinx had smeared on my face.

I wasn't a bodyguard anymore. I was the reckoning.

A man in purple robes—the Royal Technomancer—was standing at a console near the pedestal, adjusting the flow of the drain. He looked at me, startled, his hand hovering over a lever.

He was hurting him. He was draining him.

I didn't have a quip. I didn't have a clever line. I had a bullet.

I raised the pistol.

I pulled the trigger.

BANG.

The shot took him in the throat. He crumpled over the console, his blood spraying across the golden controls. Sparks flew as his body shorted out the regulation panel.

The drain faltered. The humming cable connected to Dorian's spine spasmed.

"Intruders!" the King roared, his voice shaking the walls. "Kill the filth!"

The Golden Guards raised their rifles.

But they were too late.

Behind me, the vent rained bodies.

"For the Slags!" Elara screamed, dropping onto the floor. Her metal arm hit the obsidian with a heavy *clang*.

She was followed by Jinx, Voss, and a hundred angry factory workers wielding pipes, wrenches, and mining lasers.

It wasn't a battle; it was a riot.

The Slags surged forward like a tidal wave of rust. They didn't fight with honor; they swarmed. Three workers tackled a Golden Guard, beating his helmet with hammers until the optics shattered. Jinx used his chain to trip another, dragging him into the mob.

I ignored the chaos. I had one target.

I sprinted toward the dais.

A Guard stepped in my path, swinging a shock-baton.

I didn't stop. I didn't slow down. I slid on the slick floor, going under his swing. As I passed, I hamstrung him with the obsidian dagger. He fell. I put a bullet in his power pack as I rose.

I vaulted onto the platform.

I was face-to-face with the King.

Up close, he was hideous. A patchwork of gold plating and rotting biological matter, held together by tubes and greed.

"You," Aric hissed, his red eyes fixating on me. "The Rat."

"Die," I snarled.

I didn't attack him. He was too big, too armored.

I attacked the connection.

I grabbed the thick golden cable plugged into Dorian's spine. It was hot—scalding hot. It burned my palm through my glove.

"Let him go," I grunted, pulling with everything I had.

"You cannot break the link," Aric boomed, raising a massive golden hand to swat me like a fly. "He is mine!"

"He's nobody's!"

I raised the obsidian dagger. It was volcanic glass, sharp enough to cut at the molecular level.

I drove it into the cable.

ZZZZAAPP.

A backlash of magical energy exploded outward. It threw me backward. I hit the floor hard, sliding to the edge of the dais.

But the cable was severed.

Sparks showered the platform. The golden light feeding the King flickered and dimmed.

"NO!" Aric roared, the sound tearing at the air. "MY POWER!"

I scrambled back up.

Dorian slumped forward, no longer held up by the tension of the current. The magnetic clamps on his wrists were still locked, but the life-draining connection was dead.

I reached him. I grabbed his face—his cold, metal face—with my hands.

"Dorian!" I shouted over the noise of the battle. "Dorian, wake up!"

His head lolled. His eyes were closed. His chest—the human part—was barely moving.

"Come on," I pleaded, my voice cracking. "Come on, don't you do this. Don't you dare check out on me. Not after I crawled through a sewer for you."

I slapped his cheek. Hard.

"Wake up!"

His eyelids fluttered.

The mechanical eye whirred, the aperture spiraling open to reveal a faint, flickering blue light. The human eye opened slowly. It was glazed, unfocused.

He looked at me.

He blinked. Once. Twice.

"You..." he rasped. His voice was a metallic wreck.

The air rushed back into my lungs. He was there. He was in there.

"Me," I said, choking back a sob. I tried to wipe the blood from his lip, my thumb trembling. "I told you I was coming back for the boots."

He looked down at my feet. Then back up at my face.

A slow, crooked smile spread across his lips. It was weak, but it was him. The fear in my chest finally broke, leaving room for the old, sharp banter to slide back in.

"You look..." he wheezed, "terrible."

"You look shiny," I countered, wiping a smudge of soot from his forehead. "Too shiny. We need to scuff you up."

"Behind you!"

Dorian's eyes widened.

I spun around.

The King had stood up. He had disconnected himself from the Throne. He was twenty feet tall, a towering golem of rage and gold.

He raised a fist the size of an anvil.

"I WILL CRUSH YOU!"

"We have to move," I said, looking at the magnetic clamps holding Dorian down. "How do I open these?"

"You can't," Dorian groaned. "They're hard-wired to the... wait."

He looked at his new arm. The right one. The one the King had given him.

"Symmetry," he whispered.

He raised his right hand. He placed it against the locking mechanism of the left cuff.

Click.

The cuff sprang open. He did the same for the right.

"He gave me his own codes," Dorian murmured, shaking the chains off. "Arrogant bastard."

He stood up.

He swayed, weak and drained, but he stood. He towered over me, half-naked, double-armed with chrome, glowing with faint blue light.

"Can you fight?" I asked, handing him the kinetic pistol.

Dorian looked at the gun. He looked at his metal hands.

"No," he said. "I can't fight."

He looked at the King, who was descending the steps of the throne, shaking the floor with every step.

"I can destroy."

Dorian grabbed my waist with his new arm. It was cold, hard, and terrifyingly strong.

"Hold on," he said.

"To what?"

"To me."

He didn't run at the King. He turned and ran toward the heavy blast door behind the throne—the King's personal panic room.

"Dorian, the exit is that way!" I pointed to the vents.

"We're not leaving!" he shouted. "We're ending it!"

He slammed his shoulder into the safe room door. It buckled. He hit it again. It flew open.

He threw me inside. He followed, slamming the door shut and locking it just as the King's massive fist smashed into the metal from the other side.

BOOM.

The door dented inward, but held.

We were in the dark. Alone. Breathing hard.

"Safe room?" I asked, panting. "You trapped us in a box!"

"It's not just a safe room," Dorian said, leaning against the wall, his chest heaving. "It's the armory."

He waved his hand. Magelights flickered on.

The walls were lined with weapons. Ancient weapons. Experimental weapons. And in the center of the room, humming with a dangerous, unstable energy, was a massive turbine.

"What is that?" I asked.

"That," Dorian said, sliding down the wall to sit on the floor, "is the primary coolant pump for the Throne. And we're going to blow it up."

He looked at me. He looked tired, broken, and absolutely beautiful.

"But first," he whispered, reaching out with his new chrome hand. "Check my valves. I think I'm leaking."

I fell to my knees beside him. I didn't check his valves. I kissed him.

It tasted like blood, oil, and victory.

Chapter 46: The Release

Sara

The door buckled.

BOOM.

King Aric was hitting the blast steel from the other side with the force of a pile driver. The heavy metal groaned, a dent blossoming inward like a reversed flower. Dust rained down from the ceiling, coating us in gray powder.

I didn't care.

I was kissing Dorian like he was the last pocket of oxygen in a vacuum.

It wasn't a romantic kiss. It was a collision. It was teeth and tongue and desperation. I tasted the blood in his mouth, the ozone on his skin, the sheer, terrifying voltage of the energy still crackling through him.

He gripped my hair with his left hand—the old metal one. He gripped my waist with his right—the new one.

It was cold. So cold it burned through my shirt.

"You're alive," I mumbled against his mouth, biting his lower lip hard enough to split it. "You stupid, shiny bastard, you're alive."

"Shut up," he growled.

He picked me up.

He didn't struggle. He didn't brace himself. With two metal arms powered by the dying embers of the city grid, he lifted me like I weighed nothing at all.

My legs wrapped around his waist instinctively. I felt the hard ridges of his abdominal plating against my stomach. I felt the heat of his remaining biological core radiating through his skin.

He slammed me against the wall.

A rack of ceremonial spears rattled violently, one tipping over and clattering to the floor. We ignored it.

Dorian buried his face in my neck. He inhaled—a harsh, ragged sound. He was shaking. The mighty Prince of Chrome, the statue who held the door, was trembling against me.

"I thought you were gone," he rasped against my pulse point. "I saw the vent... I thought..."

"I came back," I said, grabbing his face with both hands and pulling him back to look at me. "I told you. We finish it."

He looked at me. His eyes were wide, the pupils blown so black they swallowed the irises. The mismatched colors— the dark and the fractured blue—were wild.

"We're going to die in here, Sara," he said.

BOOM.
The door hinge shrieked. A bolt popped loose and pinged around the room like a bullet.

"Probably," I said. "So stop talking."

I reached for his belt.

I fumbled with the buckle. My hands were slick with sweat and oil.

Dorian didn't wait. He grabbed the front of my stolen shirt—the tactical gear I'd looted from the armory.

He ripped it.

The sound of tearing fabric was loud in the small room. Buttons scattered across the floor.

He stared at my chest, heaving in the cool air of the safe room. He looked at the scars, the grime, the war paint smeared on my neck.

"Mine," he whispered. It wasn't a question. It was a designation.

He kissed me again, and this time, he didn't hold back. He pushed his tongue into my mouth, tasting me, owning me.

I clawed at his shoulders. I tried to dig my nails in, but there was no skin left there. Just smooth, polished alloy.

It didn't repel me. It maddened me.

I wanted to find the man underneath the machine.

I shoved his pants down. He kicked them away, not breaking the kiss.

We were a mess of limbs and metal against the weapon rack. The world outside was ending—my army was fighting in the hall, his father was trying to smash the door down—but in here, the only war was friction.

Dorian

I was terrified.

Not of the King. Not of death.

I was terrified of my own hands.

The new arm—the right one—felt strange. It was too strong. Too responsive. I didn't have the muscle memory for it yet. Every time I touched Sara, the pressure sensors spiked.

Warning: Fragile Object. Handle with Caution.

She wasn't fragile. She was tempered steel wrapped in soft skin. But compared to me? She was breakable.

I tried to pull back, to give myself space to calibrate.

"Sara, wait," I gasped, my forehead resting against hers. "The arm... I can't feel the pressure. I might—"

She grabbed my right hand. The chrome one.

She didn't pull it away. She dragged it down.

She pressed my cold, metal palm against her bare breast.

The sensation hit my neural interface like a lightning strike. Even without biological nerves, the sensory data was overwhelming. The softness. The heat. The frantic hammering of her heart beneath the skin.

"You won't hurt me," she said fiercely, staring into my eyes. "You don't know how."

"I am a weapon," I choked out.

"You're *my* weapon."
She ground her hips against mine.

That snapped the last tether of control.

The biological imperative took over. The fear vanished, incinerated by a hunger so old and deep it predated the Chrome, the Gilt, and the Crown.

I gripped her. I let the metal dig into her skin just enough to anchor her.

She didn't flinch. She gasped, arching into the touch.

"Check my valves, Chrome," she taunted, breathless and wild.

I growled—a sound that was half-animal, half-engine.

I lifted her higher. She braced her hands on my shoulders, her nails skittering over the metal plating.

I didn't position her gently. I was desperate. I needed to be inside her. I needed to plug the void where the King had drained me. I needed to feel life.

I lined us up.

She was wet. Slick with desire and adrenaline.

I thrust up.

She cried out—a sharp, high sound that echoed off the steel walls. Her head fell back, hitting the weapon rack.

I froze, panic spiking. "Sara?"

"Don't stop," she hissed, grabbing my ears and dragging my head back down. She bit my jaw. "Don't you dare stop."

I didn't.

I drove into her. Hard. Fast. Deep.

It was clumsy. It was angry. It was the sex of two people who had spent days dancing around death and denied desire.

We moved together in a frantic rhythm. The metal of my hips slammed against the flesh of hers. The noise was guttural—pants, groans, the wet slap of skin, the creak of her leather boots against my metal thighs.

BOOM.
The door buckled again. A sliver of light from the Throne Room cut through the crack.

"He's getting in," I grunted, thrusting harder.

"Let him watch," Sara moaned, wrapping her legs tighter around me. "Let him see what real power looks like."

She was right. This was power. This was life. This was the one thing the gold couldn't replicate.

I buried my face in her chest. I licked the sweat from her skin. I worshipped the pulse in her neck.

I was a machine. I was a statue. But right now, inside her, I was burning.

And I wasn't going to let the fire go out.

Chapter 47: Worship

Dorian

I couldn't get close enough.

Physics was the enemy. There were atoms between us, microscopic distances that felt like canyons. I wanted to bridge them all. I wanted to dismantle her and rebuild her inside my own chest, right next to the mechanical heart that was stuttering a chaotic, broken rhythm.

She was gasping against my neck, her legs wrapped around my waist, her heels digging into the plating of my back.

BOOM.

The door hinge groaned, a shriek of tearing metal. Aric was getting closer.

I didn't care. Let him break the door. Let him see. Let him witness the one thing his gold couldn't buy.

I broke the kiss, my breath coming in harsh, static-laced rasps.

"The turbine," I growled.

I carried her three steps to the massive cooling unit in the center of the room. The housing was vibrating, a low-frequency thrum of machinery that shook the floorboards.

I set her down on the edge of the metal casing.

She didn't let go of me. Her hands were tangled in my hair, her eyes wild and unfocused. She was a mess of smeared war paint and sweat.

"Dorian?" she breathed.

"Quiet," I ordered. "You wanted a mechanic? You got one."

I dropped to my knees between her legs.

The floor was cold steel, biting into my knees, but I didn't feel it. My sensors were entirely focused on the heat radiating from her.

I looked up at her.

She was spread open before me, vulnerable and defiant. My new hands—the twin chrome monstrosities—rested on her thighs. The contrast was violent. Her skin was pale, soft, bruised from the fight. My hands were mirror-polished alloy, hard enough to crush diamond.

I was terrified I would hurt her.

I let my thumbs trace the sensitive skin of her inner thighs. The metal was cold.

She hissed, her hips bucking reflexively. She didn't pull away. She pushed into the cold. She wanted the shock.

"Open," I whispered.

I used the metal fingers to spread her. Gently. The servos whined—a microscopic adjustment of torque to ensure I didn't bruise the delicate tissue.

The scent hit me. Musk. Salt. The primal, iron tang of arousal. It bypassed my logic centers and went straight to the primitive hindbrain that the King hadn't managed to excise.

It was the smell of life.

Aric wanted to drain it. He wanted to siphon it off into a battery to live forever.

I didn't want to drain it. I wanted to drown in it.

I leaned forward.

I didn't start with my tongue. I started with my breath. I exhaled, the hot air from my internal vents ghosting over her wet, swollen flesh.

Sara's head fell back. Her hands gripped the edge of the turbine housing.

"Chrome..." she warned, her voice tight.

I licked her.

One long, slow stroke from bottom to top.

She tasted like victory. She tasted like everything I had been denied in my cold, sterile tower.

She screamed—a broken, strangled sound that was lost under the booming of the door. Her thighs clamped down on my head, trapping me there.

I didn't fight it. I held her hips with my metal hands, anchoring her to the vibrating machine, and I went to work.

I treated her like a lock I was picking. I found the rhythm. I found the tension point.

My tongue swirled around the sensitive node, teasing, flicking. I listened to her breathing pattern, adjusting my speed to match her gasps.

Faster. Her hips stuttered.

Harder. Her fingers dug into my scalp.

I hummed. It wasn't a vocal sound. It was the deep, resonant vibration of my chest cavity, the purr of the reactor core running at critical mass. The vibration traveled through my jaw, through my lips, and directly into her.

Sara sobbed. "Dorian, please. I can't—it's too much."

"Take it," I thought, the words unspoken against her skin. "Take everything I have."

I wasn't just pleasuring her. I was memorizing her.

I mapped the texture of her skin against my cheek. I cataloged the way her muscles spasmed. I recorded the taste of her on my tongue, encrypting the file, burying it deep in the sectors of my mind where my father couldn't reach.

If I died in the next ten minutes... if the King broke through that door and smelted me down... this would be the last thing I knew.

Not the pain. Not the betrayal.

This. Her.

She was getting close. I could feel the tension coiling in her muscles. Her breathing stopped being rhythmic and became a series of sharp, panicked inhales.

"Check the valves," I murmured against her, mocking her own taunt.

I sucked the pearl of her clitoris into my mouth. I used the flat of my tongue, vibrating it, while my metal thumbs pressed into the soft flesh of her thighs, grounding her.

She shattered.

It was explosive. Her body arched off the turbine, her back bowing. She cried out my name—a raw, guttural scream that tore at her throat.

I felt the spasms ripple through her. I drank them in. I didn't stop. I kept licking, kept humming, riding the wave of her release until she collapsed back onto the metal casing, boneless and trembling.

I pulled back, breathless. My face was wet with her.

I looked up.

Sara was staring down at me. Her chest was heaving. Her eyes were glassy, filled with tears she refused to shed. She looked wrecked.

She reached down. Her hand—shaking, grease-stained—touched my cheek. She traced the line where the metal jaw met the skin.

"You're mine," she whispered. "You metal bastard. You're mine."

I took her hand. I kissed the palm.

"Always," I rasped.

CRASH.

The door frame finally gave way. The heavy steel slab fell inward with a deafening clang.

Golden light flooded the room.

"FOUND YOU," the King roared.

I stood up. I wiped my mouth with the back of my chrome hand.

I wasn't afraid. I was full.

I looked at Sara. She slid off the turbine, grabbing her dagger from the floor. She looked ready to kill God.

I turned to face my father.

"You're interrupting," I said.

Chapter 48: The Finish

Sara

My legs didn't work.

I slid off the turbine housing, my boots hitting the floor with a heavy, uncoordinated thud. My knees were water. My inner thighs were trembling with a phantom echo of the friction that had just wrecked me.

I grabbed the edge of the machine to keep from falling.

My breath was coming in jagged gasps. I stared at Dorian.

He stood between me and the shattered door. He was magnificent and terrifying. He was naked from the waist down, his pants kicked into a corner, his tactical shirt hanging in ribbons from his shoulders. His skin was flushed, slick with sweat and my own fluids.

But it was his back that held my gaze.

The metal plating along his spine was glowing. Not the angry red of an overload, but a soft, pulsing blue. He looked charged. He looked like a god who had just finished creating a universe and was now ready to destroy one.

I felt a surge of emotion so violent it almost knocked me over. It wasn't just lust—though god knows I still wanted to climb him like a tree. It was possession.

He had unraveled me. He had taken the Rat—the girl who didn't trust anyone, who hoarded secrets like currency—and he had broken me open.

"You're mine," I whispered to his back, the words tasting like iron and salt. "You don't get to die, Chrome. You belong to me."

"COWERING IN THE DARK?"

The voice boomed through the room, vibrating in my teeth.

King Aric squeezed through the ruined blast door. He was too big for the room. He had to hunch over, his massive golden shoulders scraping the ceiling, showering us in dust.

He looked like a sun that had gone rotton. The gold plating was tarnished, streaked with black oil. His red eyes burned with a madness that made Dorian's calculated coldness look warm.

He looked at Dorian. Then he looked at me.

He saw the disheveled clothes. He saw the sweat. He smelled the sex.

The disgust on his face was absolute.

"Filth," Aric buzzed, his voice distorted by the damage to his vocal emitters. "You defile yourself with the livestock? Moments before the end?"

Dorian didn't flinch. He didn't reach for his pants. He stood his ground, fully exposed, radiating a calm, deadly arrogance.

"I was saying goodbye, Father," Dorian said, his voice smooth. "It's a human custom. You wouldn't understand."

"You are not human!" Aric roared. "You are a component! You are a spare part!"

He swung.

It wasn't a punch. It was a backhand meant to clear the board. A massive golden fist the size of a wrecking ball swept through the air.

"Move!" Dorian shouted.

He didn't dodge. He dove at me.

He tackled me, covering my body with his, and we rolled across the floor just as the King's fist slammed into the turbine.

CRUNCH.
The metal casing crumpled like tin foil. Coolant—hissing, freezing blue gas—sprayed into the room.

We hit the wall hard. Dorian took the impact, his metal shoulder groaning against the steel plating.

He was up instantly, hauling me to my feet.

"Get dressed," he ordered, shoving me toward a pile of ceremonial armor. "Find a weapon."

"What about you?" I yelled over the hiss of the leaking gas. "Put your pants on!"

"No time," he said grimly. "Besides... I think the psychological warfare is working. He hates looking at it."

He turned back to the King.

Aric was tearing the turbine apart, trying to get to us. The room was filling with fog.

I scrambled to the weapon rack. My hands were shaking, but the adrenaline was overriding the post-coital haze.

Spear? No, too long. Sword? Useless against plate.

My eyes landed on a heavy, industrial-looking device on the bottom shelf. It wasn't a weapon of war. It was a siege tool.

A Gravity Hammer.

It was essentially a rocket thruster strapped to a sledgehammer. It was meant for breaching castle gates.

I grabbed the handle. It weighed fifty pounds. I grunted, heaving it up.

"Dorian!" I screamed.

He was dodging a blow from the King, weaving with a speed that shouldn't have been possible for a man his size. The King was slow, heavy, encumbered by his own massive upgrades. Dorian was fast, powered by the residual charge of the city and... well, me.

Dorian looked back. He saw the hammer.

He grinned.

"Go for the knees!" he shouted.

I charged.

I dragged the hammer across the floor, sparks flying. I activated the thruster on the back of the head.

WHOOSH.

The hammer grew light in my hands as the rocket engaged. I swung it with everything I had.

I aimed for the King's right knee—a massive joint of gears and hydraulics.

CLANG.

The impact shook my bones. The hammer bit deep into the gold plating.

Aric roared, stumbling.

"YOU DARE?"

He swatted at me. I ducked, but the wind of his passing hand knocked me backward. I skidded across the floor, losing the hammer.

"Sara!" Dorian lunged, placing himself between me and the King.

Aric grabbed Dorian by the throat.

He lifted him off the ground. Dorian kicked, his metal legs scrabbling for purchase, but the King was immovable.

"I made you," Aric hissed, tightening his grip. "I can unmake you."

Dorian didn't struggle. He grabbed the King's wrist with both hands—the mirrored chrome hands.

"You didn't make me," Dorian choked out.

His eyes locked on mine over the King's massive arm.

"She did."

Dorian's arms began to glow.

He wasn't trying to break the grip. He was pushing energy *back* into the King. Just like he had done in the Throne Room. But this time, it wasn't data.

It was heat.

"Burn," Dorian whispered.

The King screamed as his golden wrist began to turn red. The heat transfer was instantaneous. Dorian was dumping his core thermal energy directly into his father's arm.

Aric dropped him.

Dorian hit the floor, gasping.

"Now, Sara!" he shouted. "The turbine! Shoot the tank!"

I looked at the damaged cooling unit. The gas was leaking, but the main tank was still pressurized.

I didn't have a gun. I had lost the pistol in the tackle.

I looked at my thigh holster. The obsidian dagger.

"It's glass!" I yelled. "It won't penetrate!"

"Throw it!"

I didn't hesitate. I pulled the knife. I balanced it in my palm.

The King was recovering, raising his foot to stomp Dorian into paste.

I threw the knife.

I didn't aim for the tank. I aimed for the exposed valve that Aric had damaged.

Ting.
The obsidian blade hit the valve stem. It shattered.

But the impact was enough. The valve sheared off.

HISSSSSSSSS.
A jet of super-cooled liquid nitrogen exploded from the tank. It hit the King squarely in the chest.

The gold plating hissed and cracked. The metal contracted violently. The King froze mid-step, covered in a layer of instant frost.

"Run!" Dorian grabbed my hand.

We sprinted for the broken door.

We scrambled over the debris, tumbling out into the Throne Room.

The battle was still raging. The Slags were fighting the Guards.

But everyone stopped when the King emerged from the safe room.

He wasn't dead. But he was slow. The frost covered his chest and legs. His movements were jerky, the hydraulics screaming against the cold.

"KILL THEM!" Aric bellowed.

Dorian pulled me behind the dais. He leaned against the obsidian throne, breathing hard. He was still naked, covered in dust and sweat, his metal arms glowing faint blue.

He looked at me. He touched my face with a chrome finger.

"That," he panted, a wild smile in his eyes, "was a hell of a finish."

I laughed. I couldn't help it. We were insane.

"Put some pants on, Prince," I said, shoving a dead guard's cloak at him. "We have a war to win."

He wrapped the cloak around his waist.

"Right," he said, turning to face the room. "Let's go melt him down."

Chapter 49: The Final Stand

Dorian

My father looked like a glitch in reality.

He stood twenty feet tall, encased in gold plating that was currently frosted white with liquid nitrogen. Vapor curled off his shoulders. His red optic sensors flickered erratically, casting strobe-light shadows across the chaotic Throne Room.

He was slow—the cold had stiffened his hydraulics—but he was heavy. When he took a step, the obsidian floor cracked.

"REBOOTING," Aric boomed. His voice was a digital stutter. "THERMAL... SYSTEMS... ENGAGING."

"He's thawing out," I said, tightening the guard's cloak around my waist. "We have maybe two minutes before he's back to full speed."

"Two minutes is a lifetime," Sara said. She was scanning the floor, looking for a weapon. She grabbed a kinetic rifle from a fallen Golden Guard. She checked the charge. "Cover me."

"Sara, don't—"

She didn't listen. She never listened.

She sprinted toward the King.

"Hey! Goldilocks!" she screamed.

Aric turned, his massive head pivoting on grinding gears.

Sara slid on her knees, passing directly between his legs. As she slid, she fired the rifle straight up.

CRACK-CRACK-CRACK.

Three rounds slammed into the King's groin plating. It didn't penetrate the heavy armor, but the kinetic force staggered him.

"INSOLENCE!" Aric roared.

He swung a fist down to crush her.

I moved.

I launched myself off the dais. I didn't have a weapon, but I had two arms made of the same alloy he was.

I hit him mid-swing.

CLANG.

It was like hitting a moving train. The impact rattled my teeth and jarred my spine, but I deflected the blow. My chrome fist knocked his golden arm wide.

"Run!" I shouted at Sara.

She rolled to her feet and scrambled behind a pillar.

"Slags!" she yelled. "Take the legs!"

The Army of the Rust obeyed.

Elara led the charge. My god, she was terrifying. She wielded a heavy pipe wrench in her human hand and used her metal arm as a shield.

"Bring it down!" she shrieked.

Jinx and the factory workers swarmed the King's ankles. They jammed crowbars into his hydraulic lines. They hammered at the servos. They were ants attacking a beetle, but there were hundreds of them.

Aric kicked.

Bodies flew. A man in a welding mask was launched across the room, hitting the wall with a sickening crunch.

"GET OFF ME," Aric bellowed.

Steam erupted from his vents. The frost on his armor turned to water instantly. He was heating up. The reboot was complete.

He moved faster now. He reached down and grabbed a factory worker—a woman with a sledgehammer. He squeezed.

She screamed.

"No!" I roared.

I charged again. I jumped, grabbing the plating on Aric's back. I climbed him like a mountain.

The metal burned my bare chest. I didn't care. I hauled myself up to his shoulders.

"Let her go!"

I wrapped my metal arm around his throat—or the thick bundle of cables that served as a throat. I squeezed.

My servos whined against his. It was a contest of torque.

Aric dropped the woman. She scrambled away.

"Parasite," Aric hissed.

He reached up. He grabbed me by the hair and the cloak. He ripped me off his back and threw me.

I flew thirty feet. I crashed into the Golden Throne, smashing the control console.

Pain exploded in my back. I slumped to the floor, gasping.

"Dorian!" Sara shouted.

Aric turned his attention to the Throne. To me.

"I need... power," the King rumbled.

He marched toward the dais. He wasn't attacking me. He was trying to get back to the chair. To the interface. If he plugged back in, he could drain the remaining reserves of the city. He could heal.

"Stop him!" I wheezed, trying to stand. "Don't let him dock!"

Sara stepped into his path.

She stood alone on the steps of the dais. She looked tiny against the towering golden monster. She raised the rifle.

"You're not sitting down, old man," she said. "Seat's taken."

She fired.

The bullets sparked off his chest. He didn't even slow down.

"MOVE, RAT," Aric thundered.

He raised his hand to backhand her into oblivion.

BOOM.

A massive explosion rocked the King's shoulder. He stumbled, his arm dropping.

I looked up.

Voss was standing on the balcony above, holding the rotary cannon he'd ripped from the turret.

"Denied!" Voss shouted, firing again.

The heavy rounds chewed into the King's shoulder joint. Gold plating shredded. Oil sprayed.

It bought us a second.

"Jinx! Elara! Now!" Sara commanded.

The Slags threw something. Not rocks. Not grenades.

Chains.

Four heavy industrial chains, scavenged from the drawbridge, whipped through the air. They wrapped around the King's arms and legs.

"PULL!" Sara screamed.

Fifty people grabbed the ends of the chains. They dug their heels into the obsidian floor. They heaved.

"GRAAAAGH!" Aric roared, fighting the tension.

He was strong, but physics was stronger. With his balance compromised by Voss's cannon fire and his legs tangled, the mob pulled him off balance.

The King crashed to his knees. The sound shook the foundations of the palace.

"Hold him!" I yelled.

I stood up. The pain in my back was blinding, but the rage was stronger.

I looked at the broken console of the Throne. The main power cable—the one Sara had severed earlier—was sparking on the floor. It was thick as a python, leaking raw magical energy.

I looked at the King.

He was struggling, ripping at the chains. He was going to break free in seconds.

I looked at Sara.

She was holding the line, pulling on a chain with everything she had. Her boots—*my* boots—were slipping on the polished floor. She looked at me. Her eyes were fierce, desperate.
End it, she mouthed.
I looked at my metal hands.

I remembered the files. I remembered the outpost. The King wanted to be pure metal. He wanted to be conductive.

Fine.

I grabbed the live power cable.

The shock hit me instantly. It felt like being kicked in the chest by a horse. My vision flashed white. My internal systems screamed warnings.

POWER SURGE DETECTED. CAPACITORS OVERLOADING.

I didn't let go. I wrapped the cable around my left arm. I became the conduit.

"Hey, Father!" I shouted.

Aric looked up. He saw me standing on the dais, glowing with blue-white lightning, holding the severed lifeline of his empire.

"You wanted the power?" I yelled, my voice distorting, becoming a digital roar. "You wanted the current?"

I jumped.

I leaped from the dais, trailing the sparking cable behind me.

I landed on the King's back.

I didn't grapple him. I didn't punch him.

I jammed the live cable directly into the open wound on his shoulder where Voss had shot away the armor.

"EAT IT!"

ZZZZAAPP.
The connection closed.

The entire reserve of the Palace grid—the backup generators, the emergency cells, everything—flowed through me, into the cable, and straight into the King's central processor.

Aric stiffened.

He opened his mouth to scream, but only light came out. Blinding, golden light erupted from his eyes, his mouth, the vents in his armor.

"DORIAN!" Sara screamed.

I held on.

The heat was unbearable. I could feel my own plating starting to melt. My internal fans shattered. My optical sensors blew out, leaving me blind.

But I held on.

I poured every volt, every amp, every ounce of hate into him.

Die, I thought. *Die and leave us alone.*
The King's body began to vibrate. The gold turned white. Then translucent.

Critical Mass Achieved.
The world dissolved into noise and fire.

Chapter 50: The Overload

Dorian

I was blind. My optics had blown out seconds ago, fried by the surge.

I was deaf. The roar of the energy transfer had blown my auditory sensors, leaving only a high-pitched, screaming tinnitus in my skull.

But I wasn't numb. I was a live wire.

I was a conduit for enough voltage to light the Eastern Seaboard, and I was funneling it all into the creature beneath me.

Aric felt like a black hole. He was vast, hungry, and terrifyingly open. He was trying to eat the surge. He was drinking the lightning I was feeding him, his internal capacity expanding to accommodate the load.

More, his consciousness screamed across the data link. *Feed me. Make me bright.*

He was winning.

My cohesion was failing. The metal plating on my arms was softening, turning to slag under the heat. My biological chest was cooking.

I was pouring myself into him, and he was just getting stronger. He was going to absorb the overload, stabilize the core, and then he was going to eat me.

System Failure Imminent, my internal diagnostic scrolled across my broken vision.

Then, I felt a touch.

It wasn't the burning heat of the King. It was small. Warm. Rough.

A hand grabbed my ankle.

It grounded me.

The sensation was instantaneous. The wild, chaotic electricity arcing through my frame found a path. It didn't flow into her—the voltage would have vaporized her—but the *contact* stabilized my neural net.

It acted as a focal point. A coordinate in the static.

Sara.

I didn't need eyes to know it was her. I knew the grip. I knew the stubborn desperation.

I'm here, her touch screamed. *I've got you.*

The connection cleared the static in my head. The panic evaporated, replaced by a cold, mechanical clarity.

I realized something.

The King had opened the floodgates. To drink the power, he had to lower his firewalls. He had established a direct, two-way connection between his central processor and my spine.

He thought I was just a battery. He forgot I was a terminal.

I wasn't just connected to his power supply; I was connected to his *operating system.*

I felt the Gilt flowing through his veins. It wasn't magic. It was programmable matter. It was the same alloy that made up my own arms.

And I knew the code.

I remembered the sparring matches. I remembered the way the metal stiffened when it got too cold, or seized when the torque output conflicted with the hydraulic pressure.

It wasn't a god. It was a machine. And machines could be crashed.

"You want to be eternal, Father?" I rasped, my voice fused into a metallic growl. "You want to be perfect?"

I reached into the stream. I didn't send power. I sent data.

I accessed the root directory of his armor's lattice structure.

Command Override: SYSTEM HALT.

I slammed the code into him.

I targeted the molecular vibration of the gold. I commanded the atoms to stop moving. I commanded the flow to cease.

I forced a thermal lock.

Aric's mental scream tore through my neural pathways.

NO! I AM EXPANDING! I AM BECOMING!

"No," I thought back, pushing the command deeper, hacking past his biological overrides. "You are seizing."

I drew on everything. I drew on the logic of the machine. I drew on the stubborn, immovable weight of the Rat holding my ankle.

I executed the script.

LOCKDOWN.

The King thrashed beneath me. But it wasn't a physical thrashing. It was a system seizure.

The hydraulic whine of his limbs dropped in pitch, becoming a grinding, agonizing screech as the programmable matter obeyed my command and turned rigid.

He wasn't freezing because of ice. He was freezing because I had bricked his operating system.

Tick... tick... tick...

I felt his chest plate harden under my knees. The flexibility of the living metal vanished, replaced by the inert, heavy density of dead iron.

I felt the heat dying, choked off by the sudden cessation of movement.

Please, Aric begged, his voice small now, trapped inside the shell as his own body became his coffin. *Dorian. Stop. I cannot move.*

"You're not supposed to move," I whispered into the void. "You're a statue."

I gave one last push. I poured every remaining ounce of battery power into the encryption key, locking the code so it couldn't be reversed.

ACCESS DENIED.

The vibration stopped.

The screaming stopped.

The hunger stopped.

Beneath me, the mountain of gold went rigid. The chaos of the overload vanished, leaving only absolute, terrifying silence.

I let go of the cable.

I fell backward.

I hit the floor hard. I couldn't see. I couldn't move. My systems were offline.

My biological heart was beating so slowly I could count the seconds between thuds.

One...

Two...

Three...

"Dorian!"

The voice was muffled, like she was shouting through cotton.

Hands were on me. Frantic hands. Pulling the cloak away from my face. Checking my neck.

"Dorian, breathe! Dammit, Chrome, breathe!"

I tried to open my eyes, but the lids were heavy. My optics were rebooting, scrolling lines of code across my vision.

System Critical. Rebooting...

"Is he..." I wheezed.

"He's a statue," Sara sobbed. "You did it. You shut him down."

I tried to smile. My lip cracked.

"Bricked him," I whispered. "Hardware failure."

"Shut up. Save your battery."

She rested her forehead against my chest. I felt her tears—hot, wet, real—soaking into my skin.

"You didn't die," she said, her voice fierce and broken. "You promised you wouldn't, and you didn't."

"I kept... the boots," I mumbled.

The darkness was creeping in at the edges of my mind. Not the void of death, but the heavy, gray fog of system exhaustion.

"Stay with me," Sara ordered. "Help is coming. Elara is getting the medics."

I felt her hand grip my new chrome hand. She laced her fingers through the cold metal digits.

She didn't flinch.

"I'm here," she whispered. "I'm right here."

I squeezed her hand back. It was a weak grip, barely a twitch of the servos, but it was there.

The King was offline. The city was saved.

And the Rat was holding my hand.

I let the darkness take me. For the first time in my life, I wasn't afraid of waking up.

Chapter 51: The Aftermath

Sara

The silence was heavier than the gold.

Ten minutes ago, this room had been a cacophony of screaming metal, roaring energy, and dying men. Now, the only sound was the dripping of coolant from the ruptured turbine and the wet, ragged breathing of the man in my lap.

I sat on the floor of the Throne Room, my legs numb, holding Dorian's head. He was out cold. His skin was gray, his lips cracked and bleeding. His chest—the human part—rose and fell with a shallow, terrifying rhythm.

"Don't you quit," I whispered, brushing his sweat-slicked hair back. "The shift isn't over, Chrome."

"Sara!"

I looked up. Elara was sprinting across the shattered obsidian floor. She had a med-kit strapped to her back and a squad of Slag factory workers behind her.

"Is he..." She skidded to a stop, looking at Dorian, then at the towering golden monstrosity behind us.

"He's rebooting," I said, my voice sounding like gravel. "I hope."

Elara dropped to her knees. She didn't check his pulse; she checked his neck plating. She pulled a diagnostic scanner—stolen from a dead technomancer—and held it over his chest.

"His core is drained," she said, her brow furrowing. "He's running on emergency biological reserves. We need to jump-start him."

"No," I said, grabbing her wrist. "No more power. No more currents. If we shock him now, we fry his brain. Let him rest. Just... keep him alive."

Elara looked at me. She saw the fierce, protective set of my jaw. She nodded.

"Get a stretcher!" she barked at the workers. "And be careful! He weighs five hundred pounds!"

They scrambled to obey.

I looked up at the King.

Aric was frozen in the middle of a scream. He was twenty feet of solid, gleaming gold. The liquid nitrogen had boiled off, leaving him room-temperature and eternal. His eyes were wide, staring at nothing. His hands were clawed, reaching for power he would never touch again.

"Ugly," I muttered. "But expensive."

Voss limped over. He was bleeding from a gash in his head, leaning heavily on his rotary cannon. He looked at the statue of his former master.

"Well," Voss grunted. "That's going to be a bitch to move."

"Leave him," I said. "Let him stand there. Let everyone see what happens when you get greedy."

The workers lifted Dorian onto a makeshift stretcher made of riot shields. I walked beside him, my hand resting on his cold chrome shoulder, daring anyone to tell me to step back.

We moved him to the side of the dais, away from the wreckage.

The Throne Room was filling up. The rest of the Army of the Rust had fought their way up the stairs. Scavengers, mechanics, whores, and thieves. They stood amidst the ruins of the Gilded Age, looking around with wide, fearful eyes.

They looked at the dead Golden Guards. They looked at the golden statue.

And then, they looked at Dorian.

He stirred.

A low groan rumbled in his chest. His eyelids fluttered.

"Dorian?" I leaned in close.

His eyes opened. The optics were rebooting—faint blue spirals spinning in the depths of his irises. He blinked, focusing on my face.

"You're loud," he rasped.

I let out a breath that was half-laugh, half-sob. "And you're heavy."

He tried to sit up. I put a hand on his chest to stop him.

"Stay down. You're at 1% battery."

"I need..." He coughed. "I need to stand."

"You need a nap."

"Sara." His hand—the new chrome one—gripped my wrist. It was weak, but steady. "Look at them."

I looked up.

The crowd was watching. Hundreds of them. They were silent, waiting. They were looking at the Prince who had turned his father into a statue. They were looking for a leader.

"They're scared," Dorian whispered. "They need to know it's over."

He was right. Damn him, he was right.

"Fine," I said. "But lean on me. If you fall over, I'm leaving you there."

I helped him up. It took both of us. He was dead weight until his gyros spun up, and even then, he swayed like a tree in a storm. I wrapped my arm around his waist. He draped his heavy metal arm over my shoulders.

We stood there, a battered, bloody, mismatched pair, facing the room.

Dorian took a breath. He straightened his spine. For a second, the exhaustion vanished, replaced by the steel core of the man who had survived the Gilt.

"Citizens," he said. His voice was rough, unamplified, but it carried in the silence.

The crowd shuffled forward.

"The King is dead," Dorian said, gesturing to the statue behind him. "The Harvest is canceled. The grid... is yours."

A murmur went through the room. Disbelief. Hope.

Then, someone stepped forward.

It was the High Steward, Lord Silas—the man I'd pickpocketed at the ball. He had survived the purge by hiding in a cupboard, apparently. He was holding something.

He walked up to the dais, his purple robes stained with dust. He looked at the statue of Aric, then at Dorian. He fell to his knees.

In his hands was the Crown.

It was a jagged, heavy thing made of electrum and diamonds. It had fallen from Aric's head during the fight.

"Your Majesty," Silas quavered, holding it up. "The succession is clear. The Throne is yours."

The room held its breath.

This was it. The moment of truth. The King was dead; long live the King.

Dorian looked at the crown. He looked at the sparkling jewels, the heavy gold. He looked at the symbol of the power that had eaten his humanity piece by piece.

He released my shoulder. He took a step forward, standing on his own.

He reached out with his new chrome hand.

He took the crown.

He held it up. The light from the emergency strobes caught the diamonds. It was beautiful. It was poisonous.

"Majesty," Dorian repeated softly.

He looked at the crowd. He looked at the Slags. He looked at me.

"My father believed that gold made him a god," Dorian said, his voice gaining strength. "He believed that power was something you hoarded. Something you drained from others to keep yourself bright."

He looked at the crown in his hand.

"He was wrong."

Dorian's hand clenched.

The servos whined. The blue light in his arm flared.

He didn't just crush it. He heated it.

He channeled the last dregs of his thermal energy into his palm. The air shimmered. The gold of the crown began to soften. The diamonds popped out, clattering to the floor.

Silas gasped. "Sire! That is a priceless artifact!"

"It's scrap," Dorian growled.

He squeezed harder. The metal turned red, then orange. It oozed between his chrome fingers like wax. Molten electrum dripped onto the obsidian floor, hissing as it cooled into shapeless blobs.

He held the squeeze until the crown was nothing but a twisted, unrecognizable lump of slag.

He dropped it.

Clang.
It landed at Silas's knees.

"There is no King," Dorian announced, his voice ringing with finality. "There is no Throne. There is only the City."

He looked at Voss.

"Voss, secure the perimeter. Open the food stores. Open the medical wards. Everyone eats tonight. Everyone gets treated."

"Yes, sir," Voss said, grinning.

Dorian looked at Elara.

"You have a knack for organization," he said. "Get a Council together. Representatives from every district. Slags, Chrome, I don't care. We run this city together."

"You want me to run a Council?" Elara asked, eyes wide.

"I want you to make sure no one ever builds a chair that eats people again," Dorian said.

He turned back to me.

The strength finally left him. He stumbled.

I caught him.

"Okay, hero," I whispered, taking his weight. "Show's over. You made your point."

"Did I?" he mumbled, his head drooping onto my shoulder. "Was it dramatic enough?"

"You melted the hat, Dorian. It was plenty dramatic."

I turned him away from the crowd, away from the cheering that was starting to rise like a wave in the room.

"Where are we going?" he asked.

"To bed," I said. "And not the one-bed cot. I'm taking you to the suite with the four pillows."

"I think..." he slurred, his eyes closing. "I think I broke my back."

"I'll fix it," I promised. "I'm a mechanic, remember?"

I walked him toward the exit. The crowd parted for us. They didn't bow. They cheered. They reached out to touch his arm, his cloak, his boots.

They weren't cheering for a Prince. They were cheering for the man who broke the machine.

I looked back one last time at the golden statue of King Aric. He stood alone in the dark, frozen, hollow, and dead.

"Rust in peace, old man," I whispered.

I tightened my grip on Dorian's waist.

"We've got work to do."

Chapter 52: Rust Free (Epilogue)

Sara

The toaster was fighting me.

It was an ancient, pre-Collapse model I'd scavenged from a bunker in Sector 7. It had more computing power than the Council's new tactical mainframe, but it refused to toast bread without burning the edges.

"Cooperate," I hissed, jamming a screwdriver into the heating element. "Or I scrap you for parts."

"Threatening the appliances again?"

I didn't turn around. I knew the sound of those boots. Heavy. Rhythmic. And missing the frantic, paranoid cadence they used to have.

Dorian walked into the loft.

Our home wasn't a palace. It was the top floor of the old textile factory in District 14. It had exposed brick walls, skylights that actually opened, and a floor stained with a century of industrial grease.

It was perfect.

Dorian kicked the door shut behind him. He was carrying a crate of produce—actual vegetables, green ones, not the gray sludge paste we used to eat.

He looked... different.

The polish was gone. His hair was longer, tied back in a messy knot. He wore a thermal henley with the sleeves pushed up, exposing the twin chrome arms. The metal wasn't mirror-perfect anymore. It was scuffed. Scratched. It looked lived-in.

He set the crate on the counter.

"The toaster has a primitive AI," he said, leaning over my shoulder to inspect my surgery. "It senses your aggression. You have to be gentle."

"I don't do gentle," I muttered. "I do percussive maintenance."

I tapped the toaster with the handle of the screwdriver. *Thwack.*
"See? Fixed."

Dorian laughed. It was a rich, easy sound. The kind of laugh that came from a chest that wasn't carrying the weight of a kingdom.

He kissed my cheek. His lips were warm. His metal hand rested on my waist, the cold alloy sending a familiar shiver down my spine.

"How was the Council?" I asked, leaning back into him.

"Exhausting," he groaned. "Elara is a tyrant. She forced a vote on the new water filtration zoning. She made me read a three-hundred-page report on pipe diameters."

"She's thorough."

"She's terrifying. She threatened to weld Voss to his chair if he didn't stop cleaning his gun during the meeting."

"Good," I grinned. "Someone has to keep you boys in line."

Six months.

It had been six months since the Unification that wasn't. Since the King became a statue. Since the grid went public.

The city wasn't fixed—not by a long shot. The Slags were still dirty, the Chrome was still arrogant, and the power grid flickered on Tuesdays. But nobody was being drained. Nobody was rust.

And us?

We were just... here.

Dorian moved away, rummaging in the crate. He pulled out a bag of coffee. Real beans.

"I stopped by the market," he said. "Jinx says hello. He also says you owe him ten credits for the bet."

"What bet?"

"He bet you'd blow up the toaster within a week. You have one day left."

"I hate him."

"You love him. He's your brother-in-arms."

Dorian started grinding the beans. The noise filled the loft.

I watched him. I watched the way his metal muscles shifted under his skin. I watched the way the afternoon sun caught the scar on his jaw.

He caught me staring.

He stopped the grinder. He leaned against the counter, crossing his arms.

"What?" he asked, a smirk playing on his lips.

"Nothing," I lied. "Just checking for rust."

"I'm high-grade alloy, Rat. I don't rust."

"You squeak when it rains."

"That is a lie."

"It's a little squeak. In the left elbow. It's cute."

His eyes narrowed. "I am not cute. I am a weapon of mass destruction retired to a life of domestic servitude."

He gestured to the sink.

My smile faltered.

The sink was full. Piled high. Plates, mugs, and yes, the silver ladle I had stolen six months ago and refused to return.

"Your turn," he said.

"I did them yesterday," I argued.

"You rinsed them. You didn't scrub. There is still egg on this fork, Sara. It has fossilized."

"I saved the city," I said, hopping up to sit on the counter. "I killed a Technomancer. I shouldn't have to scrub eggs."

"I held a door open with my face while being melted," Dorian countered, stepping between my legs. "And I still took out the trash this morning."

He rested his hands on my thighs. The metal fingers dug into my jeans.

"Fair point," I conceded.

"So," he murmured, leaning in close. "Dishes."

"Make me."

The air in the kitchen shifted instantly. The domestic banter evaporated, replaced by the heavy, electric heat that never really went away.

Dorian's eyes darkened. The fractured blue iris flared.

"Is that a challenge?" he whispered.

"Maybe."

He didn't back down. He moved his hands up my thighs, over my hips, slipping under the hem of my grease-stained tank top. His metal palms were cool against my warm skin.

"You are bratty," he growled, biting my neck lightly. "Disobedient. Chaos in human form."

"And you love it."

"I tolerate it," he lied against my throat. "Because the fringe benefits are exceptional."

He lifted me.

I wrapped my legs around his waist. I buried my hands in his hair, messing up the knot.

"The toaster is smoking," I whispered.

"Let it burn," he said.

Dorian

I carried her to the bedroom.

It wasn't a pristine white suite in a tower. It was a mattress on a pallet frame, covered in mismatched quilts and pillows we'd scavenged.

I threw her onto the bed.

Sara bounced, laughing. She looked wild. Beautiful. She had grease on her cheek and fire in her eyes.

I crawled over her, pinning her wrists to the mattress with my chrome hands.

"Dishes," I said, hovering over her. "Later."

"Much later," she agreed, pulling me down.

We didn't have to rush anymore. There were no countdowns. No draining batteries. No Kings waiting to eat us.

There was just this. The friction. The heat. The slow, deliberate way she arched into me when I kissed her.

I took my time. I traced the scars on her ribs with my metal fingertips. I kissed the spot where the war paint used to be.

"You know," she whispered, breathless, as my hand slid down her jeans. "The Council wants you to run for Governor next term."

I groaned into her neck. "I'd rather fight another Hydra."

"You'd be good at it. You look good on a poster."

"I'm retired, Sara. I'm just a mechanic's assistant now."

"Assistant?" She bucked her hips, gasping as I found her rhythm. " You're the muscle. I'm the brains."

"You're the trouble," I corrected.

I kissed her again, silencing the arguments.

Outside, the city was loud. The factories were humming, the skiffs were roaring, and the people were living their messy, complicated lives. The smog was still there. The metal was still there.

But the fear was gone.

I looked down at Sara. She was staring up at me, her eyes full of a fierce, possessive light.

She reached up and touched my face.

"We're okay, aren't we?" she asked softly.

I leaned into her touch. I felt the beat of my mechanical heart, steady and strong, synced with hers.

"Yeah," I said, dragging the blanket over us, shutting out the sun, the city, and the ghosts of the past.

I kissed her forehead.

"Let the world rust," I whispered. "We're just fine."